Masquerade Mistake

Sunset Bay, Book 1

Crissi Langwell

Cover & Interior Design: Crissi Langwell/Canva
Inside Art: Shutterstock
Author Photo: Shawn Langwell

ISBN: 978-1-961240-00-1

Publisher: North Coast Stories
This book is also available in hardcover and ebook.
Please visit the author's website to find out where to purchase this book.

www.crissilangwell.com

NORTH COAST
STORIES

"We are fashioned creatures, but half made up."
— Mary Shelley, Frankenstein

To all the single moms out there.

I see you. I was you.

You're doing a great job.

Claire's Super Mellow Playlist

Salt and the Sea ~ Gregory Alan Isakov

The Night We Met ~ Lord Huron

State Lines ~ Novo Amor

House of Cards ~ Radiohead

Japanese Denim ~ Daniel Caesar

Want U Around ~ Omar Apollo (Ruel)

Standing in the Rain ~ The Paper Kites

Tucana ~ Mt. Wolf

Now You Don't ~ Ocie Elliott

Wash ~ Bon Iver

When We're Older ~ James Blake

View full playlist at
crissilangwell.com/sunset-bay/masquerade-mistake

Please note:

The novels in the *Sunset Bay* series feature strong, independent women who have sex, love the word *fuck*, and face challenging issues. Triggers may include experience with addiction. Each book can be read as a standalone, and all end in a HEA.

Table of Contents

Chapter 1

The room was spinning. That's the first thing I noticed when I opened my eyes. *That*, and my pounding head. Or was it the bass from the blaring music? It took a moment to remember what happened, but it all came back in beats.

Boom. Stand up.

Boom. Shoe caught.

Boom. Falling.

"Are you okay?" someone yelled over the music.

I turned to the voice; embarrassment washed over me as I took in his appearance. Like me, he wore a mask over the top half of his face, hiding his identity. In the two seconds it took to formulate my answer, I studied his facial features around the mask; a roman nose over plush lips, a clean-shaven face with a chiseled jawline, and a concerned pair of eyes the color of deep jade. I didn't need to see his entire face to know he was attractive, or that I looked absolutely ridiculous still lying there on the floor.

But let me back up.

I'd just graduated high school that afternoon, top honors with a partial scholarship to UCSD. While everyone else had family cheering them on, I had no one. I'd told my mom beforehand about my graduation. I'd stuck the invitation on the refrigerator and reminded her every few days, and still she didn't show up. Not that I expected it. I hadn't seen my mom in days, so I drove myself to graduation, bracing for silence when I walked across the stage. Instead, I heard my best friend Maren's loud voice coming from the back.

"You fucking rock, Claire!"

How do I describe my friendship with Maren? She was the dark to my light, the yang to my yin. It was like we were two halves of one whole, with nothing similar in the other. I studied hard and finished high school strong. Maren dropped out at the beginning of the year and had been MIA the past few months. In fact, her presence at my graduation was completely unexpected.

"Where have you been?" I demanded when I finally found her in the crowd after the ceremony. She responded by flinging herself at me, engulfing me in a bone-crushing hug.

"Around," she said once she released me. I knew this was the only answer I'd get. "There's a rager across town tonight. Come with me."

"Who's throwing it?"

"Some theater guy I met a few days ago. Brad, I think. Or Brian. I don't know. All I know is that it's supposed to be huge."

I already had tickets for Grad Night—the traditional all-night sober party in the high school gym. It sounded fun at the time, but so did sitting in bed with a book in an empty house. Though, now that Maren was here, this third option sounded intriguing. Especially after she told me the theme.

"Masquerade?" I squeaked.

"Yeah, weird right?"

"Maren, how are we supposed to pull together masquerade costumes?" I asked, even as I did a mental inventory of what I had in my closet; a few years of homecoming dresses, some odds and ends in the Halloween costume box, random material from my mom's short-lived experiment with being Suzy Homemaker.

Back at my house, we pulled all these items out. By the time we were dressed, my room was trashed. But we looked incredible. Maren chose a dress I hadn't worn since junior high, which fit her wiry frame like sapphire plastic wrap. Her coffee eyes shone through a strip of black lace, making her appear all the more mysterious. With the form fitting gown and her sleek black hair, she was somewhere between dancer and dominatrix. I, on the other hand, went full princess. I had on my mother's old prom dress, an ice blue strapless ball gown with a navy cloak to keep me warm. It was so 1980s, but I didn't care. My amber eyes appeared almost gold through the black fabric of my mask, with heavy shading and black mascara that Maren had helped me apply. Finishing the look off was a silver tiara with clear glass jewels, placed on top of my piled blonde curls.

"Cinderella, I believe we're ready for the ball." Maren grinned at me through rust-colored lips, and I felt a flurry of butterflies over a night I was sure would be full of surprises.

Surprises was an understatement. Maren had taken off within the first hour, and I'd spent the rest of the night sipping a drink that tasted something like gasoline and orange juice as I pretended to have fun. The house we were at was a tiny shack on the outskirts of Sunset Bay, and full of people in various interpretations of what "masquerade" meant, including some guy in a full body dinosaur costume, with a tail that cleared the path behind him.

I sat on the edge of a dirty couch, trying not to touch the couple making out next to me as I mulled over abandoning Maren for that book waiting for me at home.

"Fuck this," I muttered, standing quickly. Unfortunately, the heel of my shoe was caught in the tulle under my dress. I pitched forward, flinging the contents of my red Solo cup.

That was the last thing I remembered before opening my eyes and looking into his.

"Are you okay?" he yelled, his voice competing with the techno music.

I know I mentioned this guy's attractiveness, but honestly, it was enough to know he was out of my league. And the mask only made him hotter. Let's just say if there were a fifth Hemsworth brother, this guy would be him. Except for the green eyes. Those were all his own, and right now they were waiting for an answer.

"I think so," I started, lifting a hand to the back of my head. There was a tender knot on my scalp, and I winced as my fingers brushed over it. My crown was tangled in my hair, and I noted the syrupy wetness within the strands. Alarmed, I sat straight up, knocking my head into his chin. He grunted at the same time I did, releasing me as he rubbed his chin.

"Sorry," I groaned, rubbing the new wound on my forehead as I inspected my sticky hand. No blood, just that godawful orange drink. I looked down at my dress, noting the dark stains spreading on the material. I moved to get up, but he stopped me with a hand on my arm.

"Easy there, Sparky. You've had a little too much to drink."

Okay, cute or not, the insinuation pissed me off. I knew my limits, and a couple sips off an awful drink wasn't even close.

"I'm not drunk," I snapped, pulling my arm from his grasp. I tried getting up again, but my shoe was still caught in my dress. Frustrated, I tore off my heels, ripping the tulle in the process. "Fuck!" Even in my anger, I realized it didn't matter. The dress was ruined, and my mom probably wouldn't miss it. She wouldn't even know it was missing if I threw it away, just like she didn't notice me. And Maren was no better. "I'll be so glad to get out of this fucking hell hole," I muttered.

"Hey, a place with free booze isn't that bad," the guy said, offering his hand again. This time I took it, flashing him a weary smile once I was back on my feet.

"Not the house," I explained. "I'm talking about this town. These people. Everything. I feel like my whole life has been on hold, and I'll be so glad to get the hell out of Sunset Bay and leave it all behind."

As I brushed past him, my bare foot slid through that stupid drink, and I flailed my arms to keep my footing.

"Sober or not, let me help you," he said, his hand gripping my arm before I could land on my ass. I sighed, letting him guide me to the front door even though I knew I could do it on my own. I took one last glance at the party behind me, and decided Maren was a big girl and could handle herself. After all, she abandoned me first.

"Are you sure you're all right?" he asked once we were outside. I shivered in the breeze, pulling my cloak closer to me. The fresh air felt good in my lungs. I breathed in deep, and even under the stench of my putrid drink-covered dress, I detected his soft scent. A hint of wind mixed with a healthy dose of sunshine and gusty dreams—at least that's what came to mind as I inhaled, and what I mentally batted away as I nodded in reply to his question.

"I'm fine," I said, looking down the street for my car. Then I groaned. Maren had been the one to drive, even though her car looked like she'd been living in it. I had no way of getting home without her.

I sat down heavily on the step, weighing my options. I could call a cab; except I had no money. I'd call my mom, but I was still mad at her for standing me up at graduation. Besides, if she didn't answer my earlier reminder texts, what made me think she'd answer now?

"You don't look fine," he said, sitting beside me. I scooted over to make room, but I didn't look at him. I could already feel the tears welling up in my eyes, and I didn't want him to see me cry. "Are you okay to drive?"

he asked.

"For the millionth time, I'm not drunk. As you can see, I'm wearing my drink." I figured if I could stay angry enough, I'd avoid crying in front of him. Wrong. I immediately burst into tears. "I don't have a ride," I finally blurted out. "I have no idea where I am, my friend ditched me, and I don't know anyone. On top of everything, I graduated today and my mom…" I wiped my face, even as the tears kept coming. This was my life. No matter what I did or who I cared about, they would always let me down. My mom was a constant in that department. And Maren, she was a mess. But was it too much to hope someone would take the time to care about me? To see me?

"Never mind, It doesn't matter." I stared up at the sky, wishing I could see the stars beyond the bright streetlights. "In a few months, I'll be out of here and won't have to worry about any of this."

He stood without speaking as I tried my hardest to pull myself together. I heard the door open, the sounds of the party invading the silence before he closed the door again, leaving me alone.

"That's just great, Claire," I muttered. "The only decent person at this party, and you scare him off." I stood on shaky legs, my head throbbing from the lump. If I walked home, how long would it take before I recognized my surroundings? Could I even walk in these damn heels?

The door opened again, and the guy was back, this time holding another red plastic cup.

"It's water," he assured me, extending it toward me. I took it, my fingers brushing his, sending a current of warmth through my hand and up my arm as I exhaled.

"Thank you." I lifted the cup to my lips, cooling myself with icy relief.

He sat next to me, his leg brushing mine. It wasn't necessarily a move, but my body reacted just the same. I liked him touching me. I didn't even know him, yet the mere presence of his leg shifting against mine was enough to make me wonder what it would be like to kiss him.

"Can I drive you home?" he asked.

I started to say no, but then I thought about my other options—of which there were none.

"I don't even know your name," I said.

"I'm —"

"Wait, don't tell me," I cut him off, laughing into my cup. "If you tell me, I'll have something to remember from this day, and honestly, I just want to forget everything."

"Fair enough," he said, touching his mask. "I guess it kind of matches the whole masquerade thing, though I think we're part of a small group that understands what a masquerade really is. Did you see the dinosaur?"

Thankfully his car was cleaner than Maren's. It also smelled like him, a scent I found more intoxicating by the minute. I tried to ignore it, but I couldn't escape the heady feeling it gave me as he navigated the turns of the neighborhood, eventually landing on a street I recognized. From there, I gave him directions to my house. But as we approached, I saw my mom's car in the driveway, and a strange car next to that. We passed the house and I said nothing to slow him down, feeling the ball of dread grow in my belly. We reached the end of the street, and he idled at the stop sign.

"Right, or left?"

"I, uh, right," I stammered. He turned right, and I realized my error immediately at the dead end. "I mean left."

He parked the car, then turned to me. "You do have a house, right?" he asked. I fiddled with my dress, then brushed at the drink stain as if it would make a difference.

"We passed my house," I admitted. He started to put the car in gear again, but I placed my hand on his arm. His skin was warm, and there was a tattoo of a palm with an eye in the center on the inside of his forearm. I was tempted to grip his arm like he gripped mine earlier. The magnetic pull between us was unlike anything I'd ever known, and I wondered if I was the only one experiencing it. He looked down at my hand, and I removed it. "I don't want to go home yet," I said. I noticed the question in his eyes, but I was afraid to let him ask it. "Can we just hang out for a while?"

He paused, seeming to mull over what I was requesting. I shook my head, offering a small laugh. "Sorry, I'm assuming you have nothing to do. You probably want to get back to the party."

"Seriously? That place is full of drunk people in masks, plus a weird dinosaur. I'm here with the prettiest girl from the party. Why would I want to leave?"

I ducked my head at the compliment, but he reached over and tilted my chin toward him.

"You don't think you're pretty?" he asked.

"I mean, I don't think I'm ugly," I said. "But I don't exactly have people lined up to date me."

Make that *zero* people. I mean, I'd had boyfriends, but not a lot of luck with them. There was my first boyfriend my sophomore year, but dates with him were hanging in his bedroom trying to fend off his roaming hands. Then there was the guy in my junior year who pressured me to put out for three months until he finally gave up trying. He dumped me for someone who would. And my most recent boyfriend, Jed Thomas, took me to senior prom and thought my cherry was his reward for the night. He stopped speaking to me after that night.

A count of three strikes. And there I was, the day of my senior graduation, my virginity still intact. It wasn't that I was saving myself for anything. It was just that, when it came down to it, I felt like there needed to be some kind of spark. The only three guys who had tried were just…boring. No substance. Their minds only on one thing.

I peeked over at the masked guy next to me, and he was looking at me like I was completely crazy.

"What?" I asked, a nervous giggle escaping my lips.

"Just that…you have to know how beautiful you are. I mean, doesn't your boyfriend tell you?"

I laughed hard at this. "Wow," I said once I caught my breath, "that was smooth. I guess this is the part where I tell you I don't have a boyfriend, and where I ask what your girlfriend would think of you sitting here, flirting with me."

His grin intensified. He leaned a little closer. "I don't have a girlfriend," he said. His hand slipped forward, then took mine. "So, mystery single girl, tell me…why are you leaving Sunset Bay, and what will you do at UCSD?"

For the next hour, I told him everything about me—except my name. I told him I was going as an English major, partly because I was good at it and partly because it was versatile, but mostly just to see somewhere new that wasn't too far from home. I would still be in SoCal, but hours away. I told him how I spent my days, which lately was just cleaning house and reading books, the latter of the two being my favorite way to pass the time.

He never once asked me about my family, which I was grateful for. I wish I'd thought to do the same, because when I did, his expression darkened.

"It's just my mom," he finally said, and both of us left it at that.

He told me about his job waiting tables, and his hopes to one day own his own restaurant. I asked if he cooked, and he shrugged.

"I'm not bad at it," he said, the same way I'd said I wasn't ugly. It let me know that he was probably great at it.

I learned that he had already graduated from my high school last year, had been away at college in Denver, but was now on break. He'd heard about the party through a friend and thought it sounded fun.

"Be honest, you were just there to pick up chicks, weren't you?" I nudged his shoulder, and he nudged mine right back.

"Mission accomplished," he joked. But then he turned serious, "Okay, honestly, I was there for a hookup. But when I offered you a ride home, that was literally all I was offering. I'm not trying to hook up with you."

"Oh." I slide my hand from his, then regret my reaction. I was stupidly giving myself away. And over what? Because the guy didn't want to have a casual fling in the front seat of his car? I had spent my whole dating life fending off casual flings. And now I was disappointed?

"Hey there, Sparky, that's not what I meant." He reached over and took my hand again, waiting until I finally looked at him. "You're fucking hot, probably way out of my league. I would nail you if I thought I had half a chance, I didn't want you to think that was the only reason I rescued you from that party."

"God, you must think I'm so pathetic." My cheeks felt flush, my ears burning. "I–"

But I didn't get to say another word, because his mouth was on mine. My mind took a while to catch up, but my body knew exactly what to do. I met each draw of his tongue, each way his teeth tugged at my lip and I nipped at his. My hands found his neck and his found my waist, and when I finally came to my senses, I realized I was cupping his face as we spoke a new language into each other's mouths.

This was what I was looking for. The spark. I didn't know this guy—I didn't even know his name—but I would be damned if I let this opportunity pass us by.

He was the one who stopped, like a brick wall in front of a racing stallion. I panted, feeling my core tighten with need in a way I'd never felt before.

"Keep going," I pleaded. I was completely beyond trying to be coy. Just his kiss was making me desperate.

Our eyes locked as we breathed heavy within the

confines of his car, and I recognized the same need reflected in his expression.

"How much did you drink?" he asked.

This time I wasn't offended. I recognized the questions he wasn't asking. *Are you in the right frame of mind to say yes? Will you regret this tomorrow?*

Would I? No. What I would regret is waking up tomorrow to the knowledge that, once again, Claire Myers had played it safe. I would regret going to college at the end of summer still a virgin, and possibly, just replaying my high school years in another location.

I would regret not taking a chance to do something a little reckless, even though I'd never been so sure about anyone in my entire life as this nameless, faceless boy in the seat next to me.

"I'm sober enough to know I want this," I said. "And I drank enough to want more."

I was all heartbeat as he pulled me on top of him. My back rested against the steering wheel, and my dress pooled around us like airy meringue. His hand tentatively touched my mask, and I jerked back, accidentally hitting the horn at the same time. My nervous giggle led to a soft chuckle from him, until both of us were unable to stop laughing. Whatever happened, it broke the tension.

"Can we leave the mask on?" I asked, covering his hand with my own. He threaded his fingers through mine, then brought them to his lips.

"So you can forget this night?"

I shook my head. "I have a feeling I'm never forgetting this night. But the mask, the fact that you're a stranger, that I don't know your name... The mystery adds something to this, don't you think?"

He smiled, then cupped my cheek.

"How will I call you tomorrow, then?"

"You won't," I said. "Why would you? You'll be in Denver, and I'll be in San Diego. I plan to leave everything behind. I mean..." I paused trying to find a polite way to say it. "If I get to know you, I—"

"It's okay," he said, his lips curving into an irresistible grin. "I get it. But tonight, I get you— Miss Whatever Your Name Is."

I tilted my head back to laugh, but he caught me. Pulling me to him, his mouth crushed on mine. His fingers fumbled with my zipper, then the cool air of night caressed my naked skin. His warm hands covered my breasts as his kiss deepened, and all my senses came alive. It was like my skin was one continuous nerve ending, and every place he touched left goosebumps and tremors in its wake. I felt him harden, the thick denim of his jeans and my thin cotton panties the only barrier between us. I moved against him, feeling as daring as I did nervous, and he groaned against my mouth.

"You don't know what you're doing to me," he said,

his voice husky as his fingers wove through my messy hair.

"I have some idea," I murmured. My lips ached from the forcefulness of his kisses, and I longed for so much more. With a swallow of courage, I cupped his package through his jeans, then raked my finger across the material covering his hardened bulge.

"Fucking hell." He ground himself against my hand as his finger brushed aside my panties and found my slick slit. "You're so fucking wet."

I moaned at his touch, my whole body coming alive at the realization that we were doing this. I was both excited and scared out of my mind. Would it hurt? Right now I wasn't sure I cared. I wanted him in me, to relieve the deep ache in the center of my core. It felt like I would explode if he didn't remedy it immediately.

I undid his zipper, then grasped his unsheathed cock. It wasn't the first cock I'd ever held, but goddamn, it was the nicest. It filled my whole hand, and I raked my fingers over the smooth, hardened curve. He groaned; head tilted back as I continued my exploration. Looking it his masked face, I was overcome by the eroticism of this moment. It was like something straight out of *Fifty Shades*. At least it seemed that way through my lack of experience.

His finger penetrated me, and I yelped in surprise. He stilled, pulling back and looking me in the eye.

"Is this okay?"

I nodded, unsure how to even form words. I'd gone this far before, but the fullness of his finger was unexpected. And if it felt this tight, how was I going to take the fullness of him?

"It's good," I assured him, then moved my hips so that his finger slid in further. Holy hell, it felt good. I panted against him as he withdrew, hovering at the edge.

"More," I breathed, guiding my hips against his hand. He curled his fingers inside me, the heel of his palm brushing against my clit as he rolled my nipple between two fingers. He captured my nipple in his mouth, and a warm sensation bloomed at the top of my head before cascading down my body in waves as I gripped his shirt.

"Oh, God," I panted as his hand kept a steady rhythm. I reveled in the intensity as I prayed it would never end. His hand eventually slowed, though, and my orgasm faded with it. His eyes danced as I moaned in protest, even as I fought for breath.

"Don't worry," he murmured, brushing my hair away from my masked eyes. "I'm not done with you yet." He leaned across me, reaching into the glove compartment and fumbling around. This time, it was his turn to groan. When he leaned back, he shot me a grin, though tinged with frustration.

"I don't have a condom," he explained. "But it's fine,

I want this to be about you."

Before I could respond, he had me on my back, my dress hiked up, and his hands clutching the sides of my panties before he slid them down.

"What do you mean *about me?* Oh!" I sucked in a sharp breath at the warmth of his mouth on my clit before he nestled his tongue into my folds. I clutched his hair as he licked me, the buildup growing with each sensitive stroke. This time, I did explode—my whole body an electrified mess of nerves.

"Please," I begged, my yearning now a full-fledged blaze.

"Tell me what you need." His mouth lapped at me as I lost all sense of place, everything disappearing as he coaxed out wave after wave.

"I need you inside me," I pleaded, my frustration mounting as he shook his head.

"I want to. God, I want to. But I can't."

"I'm clean," I promised. *I've never been with anyone else.*

He paused, the fire a living fortress between us.

"But are you on the pill?"

I considered lying. My need was that great, but I was a terrible liar. Plus, it wasn't fair to him. I shook my head no. He started to pull away, and in desperation, I held on to him.

"We'll be careful," I said. "You can pull out, and I'll get Plan B tomorrow. Just please, don't stop this."

He searched my face, and I saw my own need mirrored in his. I held my breath as he maneuvered himself on top of me. I felt the hot hardness of his cock, pausing at my entrance. For a brief second, I considered the magnitude of what we were about to do. There was no going back. Then, the pain. He thrust and I bit back a scream as something popped inside me. It felt horrible. I clutched his shirt, regretting I ever did this, but also relieved I was getting it over with.

"Hey."

I opened my eyes, and he was peering down at me, a look of concern on his face. "Are you okay?" he asked. He started to pull back, which stung like hell. I held on to him, preventing him from leaving me.

"I'm okay," I said. He brought a finger to my eye and caught a tear. The inside of my mask was wet. I hadn't realized I was crying.

"We can stop," he said, caressing my face, running his thumb over my lips. I covered his hand with my own. I shifted my hips, feeling him move inside me. This time, it felt better—almost good.

"I don't want to stop," I said. "But can you go slow?"

He nodded, leaned down and kissed me gently. He rocked against me, continuing to explore my mouth. The way his tongue danced over mine made me think of his face between my legs, which loosened me up and allowed him to slide in me a little easier. I thought maybe I might climax again, but everything felt so raw, so tight, so full. It stung as he moved, like friction on a scabbed knee. But the pain was mixed with pleasure. I couldn't help but moan into his shoulder, which made his movements quicken. This time, though, it was fine. Good, even. I matched his movements, hoping I knew what I was doing. And then he growled, pulling out and spilling his seed across my thigh. His face looked pained, intense. For a moment, I regretted the stupid masks. I wish I could see his full face.

But this wasn't forever. This was just a night. And he was just a boy who had taken something he didn't even know I'd given him.

"Did it hurt?" I asked. He laughed, then looked at me.

"Not at all. I should be asking you that. It looks like I might have torn you." Then his face took on a look of realization, followed by regret. "Fuck. Are you a–"

"It's my period," I lied. When relief flooded his expression, I knew I made the right decision. "Sorry, it's early. You're probably grossed out."

"Anyone who's grossed out by a period doesn't deserve the girl."

I swear to God, if I weren't leaving at the end of summer, this could be something.

"Do you want to grab a bite to eat?" he asked. "Or maybe stay the night with me? My mom is out of town.

You could even have your own room."

"I can't." Two words I never hated more. But if I stayed, I'd never want to leave. Not him. Not Sunset Bay.

And nothing was going to get in the way of me leaving.

I sat up and put my panties back on, then grabbed my purse as I clutched the door handle.

"Let me at least drive you home," he insisted, but I shook my head. The stranger's car in our driveway flashed through my mind. That, and the embarrassing disarray of our home. Besides, if he knew where I lived, he could find me again….

"It's not far from here," I promised. "Please don't make me show you my house."

I could see the argument all over him, but he finally nodded.

"This could have been something more," he said.

I know. I opened the door, sucking in my breath as the cool night air hit my sweaty skin.

"I'll never forget you," I promised. He caught my hand and pulled it, forcing me to move forward as he kissed my knuckles, then ran my fingers over his cheek. I caught sight of the tattoo on his inner arm. The eye in the middle of the palm seemed to watch me, and I found it comforting. I memorized every line, just like I memorized the perfect green of his eyes that now studied my face.

"You're a mystery," he whispered, "and I will spend the rest of my life wishing I could have solved you."

Chapter 2

Seven years later…

I'm racing against the clock, and it's a losing battle. Why I agreed to make "hot breakfast," I don't know.

"There's enough cereal to feed a small village, and you're scrambling eggs," I mutter, scraping hardened egg off the supposedly non-stick pan, knowing full well he's going to complain.

"Finn, get out here or you're going to miss your bus!" I yell, spooning the egg on a plate beside a blonde piece of buttered toast. At least I got that one right.

He stumbles into the kitchen, one shoe on and the other in his hand. His hair needed a trim two weeks ago, and it's hanging in his eyes.

"I wanted runny eggs, not scrambled," he says as I place his plate in front of him. I ignore his protest and grab a brush off the side table. Thank goodness for convenient clutter.

"The egg broke in the pan, so today you get scrambled. Hold still." I work at a tangle as he tries to eat, but every time I yank, egg falls off his fork and back on his plate.

"Mom!" He tries to smack the brush away, but I hold it out of reach.

"Give me one second," I say, and I'm relieved when he stays still long enough for me to make some sense of his hair. He shovels the rest of the food into his face while I fumble with the knot in his laces. We have one minute left when he's at the door, backpack on, lunch in hand.

"I love you, Finn bug," I say, holding his face and giving him a kiss on the nose. He squinches into a toothless smile, and I know one day he won't let me do this anymore. Right now, I'm soaking it up.

"I love you too, Mom bug," he says, giving me a kiss back on my nose. Then he's out the door. Now that he's a big first grader, he insists that I can't stand with him outside. So I watch from the window as usual, my to-do list running through my head, even as I marvel at how fast it's all going.

The bus arrives, and while he's too old to have his mom out there with him, he turns and waves. I wave back and keep waving until the bus is out of sight, just in case he's watching.

Then it's time to work.

My craft room is an organized disaster. A large table in the center of the room is covered in book swag, all promoting B. A. Warner's upcoming book, *Midnight Fire*. Off to the side are keychains, each with charms and a tiny replica of the book. Another corner holds the resin glitter magnets I set last night. About a hundred ribbon and charm bookmarks are already in pouches, as are the wine stem charms. The early editions of B. A. Warner's book are off to the side, ready for me to package into boxes and send off to the author's street team and select bloggers who will promote the book during launch week with giveaways and hyped-up social media posts.

It's all for Bookish Magic, the business I created when I was pregnant with Finn. I'd always been a huge reader, and I started making little swag gifts for the authors I loved the most as a thank you for entertaining me. One of the authors loved it so much, she commissioned me for a book event. That event led to more authors hiring me for book swag. By the time Finn was born, I had my own apartment, steady work, and never had to worry about childcare or bills. I wasn't rich by any means, but I had enough. It all happened by accident, really, which I guess was the theme once I realized I'd missed my period.

I'm halfway through packaging the book boxes when I hear the front door open and close, followed by the familiar sound of size eight boots on the hardwood.

"Please tell me you brought coffee," I say. Maren holds up a tray with our usual iced almond milk lattes in one hand and a bag of pastries in the other. My stomach rumbles in anticipation. "I probably wouldn't eat if it weren't for you." I get up and follow her to the kitchen table.

"No, you'd probably eat less sweets and more vegetables. But I'm here to give your skinny ass a few curves," she says, grabbing two plates and setting a croissant on each.

"You're one to talk." I lean in and smell the pastry when she places it in front of me. "Oh wow, you got the almond ones."

"Fresh baked too. I'm only here for a few minutes, though."

Maren almost always stops over at my house on her breaks from Insomniacs, the coffee shop just blocks from my house. She says it's better than eating food in her car since she hates what the ocean air does to her dark hair, which today is streaked with neon green. Why the humidity bothers her after twenty-five years of living in Sunset Bay, I don't know.

"I should probably let you know that these are bribe croissants," Maren says before she takes a bite. I put mine on my plate without tasting it and give her a look.

"How much and do I need to call a lawyer?"

"Girl, I'd bring the salted chocolate chip cookies if I

needed bail money," she laughs. "Trust me, you'll like this one."

I sit back in my chair and cross my arms over my chest, refusing to touch the payoff pastry until I know what I'm signing up for.

"So, you know my co-worker Nina?"

"The one who never gets my coffee order straight?"

"Yeah, her barista skills are lacking. But her genetic pool is on fire. You should see her cousin. He just moved to town and doesn't know anyone, and we both thought it might be fun if we set him up with someone cute and single to show him around."

"Oh, hey! You're single! You should totally show him around!" I pick up the croissant and take an enormous bite, figuring I might as well since I'm not about to do what she's asking.

"Claire, you have to date sometime. Finn just turned six, which means you've been single for…" She stops to count on her fingers.

"Almost seven years. Longer, because I wasn't actually dating Finn's dad."

"The mysterious Finn maker," she says dramatically. "Man, that kid is going to be so messed up when he eventually asks about his father, and you can't even tell him his name."

I throw a piece of croissant at her, and it lands in her hair before she can duck.

"Not funny." But really, it's something that's worried me, especially as Finn gets older. It's only a matter of time before he starts wondering why he doesn't have a dad like all the other kids, and I have no idea how to explain this. My fingers automatically reach for the opal starfish necklace at my neck, just like I do whenever I feel out of place. Maren gave it to me the day Finn was born, though she told me it was from Finn. I'd kept it on since then. It reminds me of my two favorite people in the world, and the truest family I have.

"You are not your mother," Maren says, naming the thing I'm really afraid of as I clutch the starfish. "You slept with one guy your whole entire life, and it just so happened he had really ambitious sperm. Besides, if you hadn't, you wouldn't have this amazing kid named Finn."

"You're right," I say, releasing the charm so I can squeeze her arm.

"I'm also right that you need to get out there and start dating." She shushes me when I open my mouth to protest. "I'm serious, Claire. While you're still young and hot. Otherwise gravity is going to take its toll, and, well…" She raises an eyebrow and then glances at my chest.

"Shut up!" I laugh, but I also feel flustered by her insistence. "I know you're just trying to help, but I won't put Finn through that."

Maren gives me a pointed look. "First off, what your mom was doing was not dating. It was bringing home every guy she met and staying out for days at a time. I know you, and there's no way you'd be that kind of mom. But aren't you lonely?"

"Why would I be lonely? I have Finn. And I have you. And on brief occasions, I have my mom. That's all the humans I need in my life, thank you very much." I finish my croissant and clear both of our plates from the table. Maren looks at the time on her phone before she stands, slipping her messenger bag over her head and across her body.

"So, you're not even going to consider this guy? What if I told you he has abs for days and a happy trail that leads to his…"

"Where did you see him? At the strip club?"

"Nah, it wasn't Tuesday," Maren jokes. "He came into the coffee shop."

"He came in without his shirt on?" I raise an eyebrow at her. "What kind of place are you working at?"

"He ordered his coffee black, and you know I can assess a man by his coffee order."

If I hadn't seen it with my own eyes, I would have thought she was lying. But she'd proven it with the guys she'd dated in the past. Elias had been all about the triple shot mochas, and he'd cheated on her within the first few weeks. Shane liked his cappuccinos with extra foam, and well, he swung for the other team now. And then there was Lance…

"Remember the tea drinker from Britain?"

"Oh God, do I." She pretends to faint. Until Lance, Maren thought tea drinkers were a step above cat hoarders. Then he showed her his talents.

"I didn't see you for three full weeks," I say, laughing.

"He was my first tea drinker, and he won't be my last," she promises. Lance had only been in the States for a short time, and Maren didn't have the patience for long distance. Honestly, I don't think Maren has the patience for relationships at all, since she's never stuck with the same man for more than a few months.

"Why can't *you* date your co-worker's cousin if he's so hot."

"You know I don't have time for dating right now. That's what fuck buddies are for."

I roll my eyes. Maren has been seeing this loser named Brock for the past few months, but I've never met the guy. She doesn't even know what kind of coffee he drinks, which shows how little she cares for him. Still, I wish she's settle down with someone who was worth it rather than these loser guys taking up space in her bed.

"Besides, I have a gig almost every night," Maren continues. "Which reminds me, I have one tonight at Hillside in the Marina District. It's early and family friendly, so you could totally come with Finn." A few years ago, Maren got serious about her music, never turning down a gig no matter how awful the pay was. Now she's like the Joan Jett of the local scene and has amassed a small gathering of fans. But I know Maren has bigger ideas for her music career, one that will get her out of coffee for good and into huge stadiums. "So, can you come?" she asks.

"Hmm, let's see. I have a standing date with Outlander tonight, but I suppose I could cancel."

"Girl, it's early enough that you could go, eat dinner, totally fangirl on me, and make it home in time to see Jamie's butt on your tiny phone screen. Speaking of butts, you should see Nina's cousin."

I glare at her as she walks out the door laughing.

Chapter 3

I use the time before Finn comes home to get some of my errands done. I start with the post office, lugging a dolly full of packages up the ramp. The carriers here know me by name. Sometimes this feels like my version of a social life as I make small talk with the clerk stamping my packages.

When I head for the store, the street I usually drive to get home is blocked with traffic, so I turn down a side street that will take me miles out of my way—and right near my old neighborhood.

I haven't seen my mom in months. The last time I came by this guy, Duke, answered the door, then he disappeared in a back bedroom as if he didn't want anything to do with her, either. She was lying on the couch surrounded by coffee cups filled with ashes and cigarette butts, and a few empty bottles next to a plate of food with something unrecognizable rotting on it. Across from her, some talk show blared on the TV. Between the noise, the stench of smoke and grease, and the sight of my mom's obvious deterioration, I couldn't stay longer than ten minutes.

My stomach twists as I near her house. In the months I haven't seen her, the guilt has been a constant companion. She needs help, but I don't know what to do for her. I'm mad at every way she's failed me, and her current mental state is a part of that list. She did this to herself.

I slow to a stop, eyeing the home I grew up in as I fight my nausea. Besides the overgrown lawn and the dying plants out front, it's still the same house. The peeling yellow paint on the siding. The white door with scuff marks at the bottom. The window covered with cardboard that had been broken by one of her old boyfriends during one of their fights. If I look long enough, I swear I'll see a younger version of my mom— one that hid her drug use and alcoholism behind a wide painted smile as she greeted me after school. But I always smelled the skunky scent of old beer or the burnt plastic odor from the glass pipe she hid. Even before I knew what it was, I smelled it.

Mustering my courage, I walk the path to the door, stepping over weeds growing between the cracks. I used to keep up my mom's front yard so that Finn had a place to play when we visited. But it's been almost a year since I've brought him here, and almost as long since I've pulled any of her weeds or mowed the lawn. I don't think anyone else has, either.

I hold my hand up to knock, but stop short, nerves twisting my stomach into a double knot. It's just a place. It's so silly I'm even affected this way. And yet, my insides don't get the memo. I feel like I'm twelve all over again, unsure what I'll see on the other side of the door.

I rap my knuckles on the door before I can lose my nerve. I never step inside without knocking first because I don't know who else is here. I half hope no one will answer so I can leave while feeling like I tried my best to be a dutiful daughter.

Heavy footsteps sound on the other side of the door, and I sigh as I straighten up. The door swings open, and I'm surprised to see Duke is still here. My mom isn't usually one to keep the same guy around for months at a time. With his grease-stained Henley shirt, leather vest, and long grey hair that matches his even longer beard, the guy looks something between biker and homeless— but not much different from any of the other guys she's brought home.

"Is Mom here?" I ask, even though I know she is. She doesn't have a car anymore, and there really isn't anywhere for her to go. Not even the grocery store, thanks to the automatic delivery system I've set her up on. I still get billed, which has been my one way of knowing she's alive. Or at least someone at the house is receiving them.

He opens the door wider, then nods toward the living room without saying a word. I'm not sure I've ever heard Duke speak, now that I think of it. He turns and walks away as I step into the house, just like he did the last time.

One whiff, and I know nothing's changed. There's a nauseating chemical smell, and smoke sits heavy in the air. When I turn the corner to the living room, my mom is still on the couch. If she wasn't wearing different clothes, I'd think she hadn't moved since I was last here. The TV is blasting away, and a slow trail of smoke rises from the lit cigarette on an ash-filled plate. My mom is passed out, her mouth open. I note the two empty beer bottles lying near the plate.

"Mom, get up," I say, nudging her before snuffing out the burning cigarette. My knee bumps something on the floor, and I hear something roll under the couch. Leaning down, I fumble blindly until my hand closes around something glass and circular. My heart sinks as I stare at the crack pipe in my hand.

My mother makes a small noise, and I pocket the pipe quickly. Her eyes remain closed, but she smacks her mouth. She's wearing shorts and a tank top, and I can tell she's lost weight by the way her knees jut out and the gaunt look of her cheeks. Her sallow skin appears like worn paper and her stomach protrudes like a small melon, making the rest of her body appear that much more skeletal.

I turn off the TV and can suddenly think. It allows me the space to take in the mess around me.

"Mom," I try again, this time shaking her shoulder. She's so tiny now, her whole shoulder bone fits in the palm of my hand. I feel like I could break her. She remains asleep.

I leave her be and start picking up things in the living room. I only have a few more hours before Finn is out of school, so I don't plan to stay long. But the least I can do is straighten up.

I bring the empty bottles and dirty dishes into the kitchen, and exhale at the sight. More dishes are piled in the sink, crusted with moldy food. To-go containers litter the countertops. The floor is sticky, and I regret the cute Mary Jane shoes I wore today. Grease streaks run down the walls, and something furry disappears behind the water heater. When I take a closer look, I see rat droppings and a hole that leads to the covered porch.

I get to work scraping the plates and stacking them, then scrubbing the sink before filling it with water. I work in batches—filling the dish rack with clean plates and then drying them before putting them away. I go through the fridge too, throwing full containers of food in the garbage as I hold my breath, then dragging the garbage bags to the can out back. Before I leave the can, I pull the pipe out of my pocket. I bury it down deep into the trash, hoping it will remain there until the garbageman collects it.

Back in the house, the dishes and counters are as clean as they're going to get. I wring dirty water from the mop before tackling the floor one more time. By the time I'm done, the house looks somewhat decent, and my back and legs are killing me. I put on a pot of coffee, breathing in the earthy aroma while I wait. Then, with a steaming cup, I return to the living room.

My mom's eyes are closed, but when I wave the cup under her nose, her mouth twitches. She opens her eyes partway, but it's a struggle.

"Hey there, baby," she slurs, then groans as she moves to sit up. Her thin hair is piled on the top of her head, with a few knots at the back. I hand her the cup, fighting the urge to run a brush through her hair. Like she's the child and I'm the mom she was supposed to be.

"Drink. It will help."

It's black and probably too hot, but she drinks it anyway. After a few sips, her eyes cross a few times before focusing back on me.

"Did you bring Finn?"

"He's still in school," I say, even though we've had this conversation before. I told her to get clean and start taking care of herself, and I'd think about letting her visit

Finn.

"Next time," she says. I want to argue with her, to remind her of my boundary. But the state she's in, I know it would only upset me more.

"So, you're still with Duke."

She makes a noise in her throat but doesn't confirm or deny.

"He helps buy food," she says. I shake my head.

"No, Mom. *I* buy your food. He just eats it."

"He buys the beer and cigarettes, and sometimes brings food home from Pinko's," she says, then gives a throaty laugh. I don't join her. She's only just woken up, but I already want to go home. I pretend to look at the clock on the mantle, then stand and stretch.

"I better get going," I say. "Finn will be home from school soon, and we're headed to Hillside to see Maren sing. You remember Maren, don't you?"

She nods, setting her coffee on the table next to her and grabbing her smokes. "I thought she disappeared, off on one of her drug binges. That girl was always trouble."

"That was a long time ago," I point out. I don't point out the irony of her remark. I tilt my head toward her as she lights her cigarette. "Hey, you need to stay awake when you smoke. One of these days, you're going to burn this house down."

"And then I'll be dead, and you won't have to worry about me anymore, will you?"

I'm not shocked by this statement. She says something like this almost every time I see her.

"I don't think we have enough money in this house to cover your funeral." At this, I get one of her wide-mouthed grins. Despite the way her teeth have rotted in the front, I see the mom I knew from time to time. The one who brushed the hair from my face before kissing my forehead, and who made my lunches. The one who skipped drinking and dates so she could stay home with me to watch a movie. By the time I was fourteen, that mom disappeared completely. But for a time, I had her.

I stand, brush the few wisps of hair away from her face, and then kiss her forehead. Her skin feels like leather under my lips. "It was good to see you."

"It's good to see you too, Claire. Don't be a stranger."

I brush the tears from my face as I drive away, feeling dirty for having been in that house for so long. Feeling guilty that I'm not saving her from it. Feeling shame that I don't want to. For all the ways she's wrecked me, I'm still tethered to her by some invisible string—a bond that keeps me from severing ties altogether. I have to know she's okay, even as I resent her. And I'm not her keeper.

Why can't I just let her go?

Chapter 4

Finn swings his legs as he dips a French fry in tartar sauce. How I made a kid who likes anything made with sweet pickles is beyond me. But when you have a picky eater like mine, you learn to never question the foods he *does* like. You just keep a healthy supply of it. Or pray that the restaurant has it on hand.

Thankfully, Hillside does. They also have a killer Sonoma salad, full of apples, walnuts, raisins, and feta cheese, topped with smoked chicken. I've made a serious dent in it, while Finn has only touched his fries and not his burger. I have a feeling I'm looking at my lunch for tomorrow.

Maren is on stage, her eyes closed as she grips the microphone. Her voice is powerful enough to not even need the mic, and honestly I think this place is too small for her. But her fanbase showed up, and they're dancing at the foot of the stage while she nails every key. Every so often, she looks out at me and winks, and I blow her kisses. We're seated at the back corner of the restaurant to save Finn's little ears, but I'm thrilled when he takes time out from his French fries to watch his Auntie Maren sing on stage. She promised me tonight's performance was family friendly, and I cringe as she sings the F word for the third time that night.

"Fuck, fuck, fuck," Finn sings softly as he scoops a mountain of tartar sauce onto a tiny fry.

"Finn, sweetie, we don't say that word. And easy on the tartar sauce, that french fry looks like it needs a break."

He pops the fry in his mouth and grins, showing me a slush of fry and sauce. I wrinkle my nose in mock disgust, then show him my chewed-up salad.

"Gross!" he laughs, and I'm pretty sure it's because they're vegetables, and has nothing to do with their masticated state.

On her break, Maren says hello to a few fans before heading to our table. She grabs my fork and starts in on my salad, eating as if she hasn't had anything all day. I'm full anyway, so I push the plate toward her and nod my head, indicating she should finish it. I still have my mom on the brain, and if Finn weren't here, I'd want to talk it out with Maren—even though the story hasn't changed. My mom is a wreck, and I'm always going to be the one picking up the pieces.

"See that guy over there?" Maren murmurs, snapping me out of my thoughts. I turn my head in the direction she's looking, noticing the guy she's referring to at the bar. *Noticing* is too small a word. He's wearing a loose-fitting t-shirt, but it doesn't hide the shape of his hardened pecs or broad shoulders. His tan arms are completely covered with black and grey tattoos, only accentuating the fact that this guy is ripped. His dark hair is mussed like he's spent the day surfing, which wouldn't be abnormal here in Sunset Bay. But it's his smile that gets me the most. He has a clean-cut beard that perfectly outlines his chiseled jaw, and as he talks with the bartender, his mouth melts into an irresistible smirk, as if he's holding a secret. It makes me mentally lean in, wanting to uncover whatever he isn't saying behind that smile. Maren nudges me and I realize I'm smiling, too. I quickly break my gaze only to notice her Cheshire Cat grin. I realize immediately who he is.

"Oh no," I say, shaking my head.

"Oh yes," she answers. "That's Ethan Chance, the guy I was telling you about."

"You can't be serious."

"I'm dead serious. Look at him!"

"No, I mean you can't be serious that you brought me here to meet him while I'm with…" I nod my head toward Finn who is too busy swirling a soggy fry in tartar sauce to even know what we're talking about.

"No, you dolt. I know better than that. I brought you here so you could get a preview before you go out with him tomorrow night."

"Maren, I told you…" I stop, look at Finn. "I can't," I hiss.

"Yes, you can," she says. "I saw the look on your face when I pointed him out. You think he's cute."

"I think a lot of guys are cute. It doesn't mean I'll go out with any of them."

Maren stares at me, her eyes hyper-focusing like she will bore holes into my head. I've seen her use this look in public, and it's intimidating as hell. But I'm *mad* as hell. I match her stare, refusing to look away until she sighs.

"Just one date," she pleads. "I'm not asking anything more. Just one date, and I'll shut up for the rest of my life about your sad, pathetic, nonexistent dating life."

I mull this over. When we were kids, Maren was infamous for making promises she never intended to keep. But that was before she got sober. Now that we're older, Maren's word is solid. She'd also never do anything that would jeopardize Finn's or my safety and comfort.

"One date, and you'll lay off?" I can't believe I'm agreeing to this. I peek at the guy again, losing myself in the way his cheek creases when he smiles, kind of wishing I could get a closer look.

"I promise. Oh my God, I can't believe you said yes."

"You didn't really give me much choice," I say, wrinkling my nose. But I also can't stop the butterflies from swirling inside my belly.

As soon as Maren starts her next set, I flag the waiter for a box and the check. While I wait, I steal glances at the bar. The guy looks like an Ethan, whatever that's supposed to mean. At least he's nice to look at, which assures me that even if he's a dud, this one and only date of ours will have a nice view.

"Mom, I have to go to the bathroom."

I tear my eyes away from Ethan to see Finn clutching himself. The waiter shows up with my receipt as Finn runs from the table, and I grab the receipt and the box of food and tail after him. But Finn is too quick. I want to take him in the girl's bathroom with me, but he bolts into the boy's bathroom before I can stop him.

"Ugh, Finn," I mutter. I wait outside the bathroom, the mama bear in me staring down every man that exits while Finn takes his sweet time.

"Is this the line?"

I turn, and there's Ethan staring down at me. Now that he's close, I see that his eyes are a rich chocolate brown, and I can see my reflection in them. I stumble backwards, and he quickly grabs hold of me and keeps me upright.

"Thanks, I've only been walking for a few days now," I stammer, and he laughs at my attempt at a joke.

"They say it's like riding a bicycle," he jokes back. And then he flashes me a grin and I swear my knees go wobbly. Luckily he doesn't notice as he skirts around me and heads into the bathroom.

Finn comes out a minute later, and I tuck his hand in mine and make a beeline for the exit, resisting the urge to glance behind me.

"Damn you, Maren," I mutter once Finn is buckled into the backseat of the car. But I'm smiling. "One date. That's it. Then it's over."

Finn is hungry when we get home—big surprise—and apparently only waffles will do. With just half a salad in me, I assess there's a small pocket in my own belly for a treat. So I pull out the waffle iron and whip up a batch. As a special treat, I scoop a little ice cream on each of them, topped with a dash of maple syrup. I'm sure I'm going down as the worst mom in the world after a dinner of French fries, but I can't resist his dimpled smile as I set the plate in front of him.

"Today was fun," he says, then spoons a huge bite into his mouth.

"Smaller bites, please. And what was so fun about it?"

He finishes chewing, then wipes his mouth on his

arm. I want to correct him, but I've learned through trial and error that too many corrections make his ears close.

"I got to be line monitor at school today, and Miss Lane said I did a good job leading the class. Then at recess, Kala chose me first to be on his kickball team. We finished all our work in class so I didn't have homework. And then I got to eat French fries for dinner, and now waffles for dessert." He flashes me his gummy smile, and I can see one of his adult teeth is starting to grow in.

"Know what I loved best about today?"

"What?" he asks, his mouth full of ice cream. A little drips on the table, and he wipes it with his hand. I shake my head but laugh it off.

"I liked being with you."

"Like when we went to eat at Auntie Maren's?"

"That was Hillside restaurant, but yes. When we went to see Auntie Maren sing, and I got to sit with my favorite person in the whole wide world."

"Me?" His eyes light up as I nod. He finishes off his ice cream, then swings himself down from the chair. Carefully, he picks his bowl up and brings it to the sink. The rare gesture makes him seem years older, and I have to will myself to not tear up.

"Can I take my own bath tonight?" he asks. This was a change. Usually he argues against taking baths at all. Still, the question rocks me a little. It's just another step at him asserting his independence.

"How about this. I will let you bathe yourself, but with the door open, and only if you promise to wash really well." I know that last one was a long shot, but it doesn't hurt to try. He runs from the table before I can change my mind, though I follow him in so I can start the water and make sure it's the right temperature.

"I got it, Mom," he sighs, and I give him a sideways look.

"I said you can take your own bath. But I still get to run the water and make sure you don't make waterfalls in the bathroom." He grins, then runs to his room to get undressed. I shut off the water just as he comes back, wearing a robe and looking way too old to be my little guy.

"Okay, Mom," he says, looking up at me with exasperated eyes. It hurts my heart a little to know he wants privacy, but I guess it's all part of growing up. I'm not ready for this. I shrug my shoulders in a teasing way as I exit, and he nudges the door behind me, though I note how he keeps it slightly ajar. Both of our bedrooms are on either side of the bathroom, and I sit on my bed pretending to read a book, when really I'm just making sure he doesn't drown. He hums while he's washing, and I smile as his little voice echoes off the walls.

Seven years ago, I had no idea what I was doing. I was only eighteen when the nurse placed this tiny bundle in my arms as if I could be trusted with a human life. My mom had showed up at the hospital by some miracle, though I could smell the alcohol on her from across the room. She'd offered to stay with me, and part of me was tempted to say yes since I had no idea what I was doing. Luckily, Maren was there too, and she said she was already staying with me even though we hadn't discussed it. Between the two of us, Finn survived his first week. But once Maren left, it was just Finn and me. I remember the first night alone, feeling like a failure as Finn screamed his head off. Eventually he tired himself out, nursing noisily as he watched me with wide wary eyes.

"Look kid, I didn't sign up for this either," I told him. "But if we're going to survive this, you gotta work with me. We're on the same team, you and me. And I promise you, I will always have your back. So trust me, all right?"

And it's like this light bulb went off. He was mine. And I was his. I'd spent most of his first week feeling like I was playing defense. I was running on fumes, stunk like spit up and shit, and felt sticky and needed a shower. But in that moment, I realized we were in this together, and would be for life. I felt a huge ball of warmth expand in my chest as I watched him nurse, and I realized I'd never loved anyone or anything with such ferocity in my life.

"Mom, I'm done!" Finn calls now from the bathroom. I hide a grin as he lets me help him out of the tub and run a towel over him. His hair is wet but unwashed, so I spray a little leave-in conditioner in it.

"Haircut tomorrow, okay buddy?"

"Okay," he groans. He brushes his teeth, and I get all the spots he missed. Then he laughs as I swoop him into my arms, cradling him as if he were my little baby all over again. My big, heavy baby, that is. I drop him on his bed with a grunt, then make a show of stretching my back.

"You are growing up too fast," I say, ruffling his damp hair.

Even though he's a big kid now, he settles into bed with the blanket under his chin as I continue reading from *Mrs. Piggle Wiggle*, the chapter book we started earlier this week. It's my own childhood copy, and a little worn at that. But it reminds me of younger days when my mom stayed with me at bedtime and read me stories about a little old lady who had a cure for every ailment.

"Can I stop taking a bath so I can grow plants on my arms?" Finn asks when we're done.

"Not on your life," I say, kissing the top of his head. "Sweet dreams, Finn bug."

He burrows down under his blankets until I only see the top of his dark head.

"Sweet dreams, Mom bug."

Chapter 5

As I get ready for my date with Ethan, I realize how out of practice I am. When I say out of practice, I mean that I have no experience. Zero. Zilch. Nada. I mean, does high school dating even count? My dates in high school consisted of going out with someone who thought I was cute enough to ask. My relationships were short-lived. And dates? Beyond school dances, they usually consisted of watching movies in a public area of the house to make sure we weren't having sex. The only grown-up date I can think of is the ride home with that guy from the masquerade party, and we all know how that ended up.

Wait, do I bring condoms? No. We're not having sex. Is it the guy's responsibility if we do?

I scour my room, as if miraculously, a condom or chastity belt might appear. I don't have any kind of protection at all. Why would I? I don't date.

"Is that what you're wearing?"

I look up from the drawer I'm rummaging through to see Maren in the doorway. Then I look down at my outfit. It's a cardigan sweater with a pair of jeans and my favorite tennis shoes. I also have on my favorite t-shirt— the one that says, "Surely not everyone was Kung Fu fighting."

"We're just going out for dinner, right?"

"Right," Maren says, heading straight to my closet. "But you're not having dinner with me, you're having dinner with a guy who might want to end your drought, if you catch my drift." She starts pulling clothes off the hangers and throwing them in a pile on my bed.

"I'm not having sex with him, if that's your drift," I say, leafing through the clothes. "Oh, this one's yours. You left it here last time you came over."

She takes the black dress from my hands, then holds it in front of her. She looks at me, then back at the dress before tossing it back.

"Put it on," she commands, and I stare at her.

"Maren, you're like a toothpick. There's no way this will fit me."

"It will," she promises. "You have perfect curves, and this will show off every one of them."

"That's what I'm afraid of," I mutter. But I do it anyway. As I'm changing, Finn shuffles into the room and joins my clothes pile on the bed. He has his RC stunt car with him, and he sets to work making a mountain racing course with the pile, driving the car over buttons and zippers into pleats and cuffed hems.

"This is too tight," I insist to Maren. The dress clings to every inch of me, with a neckline that reveals a bit more cleavage than I'm comfortable with. The back is even lower, proving there's no safe way to wear a bra with it. At least my ass isn't showing, but it's shorter than my favorite pair of shorts. I start to tug it down, but I stop when I realize it just enhances the view of my cleavage.

Maren's eyes are wide, and her smile grows into something wicked.

"It's perfect, but I agree, it's not totally you."

I start to tug it off, but she clears her throat and gives me a narrow-eyed look. She tosses me a loose crop top sweater from the back of my closet.

"I did not give you permission to change," she says.

"I didn't realize I needed it in my own house." I shrug the sweater over my shoulders, and then check myself in the mirror. Surprisingly, it's not bad. The dress is still tight and short, but the sweater adds the modesty it was missing. It's definitely sexier than anything I've ever worn, but it doesn't reach Maren's level of vixen. I turn side to side, studying every angle before finally giving Maren the look of approval she's been waiting for. She slips off her chunky boots and hands them to me.

"Try it with these," she says. "They're actually quite

comfortable," she adds as I eye their platform height.

I slip them on, and suddenly my five-foot-three height is more of a five-six, and I look tall and skinny. And she's right—they're comfortable. I feel like I'm on a runway as I walk across the room, testing them out.

"You look weird," Finn says, studying me.

"Trust me, Finn, this is a good kind of weird," Maren says, ruffling his hair. I wrinkle my nose at both of them. Then I turn back to my reflection. I definitely look weird, and if I could look sexy in a pair of leggings and an oversized tee, I'd do it. But this is a good alternative.

"Hey Finnster, want to go set up the Marvel marathon while I order us pizza?" Maren asks. Finn's eyes lit up, and he bolts for the TV in the living room.

"You're a good aunt, you know that?"

"Yeah, well, there's an ulterior motive. I need him gone because you and I need to have the talk." Maren opens her purse and hands me a couple thin square packages. My face flushes as I drop the condoms on the bed.

"We're not having sex."

"That might be your plan right now, but you and I both know how Finn got here."

"Hey, if you hadn't ditched me that night, I wouldn't have ended up in a car with old what's his name."

She tries to hide her discomfort, but I recognize it immediately.

"Maren, I'm teasing. That was a lifetime ago, and both of us learned some hard lessons."

"I know," she says. But her usual fire is gone, and I feel bad. I sit on the bed next to her.

"If I could have taken away all the bad stuff that happened to you, I would," I tell her. "But if it meant taking away that night, I'm sorry, I couldn't do it. Finn is the best thing that's ever happened to me, and I give you partial credit for helping the stars align. But do I blame you? Not at all. I make my own decisions, and I was fully aware of what I was doing, even if I had no clue what would come of it."

Maren nudges me and gives a soft smile. I know her mood shift has more to do with her past mistakes than about what happened with Finn's father. There's a lot she's had to overcome, and while she's a completely different person now, I know her past haunts her.

"Forget it," she says, pulling me up with her as she stands. "I take full credit for that boy. I'm the one to blame for how awesome of a kid he is."

"You're right. I had nothing to do with it." I groan as she pushes the condoms back in my hand, though I stick them in my bag anyway.

"You don't have to use them, but it doesn't hurt to just carry them. And you know I won't judge if you *do* end up using them. The man is hot."

"Being hot doesn't mean he'd be a good role model

for Finn."

Maren shakes her head. "Claire Gertrude Myers, do not put that kind of pressure on this date."

"That is not my middle name."

"I'm serious. This is a first date, and the biggest reason you're going is to just get your head in the dating game."

"I thought it was to show him around," I say.

She waves her hand. "He's from around here."

"What?" I glare at her, and she just rolls her eyes in response.

"You cannot be a spinster forever. Besides, I didn't totally lie. Ethan moved away for a few years, but now he's back. It's possible this town has become unfamiliar and he needs a pretty girl like you to show him around."

"I'm not a spinster."

"You're headed there, sister."

I grab my purse, even though I'm now less confident about this date than ever. "So, if I'm not playing tour guide, what exactly did you girls tell Ethan about me?"

"The truth," Maren says. "That we're setting him up with a space cowgirl who knows how to use a whip."

"Maren."

She laughs, following me out the room. "Relax. I told Nina to tell Ethan that you both had a lot in common."

"And what would that be?"

She shrugs. "You both like to eat."

I'm supposed to meet Ethan at six at Coastal Plate, a new restaurant near the beach. I get there early just so I can scope out the place and am relieved to see that it's fairly laid back. The people coming and going are wearing everything from board shorts to dresses like mine, so at least I'm dressed appropriately. The fashion styles also tell me this place won't be way over my budget. I'm determined to go Dutch. I may be lacking in dating knowledge, but I do know that certain expectations may come if I let him buy my meal. No thank you. Besides, I don't need any man to think I need a benefactor.

It's about five minutes till when I start stressing about what to do next. Do I show up now and risk getting there first? Or maybe I want to. Maybe it's a power move to be the first one there.

Why do I need a power move?

"Stop overthinking, Claire," I tell my reflection in the rear-view mirror. I check my teeth, reapply my lipstick, then open my door.

Right into the car next to me.

"Damn!" I lean over to see if I made a mark, just as I feel someone's presence next to me.

"Is there a dent?"

I look up and there's Ethan, looking just as good as he smells. Seriously. He smells like he just walked out of the shower and into a forest full of citrus and pine trees.

I inhale, taking in the way his trim and muscular body fills out his classic short sleeved shirt and chinos. Now up close, I can see the intricate design of his tattoos covering his tan arms, including an incredible image of a lion woven into a variety of mandala patterns.

"Hi," he says, and I stop staring at his arms. My face heats up as I realize he asked me a question and I don't know what it was. I remember just as he leans down, his finger gliding over the small dent in his door.

"I'm so sorry," I say, rubbing at it as if I can miraculously fix it. "I'll pay for it. I can give you my insurance information. This was completely my fault."

He pauses, tilting his head. "Do I…"

My face grows even warmer as I realize he's trying to place where he's seen me before.

"Last night. Hillside." I'm hoping my clipped sentences downplay all the ways I find him attractive, including my stalking session with Maren last night.

The recognition crosses his face like a ray of light. "I remember you." He breaks into an angled grin. "What, are you stalking me?"

If my face keeps heating up like this, I'm going to have to bring a fan.

"I'm Claire," I say, and I can't help noticing the way his smile broadens.

"Thank goodness, because I thought I was going to have to cancel on my blind date so I could take you to dinner instead."

Maybe I'm supposed to be flattered by this, but it speaks volumes. He's a player. My eyes narrow, and I push my mouth into a small smile.

"I'm really sorry about your door. Get my information from Nina and I'll pay for the damage." I start to get back into my car.

"Claire."

I hate my reaction to my name on his lips. It slides off his tongue and over his lips like warm honey. I stop, face him.

"Ethan," I say, and the crease in his cheek deepens.

"I knew it was you the whole time," he says.

I search his expression, not sure if I believe him.

"My cousin told me you were nervous about meeting some strange guy, so I'm the one who suggested you show up at Hillside so you could see I wasn't some scary guy. I didn't know who you were when I bumped into you then, but the fact that you're here is too big of a coincidence."

"It's a small town," I say, "and this is currently the hottest restaurant. It's not that big of a coincidence."

"True, but Nina also told me you always wear a starfish necklace with blue opal." He reaches toward me and pulls the necklace out from underneath my sweater in a move that feels more intimate than it should. My skin tingles after his fingers leave my skin. I clear my throat, trying to hide my sudden breathlessness.

"So, you weren't going to dump me just because you saw a pretty face?"

He shakes his head. "No, but I'm glad you're you. My cousin told me you were pretty, but I had no idea."

This time, I'm flattered.

Chapter 6

I'm not good with strangers. Not in real life, and not now as I sit across the table from Ethan. We have the menus in front of us, serving as a barrier to the awkward conversations we're sure to share. So the reality of this date is hitting me hard, and I spend the longest time possible figuring out what to order so I can avoid talking to him.

It's not long enough. The waiter comes and I know I need to make a decision or neither of us will eat.

"The turkey burger and sweet potato fries," I say, and Ethan gets a bison burger with onion rings.

"And to drink?"

I'd planned on only water, but when Ethan orders a beer, I change my mind and go for a vodka soda. Maybe it will help my nerves.

I look in Ethan's direction and blush when I see his

deep brown eyes studying me. A nervous laugh escapes my throat as I give him a quizzical look. He offers a sheepish grin.

"You just seem familiar."

"I mean, we did run into each other last night when I was apparently stalking you," I say. He laughs at this.

"No, it's something else. It's probably nothing."

"Well, I grew up here, and my friend Maren says you did too."

"Maren's the one who was singing last night, right? That girl's got chops," he says when I nod. "And yeah, I went to Pacific High, graduated eight years ago."

"I graduated seven years ago from there, so you probably saw me in the halls."

"Maybe." He tilts his head, giving me a sly smile. "But if I'd seen you, I'd probably want to get to know you better."

"Sure," I laugh. "A senior going after a lowly junior. Besides, I doubt you would have seen me. I was a head down kind of student."

"So, you're a scholar. What college did you go to?"

I'm grateful that the waiter gets here with our drinks before I can answer. It gives me time to think. I don't want to call missing college a regret, because Finn is a greater gift than a degree could ever be. Plus, I've done quite well for myself without going to college. But it was a decision I never would have made for myself. Before

Finn, my plan to go to college weighed less on education and more on being my ticket out of here. And while I wouldn't give up anything about the life I have now, there are times I wonder where I'd be if I hadn't had Finn. It wouldn't be in Sunset Bay, that's for sure.

So the answer to Ethan's question is more complicated than telling him I never went. It introduces the dilemma about the right thing to do here: tell Ethan I have a kid, or don't.

I take a long sip of my drink, hoping he'll forget that he asked me about college. The vodka definitely helps loosen my shoulders, but it does nothing to erase his question. He stays silent, waiting for my answer.

"The college of life," I finally say. I don't see us having a future behind this night; there's no reason to bring up Finn.

"Ah, the best college there is," he answers, and I relax as he rolls past my omission. "I went to college in Colorado, but learned more about life from living with roommates and paying bills than I did learning about dead writers and antiquated stories."

"Hey, some of those dead writers wrote some pretty epic shit," I say.

He leans back in his chair, an amused look on his face. I feel a flame of annoyance at his apparent arrogance.

"Convince me," he says.

"Mary Shelley's *Frankenstein*," I spit out. "There are so many themes in there, and all of them point to struggles within the human condition."

"Such as?"

I think for a moment, trying to sum up one of my favorite gothic novels in a few short sentences.

"I mean, there's the theme that science and technology can go too far, which is something we're definitely seeing in the present. Think of social media and how it was created to build connections. But now, people are connecting on less of an emotional and personal level, and more as a network to further their own ambitions, be it business or just gaining a following. So I believe Shelley definitely wrote parallels about technology when it comes to *Frankenstein* and our humanity. But that's only surface level when it comes to the underlying theme of *Frankenstein*."

"And that is…" Ethan is leaning forward, completely focused on everything I'm saying—which I realize is too much.

"How isolation is the true monster. I'm sorry, I'm talking way too much, and you didn't come here for some nerdy literature lecture."

"No, keep going. I'm interested," he says. I laugh, and he places his hand on mine. It's warm and soft, and yet his grip is firm enough that I feel a sense of safety in his touch. "How is 'isolation' the monster?"

I don't move a muscle as he keeps his hand on mine. I'm slightly embarrassed how my geeky book side is coming out.

"Because isolation is at the root of everything that goes wrong in the story."

He listens intently as I describe how the doctor detaches from society as he obsesses over playing god, and then how the monster seeks revenge against the doctor after he's rejected.

"If the doctor had just shown the monster love and taken responsibility for his creation, the monster never would have lashed out."

"I think I understand," Ethan says. "So, Shelley is saying that the root of evil in this world is isolation."

"I mean, that simplifies a very complex problem, and I wouldn't say it's the root of *all* problems. But I think when someone has an emotionally negative reaction, it's generally because they don't feel seen or understood by those closest to them. People with high emotional intelligence generally have a strong support system at home."

The moment the words leave my mouth, I'm suddenly struck by a feeling I can't name. I pull my hand out from under his and flash a smile to hide this weird and sudden sentiment, which is only enhanced when I see a flash of understanding cross Ethan's face. I'm sure I'm just projecting, imagining he knows what I'm thinking. But then he speaks.

"Did _you_ lash out?"

I take a moment, processing what he's asking.

"You know more about me than you're letting on, don't you?" I finally say. I take another sip of my drink, but only because my hands are shaking.

"No," he says with a laugh. "It's just, you speak about the theme of isolation as if you know it intimately. It was a wild guess, and probably not right."

"No, it's right," I say, and I'm embarrassed by the way my eyes are filling with tears. "I'm sorry, I don't mean to get emotional. It's just that you put a name to something I wasn't quite recognizing. Maybe that's why I love this story so much, because I sympathize with the monster, even though I never really acted out as a kid."

Is getting pregnant at eighteen and asserting independence from my mom an act of defiance? Maybe. I brush that thought aside as I describe a mother who was barely home, a father I never knew, and how I basically raised myself until I moved out at eighteen.

"That's impressive. Most eighteen-year-olds are still figuring out how to not spend all their money on DoorDash and expensive toys, and you were spending it on rent and utilities. You must have landed a killer job."

"I did. I work for myself," I say, laughing when I see his eyes widen. I tell him about my book swag business and how lucky I was to start it at the beginning of an apparent book boom. "Some of my best customers are those teens you speak of, who also happen to be avid bookworms."

"No wonder you're so passionate about books," he says. "That explains a lot. I bet you were a huge reader."

"Were?" I ask. I pick up my purse and rummage inside, pulling out a copy of *For the Birds*, the current romance book I was reading. "I had a backup plan if you ended up being a complete jerk."

"I'm glad I passed the test," he laughs.

"The night is still young," I tease as I return the book to my bag. "What about you?"

"Well, I'd like to own my own bar. I actually work at Hillside, but you saw me on a night off. I'm such a loser, I like hanging out there when I'm not working." He gives me a crooked grin, and I kind of melt into his sideways smile. "My plan is to learn enough about the business working under my boss Pete and save enough money that I can start my own bar."

The waiter brings our food, putting a pause on talking. But as I take the first bite of my burger, I'm struck by how the conversation between Ethan and me has been flowing since we got here. I'd anticipated a date filled with awkward silences and forced small talk, and instead I've found someone who is interested in what I have to say. He's someone I want to get to know much better. There's still so much I don't know about him, but everything I do know, I like. He's smart and funny, and I love that he has plans for the future. Plus he's sexy as hell. It's too early to tell, but I cautiously think about what it would be like to bring him home to meet Finn.

"Now that I know what you *do* want," I say, setting my burger down. "How about what you *don't* want."

"Kids," he says.

He knocks the wind right out of me with that answer. It's not even sugarcoated. He just rips the Band-Aid off and offers me the biggest dealbreaker I have.

"Y-you don't?" I stammer. He must notice how much his answer affects me because he looks stunned as he studies my face. But he can't be more stunned than I am.

"Sorry, I should have said something a little less serious, like, I don't like Pop Tarts."

"You don't like Pop Tarts?" *Damn it, why doesn't he want kids?*

"Nope. Not even a little. I think they're highly overrated. Every time I have one, I expect so much more out of it. Like, I've put all this work into preparing it, from unwrapping it to toasting it. Then my reward is this dry sawdust thing with a tiny smear of filling. And the flavors? Don't get me started. Their idea of strawberry is nowhere close to what the real fruit tastes like."

"I think that's true of anything with artificial strawberry," I point out. My burger grows cold in front of me, but my appetite is gone.

"Let me guess, you like Pop Tarts," he says, grinning before he takes a huge bite of his burger.

"I love them," I say. "I don't think they're overrated. In fact, I think they're underrated. More people should have Pop Tarts. They should be the main course, and not some second thought food when you have the munchies." I'm not even sure I'm still talking about Pop Tarts. I'm so angry that things have turned out this way. He was perfect. And then, he wasn't.

"Wow, you're really passionate about your Pop Tarts," he says with a laugh. He finishes his last bite just as the waiter comes back to the table.

"Did you want to see a dessert menu?" he asks.

"No," I say before Ethan can respond. Then I realize I'm being rude. "Sorry, did you want anything?" *All right, Claire, he doesn't want kids. It's good I know that now and not later down the road when I might have feelings for him.*

"Nah, I'm stuffed," he says. "We'll take the check, and a box for her."

I reach for my purse as the waiter leaves, but Ethan stops me by grabbing my hand. I know I should remove my hand from his, but then he's holding it and I can't quite bring myself to break away. I can only imagine how this would feel several weeks in. I don't even know what it's like to kiss him, and I'm having a hard time separating myself from his grasp.

"I got this," he says. I start to protest, but he shakes his head. "Tell you what. If it means that much to you, you can treat next time."

There won't be a next time, though. I want to tell him as much, but then he flips his arm over, pulling my hand with his. It's supposed to be playful, but I'm focused on the faint outline of an old tattoo underneath the tangled geometric shapes of a much newer one. I lose sense of what I'm supposed to say or do, including the boundaries I should be placing, as I run my finger over the shadow of a shape.

"I covered that one up years ago," he explains, though it's as if I'm hearing him through a layer of fog. I'm too busy trying to tell myself I'm not seeing what I'm seeing. But there it is. The faint outline of a hand with an eye in the center of it.

It's him. Finn's father.

This whole time I've been across from him, and I can't believe I didn't recognize who he is. I look into his eyes, searching for the guy I met seven years ago. His deep brown irises are filled with confusion, and I realize I'm being strange. I also realize it can't be him. Finn's father had green eyes. I knew that much to be true.

"Are you okay?" he asks.

And that's when I *know* it's him. It's the same words he said to me that night, seven years ago, said in the same voice. And even if the eye color is different than what I remember, I suddenly see my son in his expression.

"Um, I'm fine," I say, dropping his arm and clasping my hands in my lap to hide the fact that I'm shaking. He's saying something, but I'm lost in a flurry of decisions I need to make without enough time to make them. I need to tell him he's a father, but I don't know if I can.

"Claire."

I look up, and I'm frozen as I see the pieces of Finn even more clearly. The shape of Ethan's nose. The crooked way he smiles. Even that goddamn crease in his cheek. It's just like Finn's. *It's him.*

"I'd like to see you again," he says.

I should say no. I should stop this now before this goes any further. I don't know if he's a good guy or not. I don't know much about him at all, except for the fact that he doesn't want kids. What am I supposed to do with that? He already has a kid, and he doesn't even know it.

I look back into his eyes, searching for the answer. I don't see it. What I do see is a possibility. He could be the man I never thought I needed.

I'm not the same girl I was when he first met me. Raising a son on my own did a fine job of erasing fantasies about Hemsworth brother lookalikes. Okay, fine. Maybe not. But my fantasies involved imaginary book characters over the real thing, because men were too much of a disappointment in real life. Still, I never lost hope that I'd feel that jolt of electricity again, the one I felt when I first looked into his eyes. The one I'm feeling now as he holds my gaze, his expression full of hope as he waits for my answer.

"Is that a yes?"

I take a deep breath, and when I release my air, a smile comes with it. Relief floods his face as I reach over and take his hand.

"Yes," I say. "I'd love to see you again."

Ethan continues holding my hand as we walk through the parking lot. My mind is pure chaos, swirling with this huge secret that will completely upend his life. But in the moments I can escape my guilt and unease, I'm anchored by his hand covering mine, recalling a time seven years ago when a stranger felt like home. I cling to this as we reach our cars and he lets go of my hand, but just long enough to free me of my to-go box. He puts it on the hood of my car as I lean against the driver's side door. Then his hands rest on either side of my head as he faces me. I'm suddenly relieved that I thought to clean my car before coming here. There's no sign of Finn anywhere.

"I am so glad I met you," Ethan murmurs, brushing a lock of hair from my forehead, and I know he's going to kiss me. It's the closest he's been to me all night, and I rest in the heady feeling I get from his proximity as I breathe him in. *Leather and pine. Summer wind. Stars and the night sky.* I inhale his scent, brushing aside my vow to be chaste as he leans closer and rests his mouth on mine.

Ethan is broad and solid. His skin is covered in ink, and his stubble drags across my skin with electrifying tingles. But his mouth is soft. Seeking. Gentle. I open my lips and his tongue slowly caresses mine. His hand moves to my jaw and his fingers graze my cheek. He was the last boy I kissed, and it suddenly occurs to me how long it's been, especially as his kiss ignites a spark in me and I feel feverish from the flame. I rest my hands at his waist, but then I cling to his back as he envelopes me in his muscular arms, deepening our kiss.

It's then that I'm transported back in time, sitting in the front seat of his car. I feel the same butterflies and recognize the familiar way he rolls his tongue over mine. He even tastes the same, an indescribable flavor I'd recognize anywhere.

We slowly break apart, and I'm sure he knows. He *has* to. And yet, his smile holds no recognition that this isn't our first kiss.

"Where have you been?" he asks, leaning his forehead against mine.

"Here in Sunset Bay, all my life," I laugh, pecking him on the mouth. Inside, I'm dying. Just as badly as I want to tell him about Finn, there are a million reasons to keep Finn a secret, mostly fueled by my pessimistic side. If I tell him about my son—*our son*—our connection will burn out faster than it began. I can't dismiss the fact that he doesn't want kids.

And in the midst of all this, my mind is haunted by the memory of my mother parading guys in and out of our house. I can't do that to Finn.

If Ethan turns out to be who I want him to be, then I'll tell him. But in the meantime, it doesn't hurt to see where this could go.

Chapter 7

Maren is waiting at my kitchen table when I open the door, a bottle of wine on the table for me, and a bottle of sparkling water for her. I love that even though she doesn't drink anymore, she still knows when I might need to dish over a glass of something yummy—in this case, my favorite sauvignon blanc from Hanna, a Sonoma County winery up north.

"Spill," Maren says, holding a glass toward me. I sigh, taking the glass as I collapse dramatically in the chair across from her. She laughs as she clinks my glass with her bubbly water. "That good?"

"You have no idea," I say. I set the wine down on the table and lean forward. "Guess who Ethan is."

She tilts her head at me, a confused look on her face. "Did we go to school with him?"

I nod. "He was a grade above us. But that's not the

important part."

I take my phone out, then open my photos. Before we said goodbye, I'd talked him into taking a selfie with me. I pull that photo up and have Maren study it.

"Who does he look like?" I ask.

She looks closer, squinting her eyes. "I think he's more of a Liam than a Chris," she says.

I laugh as I get up, crossing the room and taking Finn's school picture off the refrigerator. I bring it back to the table and set it in front of Maren. She glances at Finn's photo, and then back at Ethan's. Her eyes get wide and she snatches the photo off the table, holding it next to my phone.

"Oh my God." She looks up at me, her eyes like saucers. "It's him? Are you sure?"

"I'm positive," I say.

I tell her about discovering the tattoo, and then noticing all his features and expressions that were just like Finn's. He even had some of the same mannerisms, like how he ducked his head whenever he said something funny or how his face lit up when he knew he'd impressed me. Finn and Ethan had never met, yet they have so many similarities.

"But the only strange thing is that his eyes were brown and back then, they were green. I'm fairly certain eyes don't change color."

"It was a costume party," Maren says. "I mean, it was

a masquerade, but people were dressing up weird all over the place. He could have been wearing contacts."

I thought about it for a moment. "I guess." I peer over the table at the photo of him, still in shock that this is the same man from so long ago.

"Are you going to tell him?" Maren asks.

"No," I say, but second guess myself when I see the surprise in Maren's face. "I will eventually, but I need to feel him out first."

"I think you already felt Ethan out, and look where you are now."

I toss a napkin at her as she laughs.

"That's not all of it, though. Ethan told me he doesn't want kids."

Her smile drops, replaced by a narrow-eyed glare. She looks like she's ready to hunt him down and make him suffer. I touch her arm, shaking my head.

"Calm down. It's not like he knows I have a kid."

Maren tilts her head at me. "It was a first date and he just, out of the blue, springs on you that he doesn't want kids?" She rolls her eyes. "Players these days."

Now it's my turn to be confused. "What do you mean?"

Maren shoots me a sympathetic smile. "I keep forgetting you haven't dated in forever." She pauses to finish off her water, and then moves her cup out of the way and folds her hands in front of her. "Ethan has chosen honesty as his power move. Right out the gate, he is letting you know his intentions—that he has no plans to settle down and have a family. That way, when things start to get more serious between the two of you and he slams on the brakes, he can remain the good guy because he was honest about his intentions from the start."

"I don't think he meant it that way, though." And I don't, except what Maren says also makes sense. I don't know Ethan at all. He could totally be a player. Just because he fathered a kid doesn't mean he's suddenly a good guy.

But it also doesn't add up to the person I went to dinner with tonight.

"No, I can't believe he meant it that way. You weren't there. It was a silly comment he made, and it was just one comment."

"A silly comment that he doesn't want a kid, when in fact he is dating someone with a kid—*his* kid."

"He doesn't know that, though. Besides, it's not abnormal for a guy in his twenties to not want a family. If I didn't have Finn, I wouldn't want kids yet. Maybe not at all. I mean, do *you* want kids?"

"Why should I? I get to play aunt to Finn, then I get to go home and think only about myself."

I give Maren a pointed look, and she rolls her eyes.

"Okay, fine. Just because Ethan told you he doesn't

want kids doesn't make him some evil player. I'm still going to be suspicious until he proves otherwise, but I'll give him the benefit of the doubt."

I nod, even though being suspicious is not giving the benefit of the doubt. However, I can't help feeling the same. And yet, it's easier to believe he's a good guy. He was interested in everything I said, as if he couldn't learn enough about me—even when I went on and on about that book. If it weren't for this detail about him not wanting kids, and especially about him being Finn's father, this would be a no-brainer. But now, it all feels so complicated and strange...and exciting and hopeful.

"What if he's a good guy?" I ask, looking over my wine glass at Maren. "Like, what if this works out?" I know it sounds like a strange thing to worry about, but I'm relieved when she smiles gently at me before taking my hand.

"You deserve happiness too. But for now, just have fun. Don't think too hard about it. Be yourself, because any guy who falls in love with Claire Myers is one lucky son of a bitch, especially if he gets the Finnster as part of the deal. Speaking of which, when are you going to tell Ethan?"

"I don't know," I admit. "I wasn't actually supposed to like him. I thought this would be a one and done date, and I could go back to my single mom routine. But the fact that he's Finn's dad changes everything, so I hadn't really thought that far ahead." I look at Maren and wince. "I feel like a bad mom for not telling him I have a kid. I mean, besides the fact that Finn is his. I didn't even bring my son up."

"It's kind of hard to let someone know you have a kid when they tell you they don't want kids," she points out.

"Yeah, but I made that decision early on, when I thought we weren't going to see each other again. And now…" I shake my head. "I never thought I'd be in this position. I swore I wasn't going to date. Now, I not only have to figure out how to split my time between being a mom and getting to know Ethan, but also figuring out how to tell someone I have a kid—especially when that person doesn't want kids. It could be the one thing that makes him not want to see me, and the fact that it matters makes me feel like an idiot." Saying it aloud, it sounds even more horrible. "I mean, what's my motivation for not telling him? Is it to protect Finn? Or is it to protect me from rejection?"

"It's okay if it's both," Maren says. "You're human. No one wants to be rejected. But if he does reject you because you have a kid, then forget him. No one is worth it if they can't accept you're a package deal, even if the guy is Finn's father."

"And there lies the most complicated part. I can't just forget him." I bury my head in my folded arms on the table. "What am I going to do?"

"For now, you're going to say goodnight and go to bed. You need rest."

I lift my head. "But then what? Should I tell him now? Or wait?"

"You should do what makes you feel most comfortable. Do you think it's better to let him know about Finn from the start and see if he bolts? Or do you think it's better if he gets to know you as Claire before learning about Finn?"

I think for a moment. Both decisions sound right. "He deserves to know he has a son," I say slowly. I can't shake the unease that settles inside me as soon as the words leave my mouth. "But I can't tell him, not yet. If he finds out and then bolts, I don't think I can handle it." I mull it over a moment longer, still unsure. Wincing, I look back to Maren. "I think I need to see if he's a good guy first. Even if he's Finn's dad, my priority is my son."

Maren squeezes my hand. "I think you're making the right decision. Who knows? All of this could work out."

Maren leaves a little while later, and I sit by myself at my kitchen table looking at both Ethan's and Finn's photos, side by side. There's one other complication I haven't been able to talk about, not even with Maren. I've barely been able to think about it, it's so scary. But right now, my mind loosened by several glasses of wine, the biggest fear I have floats to the top of my thoughts.

I've spent all of Finn's life being the one he comes to for everything. Sometimes it was hard, especially when he'd go through weird phases. Like now, when he thinks he needs independence from me. But one thing is true— I've never had to share him. I've never had to consult with someone else about how to raise him, or what kind of foods he should eat, or if immunizations are a good idea or not. I've been able to make all these choices for him on my own. Even if there were times I lost my cool or felt overwhelmed, I feel like I did a pretty good job raising him without anyone else to help.

My fear is that Ethan will step into our lives as Finn's father and completely take over. I remember a few of my mother's boyfriends who tried to step in as a parent, and how angry that made me feel. I don't want Finn to feel like he has to answer to some guy who missed the first six years of his life.

But even more, I'm afraid Finn will love Ethan…more than he loves me. That's what will hurt the most.

It's just after midnight when I finally head to bed. With everything I've learned, plus half a bottle of wine, I'm feeling the late hour. I wash the makeup from my face, pausing when I hear my phone ding.

Ethan: Goodnight Claire, I can't wait to see you again.

It's been a while since I've dated, but I'm pretty sure the rules haven't changed. No one texts the same night as a first date. Right? Knowing she's still up, I text Maren just to be sure.

> Maren: It's one of the dating commandments. Thou shall not text immediately after first date.
>
> Me: So, it's a bad thing?
>
> Maren: No, it's good. It means he's into you and isn't afraid for you to know.

I lay my head on my pillow, a wide smile on my face. *He likes me.* This could actually be something, if I just turn off my brain and let my heart lead for a while.

I tap into my phone.

> Me: Goodnight Ethan. Sweet dreams.

Chapter 8

At some point in the night, Finn found his way into my room. I wake in the morning at the very edge of the bed as he sleeps sideways, his feet pressed into my back. How he managed to take up the entire queen-sized mattress without waking me is impressive. He moves in his sleep, stretching his legs even more so that I have to brace myself to stay in the bed.

"Come on, Finn," I mutter as I pry his feet off me. He murmurs something incoherent, staying asleep as I roll him toward the middle of the bed. I can smell the brewed coffee in the kitchen, thanks to the auto timer on my coffeepot. But before I get up to grab a cup, I linger for a moment to watch my sleeping son.

All this time, I only saw myself in him. Now, his long lashes brushing the top of his cheeks, I see the hidden parts of him, features I never noticed before—features that remind me of his father. Staring at my little boy, it's hard not to feel like I'm looking at a stranger. As soon as I think it, I want to bat the thought away. Of course Finn isn't a stranger. He's my everything, my little guy. I know him like he's an extension of my soul. And yet...for the first time I'm seeing the portion of him that isn't me, the parts he shares with another human on this earth.

A grain of despair gathers volume in my belly, rolling about as it grows into something bitter and unrecognizable. It's ridiculous, really. Did I actually believe Finn was made up of 100% of my DNA?

Is Finn curious about his dad?

All the fears I had last night drape over me like a shadow, leaving me cold as I watch Finn purse his lips in his sleep. The selfish part of me wants to hide my son away, to protect him from anyone who might jeopardize the life I've created for both of us.

But I'm still questioning who I'm protecting—Finn or me?

I leave Finn in bed, padding to the kitchen to pour myself a cup of coffee. As I sip the hot beverage, I recall the four words Ethan said that pained me then, but now offer a nugget of hope.

I don't want kids.

At the time he said it, I saw any kind of future with him go up in smoke. Now, I see it as a beacon that he won't try to take Finn away. Maybe. I think. At any rate, it's all I have to cling to.

I'm tempted to just call the whole thing off and cut him loose. It would be better to end things now before we develop stronger feelings. Then Ethan can live his happy, carefree, childless life, and Finn and I can go back to the way it was before I entertained the idea of potentially bringing a man into our lives.

Then I think again of my own father. There's little possibility I'll ever know who he is, and while I'm fine with that, there's a small part of me that wishes I had the chance. Would I recognize our shared features? Does he tell jokes, or is he serious? Does he have another family? Do I have any brothers or sisters? Is he the kind of man I'd want as my father? Judging by the guys my mom brought home, it's doubtful. But what if he was the one exception? I'd never know.

Finn has the chance to know. Even though I feel selfish about sharing him, I know I can't deny Finn this chance to know who his dad is. I mean…within reason. I still want to make sure that Ethan isn't some asshole who will ruin our lives or break our hearts, which is why it's still important I get to know him first.

But before I can do that, I need to understand why he doesn't want kids.

Insomniacs is packed for a weekday morning; you'd think people would be at work or school. Every table is filled with couples or groups clutching froth-filled mugs, the din of conversation mingling with the shush of espresso at the barista station and the triphop jazz playing softly from the speakers. I get in line, peeking around the guy in front of me to get a good look at Nina who's busy ringing everyone up with a bored look on her face. Today, her platinum hair has neon pink streaks in it, the same color as her impossibly long nails. I look at my own nails, bitten short with chipped green nail polish, and feel my lack of style to the full. Of course, I don't have to struggle typing.. But neither does Nina, from the looks of it.

I reach the front of the line, and a flicker of interest crosses Nina's expression. It's just a flash before the apathetic look returns to her face. But it's enough to recognize her curiosity about how last night went Ethan.

"I'd like a honey lavender latte with bee pollen," I order. "And I'd like to talk with you when you're on your break."

Nina taps her long nails on the counter, and for a moment I think she's going to say no. I glance at the coffee station where Maren is working, and she shoots me a questioning look. I hadn't told her I was stopping in, mostly because I was so nervous about it to begin with.

"My break is in forty-five," Nina says, bringing my attention back to her. "But I'm eating while we talk." She smirks, and it's possibly the first time I've ever seen her smile…if you can call it that. "I wondered if you'd come talk with me." Then she looks at the person behind me, dismissing me to wait for my coffee.

I manage to snag a table just as a couple is leaving. They left rings of coffee on the surface, and I set my cup down to find napkins, but Maren beats me to the punch.

"So, getting the inside scoop on lover boy, huh?" she asks as she wipes down the table.

"Kind of."

"Well, good luck." Maren tilts her head at Nina, then rolls it back to me. "She's already messed up five people's orders, and they of course are blaming me for the mistake." She nods at my latte. "She entered that one in as a raspberry mint mocha. But I have a feeling she did it on purpose."

"Thanks for saving me," I say, wrinkling my nose. "But why? Does she hate me?"

"Nah, Nina doesn't care enough about anyone to hate them. I think it amuses her." Maren looks back at the coffee station. "I better go. Good luck. Tell me what you find out."

I actually don't want to ask Nina too many questions about Ethan. Knowing Nina, she'll put a damper on any kind of feelings I have for him. Besides, I'd rather Ethan *show* me who he is than get a second opinion. But there's one question I can't bring myself to ask him.

For forty-five minutes, I nurse my coffee as I stare out the window, ignoring the searching glances of other coffee lovers looking for a place to sit. Even when my cup is empty, I pretend to drink only so I can avoid looking like a table hog. It's my downfall, and I know it. I care too much about people's opinion of me, even those I'll never see again.

Which is why my mouth feels dry and it's hard to swallow when Nina plants herself at my table, plopping a breakfast sandwich in front of her that she picks at piece by piece with her chopstick fingernails. She doesn't say anything, leaving me to scramble for what to say.

Here's the thing about Nina. She only knows me as Maren's friend, and that's it. I don't even think she knows I have a kid. Or maybe she does. Maybe she'll say something to Ethan before I have a chance to say anything, and it will ruin any chance I have of getting to know him better. I study her, trying to gauge how much she knows.

"What?" Her eyes narrow, and I realize I'm staring at her like a psychopath.

"I have a son," I blurt out. Nina's eyebrows raise up, and I mentally shoot myself for saying anything.

"And you're telling me this because…"

I sigh, realizing honesty is probably the best path to take.

"Because your cousin told me last night that he

doesn't want kids, and he doesn't know I already have one."

She nods slowly, but a look of understanding washes over her face.

"Look, I'm not ready to spring this on him," I say, and then ignore her questioning look as I continue. "But after last night's date, I think there's some potential between us. If I'm right about our connection, I need to know why he doesn't want kids."

"And you think I know something," Nina says, looking down at me through her hooded ice-blue eyes.

"I was hoping you did."

She leans back in her chair and eyes me. It feels like I'm the subject of an evaluation or something, like I'm being appraised for my worth. I'm irritated that she's being so coy, but I hide my feelings and wait out her dramatic assessment.

"Have you ever watched those Lifetime dramas where the dad has two complete families, and neither one of them know about the other?"

I feel numb as Nina shares how Ethan discovered his dad's other family—a girlfriend and two daughters in North Carolina. Because he traveled for work, he was able to explain the long absences.

"Uncle Tom is my dad's brother, and even we didn't know about it," Nina continues. "My uncle denied it, of course. Told Ethan he was a confused twelve-year-old.

But by that weekend, he disappeared and none of us ever heard from him until my Aunt Stacy received divorce papers."

"Oh my God, that's awful," I breathe.

"It gets worse. Uncle Tom had supported the family, allowing Aunt Stacy to stay home. When he left, he stopped contributing too. With no job skills or experience, Aunt Stacy could only find minimum wage jobs those first few years. She and Ethan lost their house, their car, and almost all their belongings while Aunt Stacy struggled to keep things afloat. They moved in with our family for a time, but it's not the same, you know? She sued for support, but you can't get money out of someone who works under the table and keeps moving locations. Last I heard, Tom and his other family moved out of the country, though none of us know where."

"And because Ethan's dad failed him, he doesn't want kids," I murmur. I think back to the way I spilled my guts to him last night, telling him about my mother. We had all this talk about Frankenstein and the theme of isolation, and he never once brought it up. "Why didn't he just tell me?" I ask Nina.

"You think one date with him will get him to spill his dark past with you?" Nina rolls her eyes as she huffs a laugh.

"I'm not being an egomaniac," I say. "It's just that I was sharing about my own messed up childhood, and..."

"And he doesn't talk about this with anyone," Nina finishes. "As soon as it was clear that his dad was gone for good, Ethan shut up about it. He's never mentioned his dad since. He won't talk about it with his mom, my dad, or even me—and we were close growing up. So it's not surprising that he never told you."

"This complicates everything," I mutter.

"Because of your son?"

No, because of *our* son.

"I just never would have guessed this." I run my finger along the rim of my empty glass before looking back at Nina. "Look, please don't tell Ethan I have a son."

Nina's eyes narrow, but I shake my head before she can speak.

"I'm going to tell him. He deserves to know what he's getting into before we go any further, but I think it needs to come from me."

Nina continues to eye me, but then her face relaxes into an eyeroll. "I'm not going to tell him, so chill. We're close, but he lives his life and I live mine. Besides, it was my idea to connect the two of you. I'm tired of him dating the same girl over and over again."

"What do you mean?" I ask.

"You know…tall, beautiful girls that could pass as models."

"Wow. Thanks."

"Not that you're not pretty," she continues, but the grin on her face shows she's not the least bit sorry. "It's just that fashion isn't your strong suit."

I look down at my yoga pants and sweatshirt, then back at her.

"Fine. So, why me?"

"Because the girls he picks have nothing going for them but their looks. They're pretty, but nothing to get attached to. It's why he picks them. He doesn't want to fall in love. But you're different. When you come in here, it's to read a book or work on a project. I never see you zoned out on your phone or trying to get attention."

I know that's another slam at my outfit of choice, or maybe even the messy bun piled on the top of my head, but I don't interrupt. This is, so far, the nicest thing she's ever said to me.

"I'm tired of Ethan pushing people away because he's afraid of rejection. He's never going to get over the loss of his dad until he lets other people in, and I have a hunch you're the person that can do it. The fact that you have a kid makes it even more perfect. So, no, I'm not going to go running my mouth." Nina picks up her empty plate and stands. She turns to leave, but then looks at me over her shoulder. "Whatever you do, don't sabotage a good thing with him. Ethan is the best guy there is out there, and if you hurt him, I'll slip laxatives in your coffee."

I don't stick around once she's gone. The cafe isn't any less crowded, and I still have a few more things I want to do before Finn gets home. But Nina's words stick with me, mostly how different I am than the girls Ethan usually dates. If that's the case, why is he still interested? Or maybe this is just a game to him. Could he be luring me in only to toss me aside when things start feeling more serious?

Last night's date was incredible. It felt like we really connected, even when I was determined that we wouldn't. But I have nothing to compare it to. If Ethan is a player and I'm just this week's token girl, I won't even know the signs to look for.

I have my secrets, and I realize now that I'm not the only one.

Chapter 9

The yellow school bus slows to a stop in front of the house, and I watch from the window as Finn hops down the steps and runs up the walkway. I'm still buzzing from my informative coffee date with Nina, and after spending the rest of the afternoon cooped up in my office, I think a little sunshine might do Finn and me good. Besides, Maren gets off work soon and I know she's dying to find out what Nina said.

Finn bursts through the door, a huge grin on his face. "Mom! Guess what?"

"What?" I envelop him in a hug and kiss his sweaty hair. He pushes back, then slips his backpack off his shoulders, letting it drop to the floor.

"I got to be kickball captain today and I picked all the best players, and our team kicked the other team's butt!"

"That's great, Finn! Can you pick your backpack up

and put it in the corner? Do you have any homework?"

He rolls his eyes as he shakes his head, then he kicks his backpack until it's in the corner. He also kicks his shoes off, but those he leaves in the middle of the floor.

"Don't get too comfy," I say. "We're heading out in a few."

"Aw, Mom. Where?"

"To the store," I say, then try to hide my smile when he collapses in a whining heap. "I'm kidding. We're meeting Maren at the park."

He perks up, even though I'm sure his heart was set on parking himself in front of the TV. With any luck some of his friends will be there, giving Maren and me the privacy we need.

Finn puts his shoes back on while I pack some snacks and juice boxes. He beats me out the door, and I balance all our things as I lock up.

On the way, Finn fills the car with stories about today. How the teacher gave them ten extra minutes of recess. How Brie took five bathroom breaks before lunch. How Jace traded him a pack of Oreos for his chips. I let him go on, knowing full well that one day he won't be so enthusiastic about talking with me. My mind wanders as he's talking, recalling times in the car with my own mom and how there was something magic about that space. She called it "The Car of Secrets," where we could talk about anything and everything. Really, it was about having my mom all to myself. No distractions. None of her boyfriends. Just me and her, talking as if this were something we did all the time. The spell would break once we left the car, and we'd go back to living our fractured relationship. But in those moments between Point A and Point B, my mom was my friend, and everything felt right with the world.

We reach Del Mar Park and Finn is already unbuckling his seatbelt as I pull into the parking space.

"Finn, I told you to wait until the car has stopped moving," I say, but he's already out the door and running toward the playground before I can open my door. I can't stay mad long. As I grab our things from the seat next to me, I see he's already found one of his friends.

I spread a blanket out on the grass, and settle with the book I'm reading, all while keeping one eye on the playground. I'm sure Maren won't be here for another thirty minutes or so, giving me enough time to maybe get to the first kiss of the story, and maybe a little…further. God, I love romance books. My love life may have been non-existent since Finn came along, but thanks to books like this, I at least get the thrill of the "meet cute," the chase, the longing, and then the satisfying coming together. The sex scenes don't hurt either. But really, it's the stuff that happens in between, all the reasons the reader can't stop reading until it's certain they'll end up as a couple. They always do, of course. But it's the buildup I live for.

"Let me guess. *Frankenstein*."

I slam the book shut and look up as Ethan kneels in front of me. He's completely sweaty with a huge grin on his face, his hair sticking to his forehead in adorable curls.

"Not exactly," I say, trying to hide the book under my hand.

Nina's voice plays in the back of my mind, *He doesn't want to fall in love. That* paired with the fact that he doesn't want kids—those should be two red flags. And yet, everything evaporates except for his smile and the butterflies swarming in my belly.

Ethan picks my book up and his grin widens as he takes in the cover—a shirtless male with rock hard abs, offering a sultry look. But I'm too busy looking at the shirtless man in front of me, sweat pouring down his chiseled muscles, and the allure of the tattoos covering his arms and chest. I want to run my hands over the designs, see if I can feel the raised lines beneath my palms, press my body against his sweaty chest.

"Is it good?" he asks.

"Oh yeah." Then I look at his face, and I know my own is bright red. "I mean, it has a great storyline. It's very sweet."

"Uh huh." He laughs as he puts the book down.

"What are you doing here?" As soon as I ask it, I want to fall through the earth. It's not like I own the park or anything. But all I can think of is Finn playing several yards away, and how I'm not ready to tell Ethan about my son…or that he's *his* son too. Even more, I don't want Finn to see me talking to Ethan. *We're not doing anything, just talking*, I remind myself. However, it doesn't stop the visions of my mom talking to some random dude while I played by myself at the playground. Inwardly, I pray that Finn will be too busy playing to notice.

If Ethan notices my awkwardness or inner turmoil, he doesn't show it.

"I just finished a game of hoops," he says, nodding toward the basketball court. I glance where he indicates and notice a few players still shooting around. Even more, I notice a group of girls on a bench near the courts, obviously ogling the guys. I'm even more haunted by Nina's words, and part of me wishes I'd never talked to her.

He's here with you, not them, I remind myself. And even though it's true, I can't help feeling like some naive lovesick girl. I don't even know Ethan. What's to say he's not charming to every girl he's around.

"Hey, where'd you go?" He brushes my cheek with his finger, and the gesture is so familiar, as if we've known each other for long.

"I'm just…I'm glad to see you," I say. I relax into his smile, but I feel a flutter of panic when he looks at my lips. *Oh God, he can't kiss me. What if Finn sees?* But he doesn't. Instead, he touches his lips, and then touches mine before standing. I feel equal parts relief and disappointment. There's something intoxicating about his scent, how the smell of his sweat pulls at something deep inside me. You can't get that kind of sensory overload from a romance book, that's for sure. "I'd stay, but I have work in an hour and probably smell like shit."

"You don't," I say, and my cheeks blaze as he reveals that crease in his cheek.

"You should stop by tonight," he says. "Come get a drink."

More than anything, I want to get that drink. Then I feel the guilt wash over me. How can I be this selfish? We just went out last night. Probably every other girl he's dated would say yes. But I'm not every other girl, I'm a mom.

"I can't. I have a deadline to meet and will probably be up all night."

"Fair enough. I have a rare night off this Friday, though. Would you like to go out again?"

"She'd love to," Maren says behind us. I turn and glare at her, then try not to crack up at the feigned angelic look on her face. "Hi, I'm Maren." She shuffles the tray of iced coffee to reach over and shake his hand. "And you must be Ethan. I've heard a ton about you."

She plops down next to me, handing me a coffee as I bite my lip, unsure whether to completely die or just evaporate into thin air.

"You have, have you?" Ethan's smile tugs at his mouth, and I bury my face in my hands. "I recognize you. You play at Hillside, don't you?"

Maren nods. "I've seen you there too. Nice to officially meet you. I hope to see more of you around." She looks from Ethan to me, then at Ethan again.

"Me too," he says, also looking at me.

"All right, fine. I'll go out with you on Friday," I say, but I laugh when I do.

"Great, it's a date." Ethan glances at the time on his phone and stands. "I've gotta run, but I'll text you later for your address."

Both Maren and I watch as he runs off, the muscles in his back rippling, his calves rock solid with each step.

"Holy fuck, that man is hot," Maren breathes.

"I know." I moan, then let out a shaky breath of air that I hadn't known I was holding. "Which is why I really need to break things off now."

"What?" She hands me my iced coffee, all while shaking her head. "You're crazy, Claire. You should be following him home so you can officially end your dry spell."

"Ha ha." I sip my iced mocha, even though I've definitely had enough coffee today. I note something extra in there alongside the dark chocolate, and I tilt my head as I try to figure it out.

"Orange," Maren answers before I can ask. "It's this new thing we're doing, kind of like those chocolate oranges you can get during the holidays."

"Well, it's delicious. Do more of these."

"Sure. Now spill."

I tell her everything Nina told me, including the part about Ethan's absent dad, though I feel bad divulging it. It's not my secret to tell, especially when he never told me. But Maren's good with secrets, and I need to tell someone. I also confirm that Ethan might be kind of a player, just like Maren suspected.

"What did he do?" Maren's eyes narrow, and I can practically feel the fire of her protective anger.

"I haven't seen it with my own eyes," I admit, "But Nina spelled out his dating habits before he met me. Why should he change now when he doesn't even know me?"

"That's why he needs to get to know you," she says. "Then he'll fall madly in love with you and live happily ever after."

"Until he finds out I—we—have a kid," I say. I hang my head. "All of this is too much. And Friday! What am I supposed to do about this Friday?"

"Wear something sexy so that he's tongue tied when he comes to your door."

"That's just it," I say. "He can't come to my door. Finn, remember?" I glance at the playground as I say it. I recognize Brie in the sand box with Finn, and I can't help but notice how much attention my son is paying to her as she helps with a mound of sand in front of him.

"Right," Maren says. "I mean, I could take him to my house for the night. It's not childproof or anything, but it's safe."

"He's beyond the childproofing age, goof," I say, even though I think she's kidding. "But he's never slept away from home. Besides, there are signs of Finn everywhere at my house. Photos, his toys, artwork on the fridge…. I doubt I can erase all that evidence of my son in just a short week. And even more, what happens if Ethan shows up unannounced? What then? If he knows where I live, it's just going to spell disaster." I can feel the knot in my stomach grow by the second. "I need to break this off before it gets bigger than it needs to be."

Maren looks at me, and I wait for the judgment. Instead, she takes my hand.

"You're scared, aren't you?"

"Terrified," I say. And as I say it, I realize this is the biggest feeling I have. I'm not just scared of who he is and what this means for Finn and me, but I'm also afraid I'll fall for him so completely, I won't be able to see my way out of it. I tell all this to Maren, the truth spilling out of me as fast as I feel it.

"I've done this for so long on my own," I say. "What if I become dependent on him?"

"You might," Maren agrees. "But knowing you, you

won't lose yourself completely, no matter how hard you fall in love." She lets go of my hand and leans back on the blanket. She's about to say something else when Finn runs up, launching himself at her.

"Aunt Maren! Are you coming over tonight? Are you bringing pizza?"

"Is your mom still trying to get you to eat healthy stuff?" she asks. Finn nods.

"Last week it was broccoli every night."

"It was not," I protest. "That was only two nights, and you didn't eat any of it."

"You put it in the brownies," he says, digging through the bag of food I brought. He pulls out the cheese and crackers snack pack, bypassing the grapes and leftover brownies. Maren picks one of the brownies up and inspects it.

"Claire, you need help," she says, holding the brownie by two fingers as if she'd found it on the bathroom floor. I snatch the brownie from her hand and take a big bite of it.

"It's delicious," I say, my teeth probably as full as my mouth. She grimaces with a disgusted laugh.

"Finnster, I can't come over tonight. But how about this Friday you and I pull an all-nighter with pizza and soda, and maybe even some broccoli-free brownies."

"Yeah! Are you sleeping over?"

"Yup. Your mom needs a night off to think about

what she's done." She raises her eyebrow at me. "Ruining brownies. That's a sin."

I have a million arguments about her plans, but I keep them bottled until Finn rejects the rest of the food I packed and runs back to the playground.

"An all-nighter? I am not staying out all night. I'm trying to find a way to break things off with Ethan, and you're not helping."

"Do what you want with the time, I don't care. But you are not going to be at your house. I'll take over Finn duties at your house, and you can bachelorette it up at my place. Just change the sheets when you're done, all right?"

I wrinkle my nose at her, even as the idea of what she's suggesting sends a thrill through me. But no. That's not going to happen.

"I'm calling off the date, so you're off the hook," I say. She rolls her eyes.

"Did you ever think that maybe I like hanging out with your progeny? I don't care if you go out with Ethan or not, tell me you don't need a break."

"But my swag orders! I have so many packages I still need to complete."

"They'll be there on Saturday when you come back. Come on Claire, live a little. You can stay up all night watching Netflix. Or you can turn off everything and listen to silence. Or, I don't know, you can stop being such a prude and have an enjoyable night with Ethan, whatever that means for the two of you. Finn is old enough for an overnight with his Aunt Maren. You've been a mom without a break since Finn was born." She gives me a pointed look, and I know my lecture is over. Even more, I know she's right.

"Fine," I say, then laugh as the serious look on her face dissolves into a smile.

"Oh my God, we have so much to do before then," she says.

"Like what?"

I'm not sure I like the look in her eyes as she says, "You'll see."

Chapter 10

"I never said I'd go out with him. Ow!"

The fact that I'm here without pants and spread eagle, while Maren sits across from me in a chair, is a testament to how close we are as friends. The fact that some woman is ripping hair off my asshole during an appointment Maren forced me to attend is a testament to what an *awful* friend she is.

"Fuck!" I yell out as the woman rips another strip off me.

"That was the last one," the woman assures me as I death grip the table.

"I hate you," I hiss at Maren as soon as the woman is out of the room.

"You just wait until you experience the smoothness of a waxed box," she says with a knowing smile.

"Don't tell me you do this too." I retrieve my pants

and start dressing.

"Wanna see?" She starts to unbuckle her pants, but I stop her.

"Thanks, but no thanks," I laugh, cringing as I pull my underwear on. Much to my relief, it's not as tender as I think it will be. I'm definitely aware of *down there*, though. My eyes widen at the sensation of skin against skin, and an airy feeling that goes with it.

"It's like being naked all the time," Maren says, and I nod in agreement.

"I definitely get the appeal. But I'm serious, no one is going to see this but me…and you, I guess."

"You're prepared, just in case," she says, swinging her purse over her shoulder as she leads the way out of the room.

Maren insists on paying since she's the one who made the appointment. I let her, figuring she owes me for the torture.

"You can pay for your new clothes, though."

I argue that I don't need any, but we still end up at The Mermaid's Lagoon, a posh clothing boutique in upper Sunset Bay. At least I thought it was a clothing boutique.

"This is a thrift store?" I say, my eyes widening as I take in the racks upon racks of gorgeous name brand clothes surrounded by display tables of sparkling jewelry. Hanging from the ceiling are multiple chandeliers adorned with lights. The place looks like it belongs in a magazine, and definitely not like a store that holds people's second-hand clothing.

"This is Sunset Bay's hidden secret," Maren says. "It's where all the rich people discard their barely worn clothes so that regular people like you and me can snatch them up and look like a million bucks. How this hasn't ended up on everyone's radar, I don't know. I just discovered it a few weeks ago, and I don't think I'll ever buy a new outfit again."

"You're just telling me about this now?" I say, pulling a pair of Brunello Cucinelli denim trousers from the rack, and I nearly choke at the price. "$500? For a pair of jeans?"

Maren peers over my shoulder, then checks the waist for the original tag that's still attached. My eyes widen. Brand new, these jeans cost $1,500.

"Who in their right mind buys jeans for this much?" I ask. "I don't even think my car is worth this much."

Maren takes the jeans and puts them back. "Those ones are a bit pricey, but this store also has designer clothes in your budget. I promise."

Thankfully, she was right. For the price of a patch made of Brunello Cucinelli denim, I walk out of there with three new blouses, two camisoles, a pair of high waisted bootcut pants, and a flirty dress that may or may not be what I wear on Friday night. When I'm alone.

Doing nothing. Definitely not dating Ethan.

Maren has to work the next few days, so she sets me up with a hair and nail appointment, along with brow shaping. I thought my brows looked fine before, but when done, I feel kind of like a supermodel—which is ironic, given Ethan's dating record. It's not that I want to be like any of the girls he's dated, but it's nice to be a little more glamorous than my usual yoga pants and sloppy bun.

Over these last few days, Ethan has been texting me too. He can't possibly know my hesitation, and yet his frequent contact seems like a lure to keep me from bowing out. It's working. I haven't told him I'm not going, and by Friday afternoon, it's pretty much a given that he's taking me out—especially when I give him Maren's address.

"I feel like such a liar," I say, sitting in a booth at Insomniacs while Maren takes her time cleaning the table next to me. I'm wearing one of the camisoles we bought a few days earlier, and I sip my iced almond milk latte carefully so I don't splatter the tan liquid on the designer top. I wrinkle my nose at the taste. A new guy is working the coffee bar today, which explains the less than stellar ratio of espresso to milk. But I'm relieved that Nina isn't here. For some reason, I can't face her on the day I'm going out with her cousin, even if this was her idea all along. It's enough that I'm going, even if I'm pretending to live in a cramped one-bedroom apartment full of Maren's guitars and dark style.

"You're not lying," Maren says. "You're protecting your privacy."

"No, it's still lying."

She shrugs, as if lying is no big thing. There was a time when it wasn't for her. It's different now. She's as honest as the sea is wet, sometimes blatantly so. I guess it's part of her recovery, but we don't talk about that much.

Still, I find it amusing that she's encouraging me to lie. The only reason I'm not turning back is because all of this is for Finn. If Ethan doesn't check out, he'll never have to know about his son.

"After work I just have to grab a few things from my apartment and then I'll be at your house," she says, looking over her shoulder toward the cash register. Her boss is there, shooting daggers at Maren. "Crap, I have to go. Just be ready when I get there, because there won't be much time." She rushes off to the counter, and I sit back in my booth and sip my latte. My phone dings and I look at it, smiling when I see Ethan's name pop up.

Ethan: I can't stop thinking about tonight.

I cover my mouth, hiding the grin that won't quit on my

face. For all the ways I need to play it cool around him, I'm already failing—and he's not even near me.

> Me: You mean when we go to the bookstore and I read you passages from Frankenstein?
>
> Ethan: Honestly, that sounds kind of erotic. Is that weird?

I grin. To be honest, I'd find it erotic if he read passages of his favorite book to me. Does he have a favorite book?

> Me: Careful there. I may just hijack this date.
>
> Him: I have a feeling I'd be fascinated by anything you want to do.

"Quit texting and go get ready," Maren hisses at me on her way past my table. I smother my smile, type back a quick smiley face, and book it out of there.

I still have an hour until Finn's bus gets to the house, so I take my time getting ready. I take a long shower and exfoliate every inch of my body. After blow drying my hair, I curl it into soft mermaid waves. I apply shimmering pink eyeshadow to my lids, then line the edges to give them a dramatic look. A little mascara, some blush, and lip gloss, then it's time to get dressed. I settle on the dress I bought this week, but pair it with chunky boots—ala Maren style—just so Ethan doesn't think I'm some feminine flower. I probably am, but I'd like to be perceived a little tougher than that.

I'm ready with fifteen minutes to spare, and I linger at the doorway of my office. There are a million things to do before Monday morning's swag shipment, but I submit to letting them wait. Maren was right, I haven't had a break in years, and one night won't kill me.

When Finn arrives home, he slumps into the house like a deflated beach ball.

"What's wrong?" I ask, roughing up his hair and kissing his forehead.

"You're not supposed to be here," he says, budging past me and opening the refrigerator.

"Sorry to disappoint," I say with a laugh. I'd be offended, but I know exactly why he's upset. Sure enough, he perks up when Maren's car rolls into the driveway, and he runs out to greet her as she balances a pizza with one hand and a bag of God-knows-what in the other.

"Do I want to know what that is?" I ask, nodding at the bag when she breezes into the kitchen.

"Nunya business," she says, skirting around me, holding the bag away. I still make out a few familiar candy wrappers through the sheer plastic.

"Have fun getting him to bed." I raise my perfectly shaped eyebrow at her, and she matches the look back at me.

"Who says we're going to bed? Speaking of all-nighters, you need to leave. Goodbye."

I shake my head, biting my smile as I watch Finn already going through the bag she's left on the table. I'm about to say something, but Maren clears her throat and points to the door.

"I'm going!" I laugh. I give Finn a sideways hug, and am at least satisfied that he leans into me. Then I grab my night bag and head out.

Chapter 11

With her gothic paintings, black furniture, and dim lighting, Maren's apartment is basically an extension of her. There's a giant poster of Joan Jett on one wall, and another with Shirley Manson of *Garbage* and Hayley Williams of *Paramore*. Several electric guitars hang like art across another wall, and her acoustic guitar is leaning against her futon as if she just got done playing it. Knowing her, she probably got in a quick jam session before heading my way.

There's also a weird smell here, faint but totally present. I asked Maren about it once, and she said it was probably coming from the air conditioner wall unit, which she only used on the hottest days.

But beyond that, the place was pretty cool. It was also totally Maren.

I realize I can't let Ethan in here. There's nothing

that looks like me here. If he comes here, he's going to think I'm some edgy musician. It's not a bad thing. It's probably way more interesting than the person I really am. But while we're trying to get to know each other, it would be stupid to offer up a false representation of who I am.

As if having him meet me at Maren's house isn't false enough…. But whatever, he'll be here in twenty minutes, and I have no backup plan.

> Me: Text me when you get here and I'll meet you in the parking lot.

I sit on Maren's low-rise couch and wait, checking my phone every ten seconds. Minutes pass by, then ten. It seems longer as I keep checking, so I get up and walk around her apartment, pretending to ignore my phone. But then I run back to check it again. No answer. I'm about to take another living room-to-kitchen stroll when my phone finally dings, and I pounce on it.

> Ethan: I'm here.

I grab my purse and rush out the door, then drop my keys as I fumble with the lock.

"Calm down," I whisper to myself as I glance over my shoulder. Below the balcony I can see Ethan's car idling in the parking lot and my stomach does a slow, nervous roll. I lock the door, checking it a few times just to be sure it's secure. When I take the stairs, it's with slow, steady steps, using the time to get a hold of my nerves. Ethan leans against his car as I reach ground level, and I take in his dark jeans slung over his hips, his button-up shirt that shows off his tattooed arms and biceps, and the way his grin leans to one side as he watches my every move.

"You're beautiful," he says, leaning in to kiss my cheek, his hand resting around my waist. My nerves remain, but something warm washes over me. Something comfortable. It's all so natural, as if we've done this a million times before. And yet, I don't think I'll ever get tired of this. I inhale his cologne, a woodsy mixture of leather and pine. When he pulls back, I look in his dark eyes and can't help but smile.

"You do too," I say, then I shake my head. "I mean handsome. You look handsome, really good."

"Thank you." He doesn't laugh out loud, but I see the humor radiating in his eyes. "So, I have a plan for tonight's date," he says, his hand at my lower back as we walk to the passenger side. He opens the door for me, and I slide into my seat. "But before we get to that, you get to pick the restaurant. Also, I'm paying and that's final." He closes the door before I can say anything, and I shoot him a mock glare as he trots to the driver's side.

"You can't pay. You paid last time, and I was supposed to pay this time."

Ethan buckles in and then rests his arm over my seat as he leans toward me.

"Right now, I'm doing everything I can to win you over. Are you really going to take that away from me?"

A small, niggling voice reminds me that he's probably a player. And yet, the earnest look in his eyes seems authentic. It's just a meal, and I do get to pick, so...

"Fine," I say. "Corner of Fourth and Sunset. You'll have to park a block away, so I hope you brought your walking shoes."

"Please tell me you're not thinking of–"

"Chicago Dogs. Yup. I hope you brought enough cash, because I plan to get two."

He gives me some serious side eye, then he puts the car in gear.

"Lucky for you, I just picked up my tips for the week. You can have as many hot dogs as you can fit in that tiny body of yours."

He pulls out of the lot, fiddling with the radio at the same time until country music fills the car. I laugh, then realize he's serious.

"I did not take you for a country guy," I say.

"Really now. What did you take me for?"

"I don't know." I study him, my eyes landing on the

lion tattoo. I lift the edge of his sleeve, a shiver going through me as my finger brushes his skin. I notice the brief goosebumps that appear on his skin, then disappear just as quickly. "Metal rock," I say. He laughs, then presses a button on the dash, and the music switches from soft country to edgy electric guitar with a beat. I tilt my head, trying to place the music.

"I give up. Who is this?"

"Primus," he says, and then the next song comes on and I know it's Tool. I definitely like this better than the country, that's for sure.

"You listen to this?" he asks. I shake my head no.

"I know it, and I like it, but it's not exactly what I listen to." I plug my phone into the car, and the music makes another dramatic change.

"Wow. Falsetto, huh? I didn't think guys could sing that high."

"It's Novo Amor," I say, nudging his knee with my hand. I linger for a moment but move my hand away before it seems too awkward. He reaches toward me and takes my hand back. I look down, marveling at how small and light my hand appears clasped in his.

"What would you call this?" he asks.

"I guess it's indie folk," I say. "But that's not everything I listen to." I take my hand away, but just long enough to switch the music again." When I put my hand back in his, Tupac blasts over the radio.

"Nineties gangsta rap?" He laughs. "You are filled with surprises. That's about as random as country and metal. Probably more."

"Probably," I laugh. "But I only listen to this when I'm alone in the car." I stop myself, realizing I was just about to talk about Finn. "Not everyone likes to listen to guys rapping about bitches and hoes," I finally say.

"And you do?" His grin is almost wider than his face.

"So, I know I'm supposed to be offended by the misogyny—and I am—but come on, how badass do you feel when you listen to this? Late at night, when I'm working on cranking out a huge order, I put on headphones and blast it. Then I feel like I can do anything."

Plus, Finn can't hear it while he's sleeping.

Ethan glances at me, then looks back to the road, shaking his head.

"You are going to break my heart," he says. His words take on a different meaning now that I know about his dad. He takes my hand and lifts it to his mouth, kissing my knuckles. Then he glances back over at me. "I just know you are."

I won't, I silently promise him, even though it might be a lie. This is just one night. One more night to find out who he is, if he's worth figuring out. If he's not, I'll cut it off. It's better to end it before we get too tangled up in whatever is happening here.

But if he is worth it…I'm too scared to think the rest.

"Break your heart, huh? Are you predicting the future? Is that what you're putting out to the universe?" *What if he's the one to break mine?*

"You're just too perfect. I find you utterly irresistible, and it scares me to death."

"Me too," I whisper. He squeezes my hand, and I realize I wasn't as quiet as I should have been, even with hip hop blaring through the car. I bite my lip, then look at him. I laugh at the same time he does. There's no need to say more.

He finds a parking spot near downtown, and we walk the rest of the way to Chicago Dogs. I'd suggested it as a joke because I didn't want Ethan to go broke over our meal. But the other part is that I really love these hot dogs. Every now and then, I skip making dinner for Finn and we'll walk to the park for a hot dog. Then we sit at the fountain, letting our feet dangle in the water while we eat.

"Okay, I have an idea," Ethan says, pulling me aside before we reach the hot dog cart. "But it's a dangerous one. Are you game?"

"It depends," I say.

"How about I put the toppings on your hot dog, any way I like, and you do the same for me."

"No."

He looks genuinely shocked at my answer. "You're

not even going to humor me?"

"No. You have no idea how seriously I take food, especially food I love."

He laughs as if I'm joking, but I shake my head.

"I'm not kidding. I'm not adventurous when it comes to food. If I know I like something, I will eat it that way forever. I don't even eat different things off the menu. There's just too high of a risk that I'll order something I don't like, and then I'll be stuck paying for something I won't eat."

"You can send it back if you don't like it," he says. "People do it all the time."

"I know, but then I have to wait for them to remake my food. Or worse, offend the waiter."

"That's literally their job, Claire. You're not going to offend the waiter."

I stare at him, knowing he's right, but determined to stand my ground on this one. "I know what I like, and there's no need to order differently."

"But these are just hot dogs," he protests.

"And I love hot dogs, and I like them my way."

He pauses, apparently deep in thought. "Okay, I have an idea." I start to shake my head, but he holds his hands up to stop me. "Just hear me out. We order two hot dogs. You make one the way you like it, and the other the way you think I'll like it. You keep the one you made for yourself, but you trade the other one for one I've made for you."

I sigh, not sure I like it, but not hating the idea either.

"If it's no good, I'll take it back," he continues. "I'll even buy you another. What do you say?"

"I guess." I try to sound as doubtful as possible, but it's not enough to keep him from rushing the cart and ordering our hot dogs. Once he does, he gives me two naked dogs.

"I'll go stand over there while you dress these. When you're done, I'll come back and have the guy dress mine."

I roll my eyes. "You better not peek," I say. As much as I hate this whole idea, I have to admit it's kind of fun.

Once he's a safe distance away, I get to work. On mine, I put just ketchup, nothing else. I'm a purist, and don't like much to get in the way of my hot dog and me. But for Ethan, I have a feeling he's more adventurous with his food. I lean over and look at what my options are. I want to add some of everything, but I feel like that's cheating. So I skip the ketchup on his, and add mustard, bacon, sauerkraut, and green onions. I'm not certain about it, but it seems like something he'd like.

Once the hot dogs are fully dressed, I walk in the opposite direction, holding the hot dogs out of Ethan's view as he approaches the cart with his two undressed dogs. I try not to look as he gets them ready, even though I'm super curious. Then I laugh as he walks backwards in my direction, so I can't see what the hot dogs look like.

"On three," he says. I'm giggling as I count down with him. When we say three, he turns around, and we both present the other with our dogs. And when I see the dog he presents to me, I'm floored. It's cheese and relish with bacon bits, nothing else—*just the way Finn likes it.*

"Not even close," he says with a laugh as he takes my hot dog, then wrinkles his nose as he sniffs the sauerkraut.

"I guess you're not a fan of fermented food," I say with a laugh, still in shock over the hot dog he handed me.

"I've never had it," he admits. After a moment of hesitation, he takes a bite. His face relaxes as he chews. "Not bad." He takes another bite, and then nods at the one in my hand. I notice that the other one he's holding looks exactly the same as the one he gave me.

"You made my hot dog the way you like it, I take it." I try to sound nonchalant, but inside I'm all over the map. If Ethan and Finn have never met, how can they have so many similarities? This has to be a sign.

"I know, not super original. But it really is the best way to eat a hot dog."

"I disagree," I say, holding up the dog he made for me, then making a show of scraping off the relish. "Now it's perfect." I bite into it and it brings me back to being here with Finn, eating the rest of his hot dog when he got bored of eating and wanted to run around. Even with the essence of pickles all over it, it's pretty tasty. "You did good," I say, mouth full of food. I swallow. "Better than I did, at least. You must have me all figured out."

"Not completely." He nudges my knee with his. "But the second part of our date could help with that."

We finish eating, and I pull a baby wipe out of my purse to clean my hands. I offer the package to him, and he accepts, but he's obviously amused by it.

"What, you don't carry hand wipes everywhere you go?" I tease. I realize my mistake, though. What other twenty-something carries baby wipes around...unless they have a, you know, baby? Or in my case, a kid who likes to touch everything.

"It's not a bad idea," he says, rubbing his hands together. He smells them. "Lavender and baby powder. Interesting."

"I mean, you could go on smelling like mustard and sauerkraut." I lean into him, and he leans back.

"Nah, baby powder is way better."

We stand, and he laces his fingers with mine. My heartbeat picks up, recalling the end of our last date. Is he going to kiss me now? I want him to, but I'm also hyper aware of my breath, wondering if I'll taste like hot dogs.

He doesn't kiss me. Instead, we walk down the street, our hands linked together like all those couples I've walked by in the past. I forgot how this felt. I'm not sure I ever knew how this felt. Ethan is still so much of a stranger to me, and yet I feel like I belong to him and he belongs to me. Beyond Maren and Finn, I don't think I've ever felt a sense of belonging with anyone. Not even my mom. Especially not my mom. But here, my hand so casually woven with Ethan's, I feel connected—like a missing part of me finally found its way home.

He slows as we near Literati, the bookstore I visit basically every week.

"Here?" I grin, not even trying to hide how excited I am.

"I had a feeling you'd like this," he says, squeezing my hand. He lets go and opens the door for me, following me in. "There's a catch, though."

"Please tell me it doesn't involve me reading *Frankenstein* to you in a dark corner."

His eyes widen, then he breaks into a wicked grin.

"Now that you mention it…"

"No," I laugh. "What's the catch?"

Ethan looks around us, taking in the rows upon rows of bookcases filled with books. "The catch," he says, "is that you and I are going to pick a book for each other."

"Are you serious? That's a catch?" I bite my lip, already mulling over several titles in my brain. He has no idea what he's in for. "Are there rules?"

"None," he says. "Pick anything, and I'll read it."

He leaves me to wander around the store, and I pause in the very center, deciding on the direction to go. Mostly I'm distracted by the direction Ethan headed in because I'm so curious about what he'll choose for me. I know this bookstore like my own neighborhood, and I can tell which genre he's looking at just by the row he visits. He slips down the science fiction row, and I hold my breath until he travels to high fantasy. He isn't much of a reader, so I'm nervous about what he'll find among those books. It could either be really good, or really, really long and tedious.

My distraction isn't helping my own search, so I disappear upstairs to my favorite section—romance. I'm not fooled by Ethan's plan. Whatever book I choose for him will say *novels* about who I am. Books are such personal things, and I take that very seriously—not just because it's my job, but because I love reading books. I can think of several dozen novels that kept me up late, reading until daylight. But my favorite books to read are ones with love stories, and what better way to let Ethan get to know me than to reveal my sappy, lovesick, romantic side?

But then I have an even better idea.

I'm still determined to hold Ethan at arm's length, but my resolve is weakening. There's a huge possibility that there's something here worth pursuing. And if that's the case, he's going to meet Finn one day. I'm still worried about his aversion to kids, but what if I can find a book that will introduce the idea first—like a love story that includes a child the father doesn't know about? Ethan's experience with his own dad obviously shaped his idea about having kids. But that's what makes a book like this even more perfect—what if the love story is so compelling, it changes his mind about being a dad? If Ethan and I don't work out, then whatever book I choose can just be a book, no hidden agenda. But if Ethan turns out to be who I think he is, I can use it as a tool to start the conversation.

It's such a perfect solution to my dilemma, especially since Ethan is the one who thought of this whole book swap first.

I scroll through the shelves of romance books. What I love about Literati is how generous they are with their romance section. So many other bookstores limit their romance books to a few shelves in the back. But at Literati, almost the entire upstairs is packed with romance books with all different levels of heat. They also have trope cheat sheets on the wall with staff recommendations for people looking to read a certain kind of romance. When I can't find the book I'm looking for on the shelf, I head to the wall guide, scanning until I finally come across a few recommendations for *secret baby romances.*

Secret baby romance. God, just seeing it named that

makes me feel so wrong. I have to keep reminding myself that I'm not playing games, but just being extra cautious.

I pick one of the tamer suggestions titled *By the Bay*, which seems fitting since we live by the ocean. I locate the book on the shelf and thumb through it. The story is kind of like mine and Ethan's real-life story, except the couple is dating and things have been rocky. They break up, but soon after the girl discovers she's pregnant. She moves to her aunt's house in Georgia where she has a baby girl and raises her on her own. The couple reconnect years later, and the guy doesn't realize the child is his daughter until he figures it out on his own.

I flip to the end, relieved to see there's a happy ending.

My phone buzzes and I pull it out, smiling when I see a picture of Ethan looking back at me. He's holding a bag next to his cheesy grin, and I know my book is in there.

Holding *By the Bay* in my hands is like holding a grenade. I still have time to put it down and go for a more generic romance novel. I mean, what if he figures out the truth while reading it, before I even have a chance to ease him into it?

But what if this is the key to starting the dialogue? Books are powerful, with stories that can change lives and shift ways of thinking. I can't help thinking of *Frankenstein*, how it not only shifted society's thinking about the role science can play in creation, but also helped people realize that ignoring tough issues only makes them bigger.

By the Bay can be my *Frankenstein*. If I believe Ethan could be a part of Finn's life, I need help tackling the ghosts of his past, and this book could be the answer. It's a stretch, I know, but I need to have faith.

I look at the book again, and suddenly it feels less like a grenade and more like a seed that's ready to sprout.

I tuck the book under my arm so I can text while walking down the stairs.

Me: Just finished. Heading to check out now. Meet you out front.

Ethan holds my hand as we walk to the beach. The glowing fire pits dot the upper portion of the beach, surrounded by people drinking and enjoying the warm night. Every few minutes, a new star appears in the rouge sky. The sliver of moon descends toward the ocean, followed closely by Venus. It's a magical night, and I feel warm all over, starting with my hand resting in Ethan's.

"We should probably swap books before it gets too dark," I say, my heart pounding as I grip the bag in my other hand.

"You're right," he says, pausing at a spot and then motioning for us to sit. I clutch the bag in front of me as

I sit cross-legged in the still-warm sand. The ocean laps at the shore in front of us, and I recognize how rare this moment is for me. Usually at this time, I'd be up to my eyebrows in projects while Finn falls asleep. I can't even remember the last time I was on the beach past dark because it just isn't convenient when you have a kid. I mean, it could have been. We could have skipped a bedtime here or there. Finn would probably love to see how the moon looks as it dips into the ocean, or how the stars look when they first appear at night.

"You first," Ethan says, dragging me out of my thoughts as he nods at my bag.

"What? It was your idea!" I'm suddenly full of regret. Why couldn't I have gotten a book that meant nothing? No message, no hidden agenda, and no secret baby?

"I just think the best should go last, is all," he says, his mouth curving into a crooked smirk. I nudge him in protest, and he laughs out loud. "Okay, honestly it's because I had no idea what to get you, and I need a clue from whatever book you chose for me to see if I was on the right track."

"You were supposed to choose a book that you wanted me to read," I remind him.

"Hello, have we met?" he asks, lifting our hands so he can kiss my knuckles. I shiver as his lips touch my fingers. "Ethan Chance, non-reader. But something tells me you're going to turn me into a bookworm. Now show your cards, Claire."

I hold my breath as I hand the package over. A million thoughts are going through my mind as he opens the bag, including the kind of message he'll get once he realizes what it's about. It occurs to me that there are more meanings he can draw from this book than figuring out he has a son. He could think I want his baby now, for one.

Oh God. I messed up.

"Interesting choice," he says, looking at the cover. There's a couple on the beach walking hand-in-hand, and on the sand next to them is a teddy bear, symbolizing the secret child. Forget the secret message—looking at it now, it seems like the cheesiest, lamest book I could have picked.

He flips the book over and reads it, holding his phone flashlight up so he can see the words. When he's done, he turns off the flashlight and looks at me. I'm holding my breath so he can't tell how nervous I am.

"Of all the books I would have chosen, I'm not sure I would have picked a romance," he says, laughing.

"I figure it's a good way to learn about what I do," I say, then my eyes widen as I realize the implication regarding babies. "I mean, the work I do with romance authors. It's a crazy popular market, and romance readers are devouring books like these, along with the swag that gets sold with them. It's allowed me to have my own business all this time, and I'm so grateful for that. But I also love reading romance. So I thought I'd start you off with something light like a…" I take the book and flip through it for a second, then hand it back to him. "Yeah, I thought I'd start you off with a sweet romance before I get you into something a bit more, uh, naughty."

"So, sweet romance means…" He tilts his head, pausing.

"No sex," I finish for him. "At least, not anything that's described."

He hands the book back to me. "I want the naughty one."

I laugh, then push it back in his lap.

"Sorry, Sparky. You have to start with the fade-to-black romance books, just like the rest of us. Now, what did you get me?"

He hands me his bag, and I open it up. When I pull it out, I squeal. It's the latest Amanda Loring book in her *Throne of Roses* series.

"I take it I did good," he says, rubbing his ears with exaggeration.

"You mean, the store clerk did good," I laugh. But I'm not mad about this at all. "This just came out last week, and I haven't had a chance to get it yet." I close the book, then turn to the back cover, reading the synopsis I practically know by heart. Then I open the book again. "It's been a nice date, Ethan. We should probably call it a night."

He snatches the book from my hands as I laugh, and he holds it out of my reach.

"Hey, that's mine," I squeal.

He peers at the bare-chested man gracing the cover, then back at me. "I don't know, maybe I should return it. If your novels have guys like that on it, I don't stand a chance."

I tilt my head, giving him a once over. "I think it's a draw," I say. He smiles at me, then takes the book and places it next to the one I got him.

"Good answer," he murmurs.

My breath catches as he gets closer. Even though we're past our first kiss—seven years, if we're being technical—my nerves mix with excitement, leaving my body tingling in anticipation. He presses his mouth to mine, and I swear there isn't a romance novel in the world that can make me feel this way. Everything disappears, and it's just us. One hand in my hair, the other holding me up as he leans into me. His mouth equal parts hard and soft, demanding and questioning. He moves to caress my cheek and I make a small sound in the back of my throat, tilting my head to capture more of him. He's warm and comforting, and I lose myself a little more with each second we're connected. I could write a novel about this, just the kiss and nothing else. It's almost surprising when he pulls back and I open my eyes.

My soul returns to my body, and I can't believe I've lived this many years without him as my air.

"I want to know everything about you," he says, his hand still on my cheek as he searches my eyes. "Your favorite color, what you dream about at night, what you ate for breakfast. Leave nothing out."

I tell him everything that isn't Finn. I tell him about living with my mother and how I raised myself. I share my hopes of traveling the world one day and seeing places I've only dreamed about. I tell him about my friendship with Maren, how I join marches to fight inequality regarding race, gender, or orientation, and how I sometimes think I could write a book instead of just reading them. And my favorite color is blue.

He tells me how he barely graduated, but got into college on a football scholarship, which explains why he's so ripped. He surfs almost every morning, and most evenings are at Hillside. In between that he's either playing basketball with friends, running, or playing video games. Or all three. I note that he says nothing about his father, feeling a twinge of guilt that I already know.

"Wow, you're pretty active," I say. "Aren't you exhausted?"

"Not really," he says. "I guess when you do it for fun, it's not tiring at all. But what about you? I know you have your book craft business, but what do you do for fun? Besides picnics at the park."

I give a weak laugh, trying to buy myself time. What *do* I do for fun? Rush in the morning to get Finn ready for school. Clean the house while he's away. Work my ass off to make sure we can eat. Sign a million permission slips. Volunteer for craft days in his classroom. Take him to the doctors, the dentist, playdates, birthday parties, and occasionally to see his grandma because I can't seem to cut her out of my life.

"Stuff," I say.

"Like, top secret kind of stuff," he whispers, his eyes roaming over the beach as if we're being watched.

I laugh at him, but inside I'm at a crossroads.

Tonight has been wonderful. It wasn't over the top, and nothing huge happened at all. It was just a night full of small, thoughtful things that not only helped us know each other, but also served as a prelude to what it would be like if I were with Ethan. If he was a player before, he certainly doesn't seem like one now. Even more, I can see myself falling for him, and the wild, curious side of me wants to find out what that feels like.

But more than anything, I realize how complicated my big secret is making everything.

"There's something I need to tell you," I say, turning so I can face him. He reaches for my hands, but I keep them in my lap. "It's the biggest thing about me, and I'm not sure how you'll take it."

Ethan doesn't speak, even when I stay silent for a

moment, trying to find courage, let alone the words, to tell him the truth. I breathe slow, doing my best to hide my shaking hands from him by clasping and unclasping them. This is it. Once I tell him, he could very well break things off immediately. I have to find the right words. This might not even be the right time. I could be making the biggest mistake, or maybe it will offer clarity to what happens next.

Finally, I just blurt it out.

"I have a son."

Chapter 12

I study his face, trying to see into his mind. He says nothing at first, and all I can feel is my pounding heart. It was the right thing to do. I know this. But I also can't help feeling like I made a terrible mistake. We'd just had an amazing night, and I had to go ruin it and tell him I had a kid.

The moment I think this, I'm filled with paralyzing guilt. I'm acting like I'm ashamed of my kid, as if I'm more worried about Ethan's reaction than the existence of my son. *Our* son. It's terrible that Ethan's dad left him, and even more so that Ethan has been carrying this burden around for so long. But it's not my issue. My responsibility lies with Finn. If Ethan can't accept that I'm a package deal, he doesn't belong in our lives, regardless of his DNA mingling with mine in our son.

"What's he like?" Ethan asks.

And just like that, I let out the breath I didn't realize I was holding. I tell him about Finn's obsession with dinosaurs, and how he's bothered when people color outside the lines, and his aversion to all things vegetable.

"You hide vegetables in your brownies?" Ethan looks at me likes he's wounded.

"Well, do you like vegetables?" I ask.

"I do now. But I didn't used to," he says. "My mom used to pull the same trick, and it never worked. In fact, it made me suspicious of everything and everyone."

I wrinkle my nose, not missing the comparison. "Fine then, how did you learn to like them?"

"First, it was realizing that if I wanted to be fit and strong, I had to start eating vegetables. So I started with salads, adding things I liked to it like bacon, croutons, and bleu cheese dressing, then slowly weaning down to just vegetables. Then I started experimenting with other vegetables. I learned that I liked them roasted more than steamed, though I'll steam when I'm trying to be healthier. Oh, and seasonings. A piece of cooked broccoli tastes a hell of a lot better with garlic salt."

"And how old were you when you figured all this out?" I ask, my eyes sweeping over his firm physique.

"Not until my twenties."

I shake my head, looking out at the ocean in front of us. "Well my kid is six, and I'd rather not wait another fourteen years before he realizes vegetables are good for him."

"Then don't hide them," Ethan says. I look at him curiously. He laces my fingers through his, then shoots me a sheepish grin. "I'm not a parent, so I'm not going to pretend I know how to raise a kid. But I think if my mom stopped hiding vegetables and instead dressed them up in delicious ways, I probably would have liked them a lot sooner."

I wrinkle my nose at him, but I'm genuinely curious about what he means, especially since it might be similar to what Finn might like. "Examples, please."

"Like, covering steamed broccoli with nacho cheese, or making fun dipping sauces for roasted carrots, or even having him help you make a huge salad with all his favorite toppings."

Admittedly, my ego wants to tell him off for suggesting any kind of way to feed our son. But he also has a point. I'd tried feeding Finn vegetables straight up, and I'd tried hiding them. But I haven't tried meeting him in the middle by making vegetables fun.

"All right, I'll try it your way," I say, nudging his shoulder with mine. He nudges me back. Then his face takes on a pensive look.

"Did you make me believe Maren's house was yours because you didn't want me to know you had a kid?"

I gape at him, and his face breaks into a huge grin.

"You knew that wasn't my house?" I ask. "All this

time, and you didn't say anything?"

"I was afraid you had a boyfriend or something, but I still wanted to get to know you."

"Oh my God, you dog," I laugh. "I can't believe you thought I was cheating on some guy for you."

"You're gorgeous," he says. "It makes no sense that you don't have a boyfriend. I wanted to give you the benefit of the doubt, and I figured it wasn't my business. I couldn't help thinking you were trying to make me your side piece."

Gorgeous. The fact that he thinks me, plain Claire, is gorgeous when he's supposedly into supermodels does something to my ego. I smother a smile and focus on the part where he thought I was cheating.

"First off, ew. My mom was a great example as to why more than one man is a complication I shouldn't have. Second, I haven't dated for years because I just haven't had the time or the energy. And third, how did you know it was Maren's apartment?"

"Nina. I was with her when I pulled up directions on my phone, and she asked why I was going to Maren's house. I told her I wasn't, that I was going to yours. But I could tell Nina knew something I didn't. She's the one who suggested you might be pulling a fast one on me since Maren lives alone."

I groan. Of course Nina told him that. She was probably paying me back for keeping this huge secret from her cousin.

"Let's just say that if I were cheating on you, I'd probably tell you all about it since I obviously suck at lying."

"Just don't cheat on me, and we're good."

I bite my lip at the implications of this. Is he suggesting that we're exclusive?

"So, this kid. What's his name? Do I need to know anything before I meet him?" Ethan asks.

"Finn. And you're not meeting him." It slips out so fast, that I almost choke after I say it. "I mean, not yet. I just...I..."

"Claire, it's fine," he says, taking my hand and pulling me into his lap. I rest my head against his chest, lulled by the thrum of his heart. "I don't know how these kinds of things work. I've never dated someone who has a kid, so I'm following your lead on this. Whatever you say is how it will go. I just have one request."

I look up at him. "Yes?"

"Can I at least know where you live? I won't drop by unannounced, and I'll be as discreet as you want me to be. But I'd like to know where my girlfr—" He coughs, interrupting himself. "I mean, I'd like to know where you live." Rubbing the back of his neck, he shoots me a sheepish look. "That sounded creepy. It's just that, I like you, and I'd like to see more of you. Part of that is visiting you at your house, and you visiting me at mine. God, I don't know how to say it without it sounding weird."

I'm still recovering from him almost calling me his girlfriend. Why did he stop? I guess it's early, but I think I want the label.

"You don't sound weird," I say, pressing against him as I peer into his eyes. "I'd love for you to see my home, and I'd love to see yours."

It's late when we finally leave the beach. As we head to his car, I realize my cheeks hurt from smiling so much. It's like this huge weight has been lifted from my shoulders. He still doesn't know who Finn is to him, but the fact that he knows about my son at all is a huge step forward.

Ethan asks a few questions about Finn and what it was like to become a parent when I was so young. I answer them all honestly, describing my struggle with insecurity.

"I essentially had to learn how to parent from scratch," I say. "My mom wasn't the best role model, and I didn't want to raise him the same way. I did the best I could, but I went into it blind, not sure what the best actually looks like."

"I'm sure you did a great job. I mean, he's still alive, right?"

I laugh at this.

"Yes, but even a bad parent can keep a kid alive. It's

the stuff they do to their child's insides that matter. I don't want Finn to ever feel the way I felt growing up."

"What about his dad?"

I knew this question was coming, but it still knocks the wind out of me. I look up at him, stalling as I try to find the best way to answer.

"He's not in the picture," I say, praying he won't ask more. Ethan squeezes the hand he's holding, offers me a sad smile.

"His loss, I'm sure."

We reach Ethan's car and he leans against the passenger side, holding me against his chest. I know he has more questions than the ones he voiced aloud, and I appreciate the caution he's exercising. I can't help feeling it's one more sign that whatever this is between us will become so much more than what it already is. I look into his eyes, and cling to the warmth I see radiating back at me. It brings me back to a night like this, seven years earlier.

"I have a weird question for you," I ask. "Have you ever worn contacts?"

"Random, but not weird. Why?"

"Just curious."

"I have perfect eyesight, so I've never needed to. But I used to play around with them when I was younger." He chuckles, shaking his head. "I had this one green pair I used to wear all the time because I thought it made me look hot."

"I bet you did," I say, biting back a smile. "You probably drove all the girls crazy."

"Not exactly, I was kind of a dork around women. But there was this one time, when I—"

He stops himself, and I smack his chest.

"You can't stop there," I laugh. "There was this one time…. What's the rest?"

"You don't want to hear about it," he says. Even in the dim light, I can see his cheeks turning pink.

"I really do," I say. I press against him to stand upright, but he holds me firmly in place. "Tell me, or the night ends now."

"Oh, really? Well, in that case…"

I remain as still as possible as he launches into the story of how we met. Except, he has no idea that I am part of this story.

"I knew the guy who was throwing the party, but I wouldn't have gone if my friends hadn't talked me into it. That, and it was a masquerade party, and there's something about wearing a mask that offers an extra layer of courage. I didn't know anyone else there, and they didn't know me. But then I see this girl lying on the floor. I thought she'd had too much to drink, but she'd just fallen. The whole time all I can think about is how pretty she was, and how confident she sounded, and that if she knew the real me, she'd laugh and walk away."

"I'm sure she didn't think that," I say, breaking my promise not to interrupt.

"Maybe, maybe not. All I know is that with my mask on, I didn't have to worry about what she thought because she didn't know me, and probably wouldn't after that night. I ended up driving her home, and one thing led to another. The crazy part is, we never even learned each other's names."

"Did you ever figure out who she was?" I ask.

"No. I didn't know the first place to look. When I dropped her off, it was blocks from her house because she didn't want me to know where she lived. I figured she had a reason for keeping things secret. Not only that, it kind of made the whole experience hotter."

"Do you regret it?" I want him to say yes. I want him to tell me how this girl haunts his dreams and he won't rest until he finds her. Instead, he kisses my forehead, then rubs his thumb along my cheek.

"It was a long time ago, and we were young. You have nothing to worry about. I'm here for you, and not some girl I had a meaningless fling with."

His words are supposed to bring me comfort, but it feels like a gut punch to be referred to as a *meaningless fling*. I hope he's just saving my feelings. I hope our *meaningless fling* keeps him up at night.

"So, Claire. You said if I told you, the date didn't have to end. And since it's nearly two in the morning and all the bars are closing down, that kind of limits our options."

This time I do pull away. I look at my phone, shocked at the time. With Maren babysitting, I have nowhere to be in the morning. But I haven't been out this late in years.

"I didn't realize the time!"

"I can drop you off at your house, or at Maren's, if that's what you want. But we can also head to my house if you're up for it."

This time, I feel a jolt in my core that hasn't been affected by a person since…well, since teenage Ethan.

"I want to," I say honestly. "But I just don't, uh…"

"I'm saving myself for marriage," he interrupts. His face is serious as he says it, but he breaks into a grin when my eyes widen. "I'm kidding." He brushes a piece of hair from my face, then cradles my cheek. "I'm being selfish, but I just don't want our date to end. We can take things slow, I promise. I just want to fall asleep with you in my arms."

Why do these words make the air taste sweeter? I smile, covering his hand with mine.

"I'd love that."

Chapter 13

Ethan's home is a one-bedroom condo on the other side of Sunset Bay. It's modest in location and size, but he makes up for it with a fresh and simple style. It's clean with a masculine touch, from the grey couch to the hint of cologne in the air. On the walls are eclectic art, and I lean in to study the neon lines intertwined with the shadow of a picture.

"I got it off Etsy," he says, rubbing the back of his neck like he's embarrassed. But I think it's cool, especially since that's where most authors find me and my swag.

I can't help but think about the kind of guy Ethan is as he shows me around. There's a weight set in the corner, a bar set up by the couch, and a few plants on his back patio. It's so different from my home, which gives off the obvious vibes of a single mother who lets her kid take over the aesthetic. For a moment I wonder how different I'd be if I hadn't had Finn.

Emptier, I decide. Yes, it's been hard and I've had to grow up fast, but I think I'm more grounded as Finn's mother than I would have been in a different life.

"And this is the bedroom," he says. I glance at the closet, noticing the pile oozing out of the space just as he rushes past me to kick it all back in before closing the doors.

"Now I know how you keep your place so clean," I laugh. "You knew I was coming over, didn't you?"

"I hoped," he admitted. I took a sidestep toward the closet, and he moved forward to block me. "Don't even think of it, Sparky," he says.

I start when I hear him say that. It's *my* word. But the way he says it sends a tingle of familiarity down my spine.

Easy there, Sparky. You've had a little much to drink.

I just realized where *my* word originated from.

"What's wrong?"

Ethan drops his defensive stance and steps toward me. I mentally shake myself free from the memory.

"Nothing." I grin, attempting to prove I'm fine. But inside, I can't help but wonder if my memories from the past are going to continue to haunt our present. We only knew each other a few hours, and our shared past has affected my whole life. "I'm just relieved to see you're as human as I am," I say.

"You may end up regretting how human I really

am," he admits. "But first impressions are everything. So for now, the junk closet stays shut."

Without warning, he tackles me to the bed as I squeal and pretend to fight him off. We both slow at the same time, and then his mouth covers mine. His kiss is gentle, unrushed. His hand plays in my hair spread over his quilt, the other cupping the back of my head as his body covers mine. I clasp his bicep, then move to his back, feeling the peaks and valleys of his muscles ripple under my hands. My need burns inside me, growing into wildfire as his tongue explores mine. I'm hungry for him. But as much as I want him, I'm afraid to go to the next level. I hesitate, just barely, but enough that he breaks our kiss and looks down at me. His eyes are kind, erasing any fear that my reservations will disappoint him.

"We're just kissing," he says. "Nothing else, I promise."

I nod, and tears unexpectedly fill my eyes. I don't know what is making me emotional. It could be his tender thoughtfulness, or maybe the fact that after all these years, I'm here with him and he's everything I hoped he'd be. Whatever it is, my tears don't scare him away. He lightly brushes them with his fingers, then kisses me again. He keeps true to his word, even when I relax, opening my mouth to deepen the kiss. This time when he breaks away, I'm amused by the struggle he tries to hide. A glance below the belt, and his arousal is obvious.

"We should probably go to bed," he says, lifting off the bed. He crosses the room to his dresser and pulls out a t-shirt, which he hands to me. "I have an extra toothbrush in the bathroom drawer, if you want it."

I bite back my smile. My own toothbrush. I know it's weird to think this is such a huge deal, but it just is. Will I keep it here? Will he store it next to his?

We brush our teeth at the same time, but he finishes before I do and heads to the bedroom. I linger once I'm done, then place my toothbrush next to his in the medicine cabinet. Then I wash my face, taking my time as I study the content on the shelves in front of me. His razor and shaving cream. A brush. Some floss. Even a night guard for his teeth. Why I find the night guard adorable, I don't know.

I slip his t-shirt over my head, and it hangs like a dress. That's a good thing since the only underwear I have with me is a thong. I can't believe I brought an overnight bag, and it's sitting in Maren's living room. My bare cheeks rub against the cotton shirt, and even though I'm covered, I feel completely naked as I step back into the bedroom. Ethan is already undressed and in bed, and my eyes widen when I take in his tattooed chest and arms.

"I'm wearing boxers," he assures me. I figured he was, but he still seems so naked. I'm not sure how I'll sleep next to him all night, feeling his body next to mine.

I crawl into bed, carefully slipping under the covers without revealing my near nudity under his shirt. It smells like him. So do the covers as I pull them up to my chin. It's intoxicating.

He scoots down in bed and we face each other on the pillows.

"What's your usual night routine," he asks.

"You really want to know something that boring?"

"I want to know everything about you."

Why do his words make me feel so gushy inside?

"It starts around seven when I start to put Finn to bed." I continue with what I do every evening, from reading Finn a bedtime story to dealing with his multiple questions or requests. "Once he's finally out, I spend the next few hours in my studio. I spend a lot of my day running errands, cleaning the house, and buying supplies, so my nights are when I get really involved in the creative process."

I'd learned early on that if I want uninterrupted time with my projects, nighttime was a sure bet. The distractions were minimal, and my mind seemed to wake up once Finn was asleep and I didn't have to worry about him.

"Every night?" he asks, and I nod. He appears troubled by this. "But how do you do anything fun? Like go out on dates?"

"I haven't dated for a very long time," I admit, and my cheeks heat up when I see how puzzled he looks. "It's complicated. I have fun, but most of my fun includes Finn."

I can see the questions rolling around in his head, but he swallows them with a smile. "Okay, after you're done with your work, then what?"

"Then I'm so tired I can barely move," I laugh. "I should do a whole moisturizing regiment, but usually I just collapse in bed until my alarm goes off at six."

"Holy hell, girl. How do you manage on so little sleep?"

"I'm used to it, and I usually fit in a nap in the afternoons. Naps are highly underrated."

"I haven't taken a nap since I was a kid," he laughs. Then he scoots closer, resting his hand on my hip as our noses graze each other's. He squeezes my hip, then pulls me even closer. "But if I were napping with you, I think I could do it every day."

I swat at his hand, but don't move when he kisses me. It's soft and tender, and I know it's a goodnight kiss. He doesn't try anything else except to turn me so that I fit against him. I can feel the t-shirt riding up behind me and my skin touching his boxers. I can tell he's still turned on, but he doesn't do anything except pull me tighter against his chest.

"Goodnight, Claire," he whispers.

"Goodnight, Ethan."

I listen to him breathe, feeling lulled as it slows. Feeling safe, even though we barely know each other. Feeling like this is where I belong.

I'm the first one to wake, my eyes adjusting to the low light of morning sun streaming through the blinds, my dream running through the barrier between sleep and awake. I'd been dreaming of Finn's father. It wasn't the first time I'd dreamed of him, but it was the first that combined the boy I'd met years ago and the man that's sleeping behind me now.

I'm surprised Ethan's arms are still around me, mostly because I'm used to sleeping on my own. But Ethan serves as a cocoon, and I remain still as his heart beats against my back. I could stay this way forever, except my bladder says otherwise. I hold out as long as I can, but eventually have to maneuver out of his hold. He stirs as I do, then pulls me tighter as I try slip away.

"I have to pee," I whisper, laughing. He groans but lets go.

I finish my business, and he's still in bed when I slide back into the sheets. His eyes are closed, but he opens his arms and I fit within them, pressing my face against his chest. He smells like morning, like skin and soap and something earthy that's both comforting and familiar. His hands drop to my waist, and then to my backside, and he inhales when his hand meets skin. He starts to pull away, but I put my hand on his, leading it back to my bare ass.

He opens his eyes, and I see the question forming in his expression.

Everything feels different this morning. Last night, I was resolved to proceed with caution and to put the brakes on if anything progressed to fast. But much of that slipped away after spending the whole night in his arms. Maybe it had to do with my dream, the way he coached me through our first time together—my first time ever—and the gentle way he touched me. Just recalling it, I can feel the yearning grow inside me, making it hard to breathe unless he's breathing for me.

"Don't stop," I whisper.

"Are you saying…" He breaks off, and I nod. Then he leans in and kisses me. It's soft and hesitant, and I can tell he's holding back, that he's treating me with care in case I change my mind. I'm not going to change my mind. As nervous as I am, as much as this feels like the first time all over again, the need inside me is greater. I press into him, wrapping a leg around him and pulling him closer. It's all it takes. He flips me onto my back and claims my mouth, taking my air and giving me his. I arch my back as his hands grasp my hips, pulling me closer so that I'm flush against his solid erection. His skin is hot through my shirt, which he's now tugging at.

"I want to feel you," he says. It's a statement, not a question, and I lift my arms up so he can pull the shirt over my head. For a moment I realize just how naked I am, even though I'm still wearing a thong. No one has ever seen me like this, not even Ethan of the past. I fight the urge to cover up, though one of my hands strays near my breast. He slips his hand into mine, pulling it back over my head as he looks down at me.

"Damn, Claire. You're incredible."

His words trigger something in me, especially when I see the hungry look in his eyes. It matches my own quiet anticipation, a feeling that's growing by the second.

He lowers his head and grasps my nipple with his lips, his tongue lighting over the tip as I burn beneath him. My breath comes out in short spurts as he drags his mouth over my belly, trailing it across my hip as he pulls my thong slowly down my thighs and over my feet. I don't have a chance to process this new level of nudity before I feel his hot air at my core, soon replaced by his mouth.

"Oh, God!" His warm tongue swirls over me with wet caresses, and I swear I'll come undone if he stops. It takes everything in me to not buck against his mouth. He increases the pressure, his mouth now devouring me in ways that make me lightheaded and frantic. The warmth spreads from my core, sliding across my skin until my mind erupts and my whole body turns to flame. I cry out as the orgasm takes over, as he steadies his rhythm, as the tremors ripple over me in waves.

I can barely open my eyes as he slides off his boxers. I hear the crinkle of the condom wrapper. Then I feel him pressing against my core. My eyes open wide as he presses in, pain blending with pleasure as he slowly enters me.

"Am I hurting you?" He remains still inside me as I get used to his presence. It's tight, just like the first time. But there's no tearing. No pain that's too much. I want to feel so much more of him. I pull at his hips as I lift mine, the pain subsiding as my need grows.

"It feels good," I whisper, moaning as he starts to move. He stays slow, his hands tangling in my hair as he kisses me, as my body remains pressed against his, as we move together like it's a dance. The feel of his chest grazing against my bare breasts is more erotic than anything I've ever felt. The way his hand clutches my back as he moves against me, I want to feel him deeper. I don't know what I'm doing, but it doesn't matter. He guides me where I need to go, my skin tingling in the wake of his wandering hands.

This is nothing like our first time, and everything like it. There was only so much we could do in a cramped car, but the way he held me then is much like the way he's holding me now—his hands grasping me with calm control while his touch remains tender and slow. Like he's savoring this. Like he never wants it to end.

And yet, older Ethan has a sureness about him that young Ethan couldn't know. He whispers soft words in my ear, telling me I'm beautiful and how good I feel, sometimes just saying my name. His kisses match the urgency I feel. He moves inside me like he's known me forever. As the warm waves of my orgasm ride over me, I feel him swell while he groans against my neck. He thrusts harder as I cry out, then slows as the aftershocks make me tremble. When he's spent, he lowers onto me and rolls us to the side, remaining connected as we recover in each other's arms.

"Good morning," he whispers after a while, and I grin at him. He pulls out but stays facing me, his hand smoothing the hair away from my face before he traces my cheekbone with his finger.

"Good morning," I say. "That was incredible." I feel silly as soon as I say it, not sure if you're supposed to comment on sex or not. But he grins before nodding.

"That was everything I expected it would be, and more." He flips the covers over, and I get an eyeful of his length. He's still hard, and he grins down at himself, then back at me as he gets up.

"Potty break," he says. "But stay where you are. We're not done."

I bite my lip at his retreating back, then stretch out in the bed. I feel massaged inside and out, my muscles straining in places I haven't felt before. I'm satiated in a whole new way, and yet, the promise of more has me squirming in anticipation.

When Ethan returns to bed, he makes good on that promise. The second time there's no pain, only pleasure, and I can't help wondering why I swore off dating all these years. Maybe I was waiting for him. Whatever it was, I'm glad I'm here now. There's no place else I want to be.

Chapter 14

Ethan and I fall into an easy new rhythm. Almost every day, he shows up at my house about an hour after Finn goes to school, and we lose ourselves between the sheets until I have to tear myself away for work. Even then, he stays with me for a few more hours, helping me with projects or playing chauffeur while I run errands. Before Finn is home from school, Ethan leaves for his own job, and I'm left with a permanent smile on my face.

We never mention the book I picked out for him. I have no idea if he's read it or not, and I'm afraid to ask. I feel like my secret will spring out at him within the pages—like one of those pop-up books—and the more I get to know Ethan, the more I'm afraid of telling him the truth. I know I need to tell Ethan that Finn is his son at some point, but I'm not sure how. And as much as he's passed Finn's photos on every wall, on my fridge, and on the mantle above the fireplace, he's never once figured out that he's Finn's father.

At the very least, I keep waiting for Ethan to ask about meeting Finn, even though Nina's story about his dad tugs at my mind. It's been weeks since we started seeing each other, and besides the day I told him I had a son, he hasn't offered any sign of wanting to meet Finn. Still, I keep hoping his feelings for me surpasses the ghosts of his past. We spend just about every moment of our free time together, getting to know each other inside and out, and the whole time I have this huge question in the back of my mind and I can't ask it.

"Just ask him," Maren tells me. She's at my kitchen table on a rare morning when Ethan isn't there. I feel bad because my mornings after Finn leaves are usually reserved for her, but I've been so wrapped up in Ethan, we haven't hung out much except when she offers to watch Finn.

"Ask him what? If he'd like to be my baby daddy?" I take a piece off the croissant she brought me and stuff it in my mouth.

"He already is, doofus. I mean, ask if he'd like to hang out with you and Finn so he can meet the kid."

"You make it sound so simple." I sigh, finishing off the croissant, then reaching for another. I know I'm stress eating, but I can't help it. The thought of Finn and Ethan together makes me equal parts nervous and excited.

"It *is* simple," she says, taking the croissant out of my hands and putting it back in the bag. I pout as she puts it out of reach. "The croissant isn't going to make things better."

"It makes *me* feel better."

"No, it will make you sleepy in an hour, and you need your wits about you. You need to talk with Ethan tonight. Tell him you want him to meet Finn."

"Why tonight?" I eye the croissant bag longingly, even though I know she's right. Eating my stress isn't the answer.

"Because the longer you put this off, the more you'll overthink it. The more you overthink it, the better chance you have of screwing this up. And Claire, you don't want to screw this up. I've never seen you so happy."

I smother my smile, but it's cresting over the hand covering my mouth, into my cheeks, and oozing out of my eyes to the point that Maren shakes her head. But she's smiling too.

"It's your fault," I say, which is what I've been telling myself for all the weeks I've neglected our friendship.

"I'll take some of the blame, along with Nina. But I think the two of you have the most to do with it." She nudges my shoulder with her fist. "I'm thrilled for you, which is why I want to see this work. The only way this will work is if you let down all of your damn barriers and let this guy fully in. That starts with letting him see Mom Claire, not just Sexy Claire."

"But Sexy Claire is so much more fun."

"Mom Claire is fun, too, just not as scandalous. Trust me, when Ethan meets Mom Claire, he's going to beg to be Finn's baby daddy."

"That's not funny." My smile drops as my heart skips a beat. Maren smirks at me, and I groan. "See, I can't even joke about it. Ethan is going to totally lose it when he finds out we had a kid."

"Or he's going to be thrilled."

"Right. Especially since he told me he's never having kids." I drop my head in my hands. Maren reaches over, removing my hands from my face.

"Claire, people change. Besides, you're not asking him to be anything. You're just asking him to meet your son. It's a normal part of dating a single parent. He's gotten to know you as Claire. Now he gets to meet the most important person in your life. If you really want to see if he's daddy material, he needs to at least meet your kid first."

I mull this over, even though there's really no mulling to do. She's right. The longer I put this off, the more painful it's going to be. If I know Ethan—and I think I have a pretty good idea about him—there's going to be one day when I tell him about Finn, and then invite him into our son's life on a larger level. But the longer I put this off, the worse I'm going to make it. He needs to meet Finn, and soon.

I stall for a few more days, which of course, leads to a whole lot of overthinking. I've run through scenarios that include Ethan proposing marriage right on the spot or disappearing from my life forever. I even imagine him figuring out who Finn is and suing me for custody. I realize I'm getting nowhere by making up stories about what he'll do. Besides, I've already gone through the worst of it in my imagination, so I might as well get it over with in real life.

Maren offers to stay with Finn so that Ethan and I can go to the movies. I'd considered just having him pick me up at my house so that I can get the meeting part out of the way. But I'm a planner. I need just as much time to get used to this idea as he might. Maybe more.

I rehearse what I'm going to say on the drive over. *Ethan, I'd love for you to meet my son, the fruit of our loins.* Ew, gross, no. Plus, I can't tell him the relation yet. *Ethan, I think it's time for you to meet my son, a boy who looks just like you, totally a coincidence.* What is wrong with you, Claire! *Ethan, it's time for you to meet Finn, which will bring us to the next level, and...*

By the time I get to his house, I am completely jumbled with all the wrong words, and nowhere closer to finding the right ones. Never in my life did I think I'd be in this position, and now that I am, I feel like the last leaf on a tree in a windstorm.

"You look stunning," Ethan says as he opens the door, his eyes roaming over me.

I'm immediately struck by two things. One, my nerve to bring up meeting Finn completely evaporates. Like, poof, nerve gone. Two, Ethan looks incredible. I mean, all he's wearing is a pair of jeans and a fitted button up shirt. But we haven't gone on a real date since we went out for hot dogs, and I'd gotten used to his laid-back look. Not that there was anything wrong with that. I kind of loved his sweatpants and t-shirt look he rocked in the mornings. But right now, I feel lightheaded seeing the way his shirt accentuates his broad chest and strong arms. I almost regret going out.

Then he grins at me, and it's the same sheepish grin Finn gives me when he knows he's in trouble but is trying to be cute to get on my good side. It works every time with Finn. On Ethan, it's damn near irresistible.

"What?" I ask.

"It's just, I'm tempted to call off the whole movie and take you immediately to bed."

Even though I'd already been thinking the same thing, I shake my head, pushing my hand on his chest as he moves toward me.

"Oh, no. Not happening. I spent way too long getting

ready for you to just strip me naked." It's the truth. I'd squeezed myself into a pair of tight jeans and paired it with a loose backless halter top that dips dangerously low in front. There's a lot of tape holding this top in place, and I'm not about to have him ripping it off before we have a chance to go out. My hair is curled in mermaid waves that frame my face, and my eye makeup is especially on point. We are going out, even if I'd love nothing more than to press my naked body against his.

He groans, but the smile on his face admits defeat. Still, he snakes his arms around my waist and draws me close. I inhale his cologne, a blend of smoky cedar and pine, as he buries his face in my neck. And damn, he feels so good. His hands cover the exposed part of my back, and for a moment I consider letting go of my resolve. But more important than being seen is the conversation I've been putting off. If we stay home, it will never happen.

He pulls away before I need to say anything, but the fire in his eyes is the same I feel inside.

"I know," I say, touching his chest. "I want it too. But if we don't leave right now, I'm going to waste this whole outfit."

"Tempting," he says, then laughs as he closes the door behind him and takes my hand.

We take Ethan's car to the movies. He holds my hand in between shifting gears, as if he doesn't want to lose contact with me. I catch him glancing at me every now, when he thinks I'm not looking. I have to fight hard to hide my smile. I like that he looks at me, that he thinks I'm pretty.

The movie is okay. I let him pick, and he chose a lighthearted rom-com that had just hit theaters. I know he did it for me, and I think it's sweet. Normally, I'd be all over this movie too. But I'm too distracted by my nerves to actually follow the plot. I feel pulled in a million different directions as I consider how I'm going to tell him, what his reaction will be, and if this is actually a smart move.

But even bigger is my fear that I'm making the worst mistake. I swore I wouldn't do this to Finn. While he's small, it was always supposed to be just me and him. Even keeping my dating life secret has taken a toll on life at home. I mean, I don't think Finn knows. But I do. I know how much I look forward to Finn leaving for school because it means I get alone time with Ethan, and that makes me feel terrible. And what is Finn thinking tonight? I know he likes being with Aunt Maren, but he must wonder what I'm doing when I'm not there.

Before Ethan came into the picture, everything was so uncomplicated. My focus was on Finn and my work, and that was it. But now I'm trying to juggle all these parts of my life so that Ethan can fit into this separate compartment. If it's this hard now, how much harder will it be trying to merge as a family?

Just that thought sends me into a new spiral. A family. I know Ethan doesn't want kids, and the trauma he went through with his own dad isn't going to go away overnight. But the thing is, he *has* a kid. And the longer I keep this secret, the longer I'm denying him the chance to make the choice for himself. But before I can tell him, he has to meet Finn. But if he meets Finn and then breaks things off, he'll shatter both of our hearts.

There's the crux of it. He deserves to know. I need to take the steps toward telling him the truth, starting with him meeting Finn. But I'm terrified he's going to let us down. I'm afraid of offering him the last part of my heart, because I don't know what he'll do with it.

I glance at Ethan now. His eyes are glassy, and I realize he's fighting back tears. I'm alarmed for a second, but then remember the movie I'm supposed to be watching. I look at the screen just in time to see a tearful goodbye between the main characters. I can't help peeking at Ethan again. The whole time I've been stuck in my head, I've completely missed out on seeing this man beside me transform from this sexy guy covered in tattoos, who has gotten to know me through hot dogs and books, to this apparently sensitive man who tears up at movies. It makes him so much sexier.

I lace my fingers through his, and his eyes dart to mine.

"Need a tissue?" I ask.

"Shut up," he says, flashing me a watery grin.

I resolve to stay out of my head for the rest of the movie, and even feel a little misty when the couple on the screen reunites at the end. But it's at the end of the movie where I see who Ethan is as he picks up our empty popcorn container and soda cup, carrying it to the garbage before we leave, even though everyone else leaves there mess for the ushers to clean up. It's a silly little thing, but to me, it speaks volumes about who Ethan is and the man I've gotten to know over the past few weeks.

Ethan chose this movie for me. He has been working around my schedule to be with me. He's respected every single one of my boundaries when it comes to Finn, and—even though he said he doesn't want kids—he's still pursuing me, knowing full well that I'm a package deal.

If that doesn't mean something, I don't know what does.

Chapter 15

"What?" Ethan sets his menu down in the restaurant, giving me a quizzical smile. I realize I've been staring. I haven't even decided what to eat yet, and I can't stop looking at him. All the nerves I felt before have made way for excitement. I can't wait to ask him to meet Finn.

"Nothing," I say, ducking behind my menu. He pulls it down before I can read the first entree.

"Claire."

"Ethan." I smirk at him, trying to play coy. I feel it's only proper to wait until we have food in front of us. But the way he's staring at me, I'm not sure I can wait that long. Thankfully, the approaching waitress keeps me from blurting out my question.

"Are you ready?" she asks.

"You go first," I tell Ethan as I speed through the menu options. As he orders, I decide on a burger with fries and a Manhattan to give me liquid courage. However, once she leaves, Ethan looks at me expectedly.

"I have something to ask you, and it's kind of a big deal." I twist my napkin in my lap, the nerves suddenly back. He sips his water, but his eyes never leave my face. "I've been waiting a while to ask you this because I needed to be sure." I pause for a moment as I consider how to frame this question. Talk about my childhood with an absent mom? Share my vow to remain single until Finn was out of the house? The fact that he's the first man I've wanted to be in Finn's life?

It's then that I notice the discomfort in Ethan's eyes. It's brief, only a fraction of a second, but I catch it. A shift in his gaze from my face to the door. The way he loosens his shirt at his neckline. How he inhales heavily as if he knows what I'm going to say.

"Thing is, I haven't dated since, well, you know. And I thought I wouldn't again until Finn was out of the house." I'm watching Ethan carefully as I speak, wondering if I'm imaging the sweat on his brow or how he's fidgeting.

"Are you okay?" I ask.

"Oh, yeah. I'm fine. It's just warm in here. Are you warm?" He looks around again, as if searching for a cool breeze.

"Not especially," I say, which is the truth. My cute top is covered up by a sweater I brought along because this restaurant must believe food is better served in the Arctic.

"Sorry, go on," he says, just as the waitress arrives with our drinks. He grabs his and guzzles half of it before I've even had my first sip.

"I guess I'm just asking if you'd like to meet—"

"I don't feel so well," Ethan says, then rushes from the table as he makes a beeline for the bathroom.

He's in there for a while. Long enough that I finish one drink, and order another when the waitress arrives with the appetizer. It's fried calamari, one of my favorites, but right now the dish tastes like cardboard. I snack on it anyway, looking out the window as I wait.

"Sorry about that," Ethan says, sitting back in his chair. I keep looking out the window, taking a slow sip of my drink. "Hey," he says, and I glance at him. "What did you want to say?"

"It's nothing." I turn back to the window. This was a mistake. Not just the whole plan to ask him to meet Finn, but all of it. I knew better. As soon as he told me he didn't want kids, it should have been over.

"Claire."

I look at him again, but this time I notice how pale his face is. Beads of sweat cover his forehead, and he dabs at them with his napkin.

"Are you okay?" I ask. I lean forward, noting the tightness of his mouth.

"I'm sorry, I don't know what's going on," he says, and I don't miss the flash of fear that crosses his face. "I'm afraid if we don't leave right now, I'm going to get sick again."

"Go," I say, not wanting to see him throw up. "Find the car, and I'll meet you there after I settle the bill." He starts to pull out his wallet, but I stop him, urging him out the door. He rushes out as I flag down the waitress and explain the situation. Luckily, they hadn't fired up our dinners yet, so I pay for what we were served and then head to the parking garage.

Ethan's driver's side door is open and he's sitting sideways with his feet on the concrete, his head hanging in his hands.

"Do you want me to drive?" I ask, placing a hand on his back. He jerks slightly, but then relaxes when he sees it's me.

"I'm okay to drive," he says. "I just got claustrophobic for a moment."

We drive in silence, the windows down and the radio off. I'm still not sure what to think. Is he sick? Or is he reacting to what I was obviously going to ask him? Whatever it is, I'm not going to find out tonight. We pull up to his house, and he doesn't even look at me as he unbuckles his seatbelt and gets out. I step out of the car, waiting to see if he'll lead the way to the house. Instead, he embraces me, giving me a kiss on the top of my head.

"Sorry tonight didn't turn out the way we planned."

You have no idea. This is a goodbye, if I ever saw one. I pull away and offer a smile, hiding the thoughts racing through my mind.

"Get some rest, okay?"

He nods, squeezing my hand before heading toward his home. He doesn't even look back at me or wait until I'm in the car.

I drive home, my mind a jumbled mess as I try to sort out what just happened. He was fine at the movies. He was fine when we sat down for dinner. It wasn't until I started to bring up Finn that he acted this way.

Suddenly, I'm angry. What did he expect would happen if he dated me? Did he believe he'd just keep dating me and never meet my son? If he has such a problem with kids, why didn't he end it the moment he found out I have one?

I pull over to the side of the road and bang my hands against the wheel. What was *I* thinking? Why didn't I end it at that moment?

Because I wanted him to meet Finn. Because I believed he'd fall in love with the son he never knew he had.

But now, it's obvious this is never going to happen unless I just rip off the damn Band-Aid.

I pull my cellphone out and touch his name. It goes straight to voicemail, and I huff in frustration, resisting the urge to throw my phone across the dash. I dial it again, and this time it goes through.

"Hello?"

His voice sounds sleepy, even though I only left him twenty minutes before. I nugget of doubt creeps into my mind. Maybe he really was sick. I bat the thought away though.

"We need to talk," I say.

"Claire, can we do this tomorrow? I really don't feel good."

"You can just listen then. I was going to ask you tonight to meet Finn, which is a pretty big deal. I haven't dated since Finn's father because I don't want to bring just anyone into his life. But you're not just anyone. You're someone I care about deeply, and I know Finn will care for you too, and..."

"Claire."

"I know if you meet him, you'll care about him too."

"Claire, let me talk."

I take a deep breath. There's so much I want to say, hoping something will click with him.

"I'm not ready," he says.

And there it is. The confirmation on what all this is about.

"Fuck you," I say.

"Claire, please."

"No, fuck you. You knew I was a mom. I was just

about to offer you the biggest part of my world, and you're not ready? I haven't been ready for six years, and tonight was the first time I thought I might be. You must have known this question was coming."

"You don't understand. Please, just trust me on this. I know I'll be ready at some point, I even thought I'd be ready when you first told me about him. But now I know I just need time. *We* need time. I want to get to know you better before we start talking family."

"I'm not talking family with you," I snap. "I'm asking you to meet my son."

"I can't," he says. "I can't explain to you why, but just trust me, okay?"

"Is it because of your dad?"

I hear his sharp intake of breath, and at the same time, I regret the words slipping out of my mouth.

"What are you talking about?" He says each word slowly, and I hear the anger behind the question.

"Nina told me," I whisper. Then the line goes dead.

I pull the phone away from my ear and look at it. I'm tempted to call him back, but I've already made enough mistakes.

When I walk into my house, I can see Maren has questions. I shake my head, not wanting to say anything.

"That bastard," she says.

"No, it's not like that," I say.

"So, he'll meet Finn?"

I take a deep breath, fighting back the tears. She takes one look at me and crosses the room, wrapping me in her arms.

"He's not worth it," she says. "He has no idea what he's missing. Finn is an amazing kid, and it's because you raised him. Any man who loves you would want to love your kid too."

"But Finn is Ethan's kid too." I wipe my face on her jacket before I think about it, then offer a shaky laugh. "Sorry, I hope that's not expensive."

"It's washable," she says. "And genes don't matter. Finn is yours, through and through. The only thing Ethan did was supply the sperm."

"God, Maren."

"It's true! You've raised this kid all on your own. You don't owe Ethan anything. He doesn't ever need to know. I say kick him to the curb and find a man who will accept that you're a package deal."

I sit down at the table, and she joins me. I use a napkin to wipe my runny nose, then another. I have a small mountain of tissues before I'm able to really talk.

"He didn't say he doesn't want to meet Finn. He just said he's not ready, and with everything I know about his past, I should have just left it at that. Instead, I asked him if it had to do with his dad."

"And how'd he take that?"

I wince, the memory of it stabbing my heart. "Not

well. He hung up on me." I sigh, wishing I could go back in time and be more understanding. "I shouldn't have gone to Nina about him. She told me things that he should have had the chance to tell me himself."

"But from what Nina said, he probably never would have told you."

"Maybe," I admit. "Or maybe he would have. It's not my choice to make. I mean, what if he found out through you that he's a father?" I groan then, realizing what I hypocrite I am. "God, I made Nina keep my secret about Finn because I wasn't ready for Ethan to know, and then I go and find out the biggest thing about him. I didn't even give him the chance to tell me."

"It's not like you knew," Maren points out.

"I know, but I should have just asked him."

"And he probably wouldn't have told you, and you'd be right here, wondering why the perfect guy isn't so perfect after all."

I bury my head in my arms on the table. "I should call him again. I should apologize."

Maren pats the back of my head. "You should give him space," she says.

I know she's right. Still, I can't help checking my phone all night long after she's gone. I busy myself with work to make up for the lack of calls. As I epoxy tiny book cover replicas, I keep my phone on a bookshelf across the room in an effort to stop torturing myself. But every notification ding, I'm racing to the shelf, hoping to see a text from Ethan. It's never him. It's no one. I am in a relationship with the app notifications on my phone.

God, when did I become such a loner? If I'm being honest with myself, it was long before Finn came along. He just became the perfect excuse to shut everyone else out.

When it comes down to it, I'm no better than Ethan when it comes to letting my past dictate my future. I can't hold it against him. Over the past few hours, I've gained a bit more clarity, which mingles with the shame of calling Ethan out before he was ready.

I mean, how many people have I told about my messed-up mom?

I told Ethan.

"But that was your choice," I say aloud in the empty room. Still, I trusted him with something I was ashamed about. I'm trying to understand his reasons for not telling me, but it's hard not to take it personally. I have to keep reminding myself that he doesn't talk about this with anyone, that it's not just me.

Besides, he still doesn't know my biggest secret. Now, I'm not sure he ever will.

Chapter 16

I don't hear from Ethan the following day, or the day after that. I've drafted about a half dozen texts to him that I immediately delete after typing, determined to not be the one who breaks the silence first.

He hung up on me. He should be the one who caves.

But it's more than pride that keeps me from contacting him. I crossed a line, and I know it. I dug where I shouldn't have been digging, and then I practically threw his past in his face. I didn't even try to understand how his father's rejection could have an effect on his life now.

Then there's the book. Now that I've seen firsthand how much his dad messed him up, I want to crawl into a hole in the earth and hide over that stupid book I picked out for him. I can't imagine what he was thinking when I handed him a book about a secret baby. My only solace is the fact that he isn't much of a reader and hasn't mentioned *By the Bay* to me once. He may not have even picked it up.

But what if he has? God, I was so stupid! How do I tell him now that Finn is his? If I get the chance, that is.

Beyond drafting unsent texts, I make myself busy to keep from checking my phone every five minutes. I pour myself into all the things I slacked off on over the past few weeks. My house is now sparkling, every single corner clean, and bags of old clothes and books are ready to donate by the door. I churn out a ton of book swag that I post on my Etsy page, and I even gain a few more clients over some new designs I put out. I help Finn build an elaborate racecourse in his room, something I've been promising to do for months and never had the time before. It's amazing how much time I have now.

I even try out a few new recipes, including interesting ways to make vegetables.

"I don't want this," Finn says, flicking roasted broccoli off his plate so that it skitters across the table. I roll my eyes as I put the vegetables back on his plate, fighting the impulse to react as I ignore his protests.

"I'm not done," I say, then spoon some "cheese" sauce over the broccoli. Ethan had suggested nacho cheese sauce, and I just couldn't bring myself to buy the processed canned stuff to put over something healthy. So I made my own vegan version using cashews and nutritional yeast.

"What is it?" he asks, inspecting the faux cheese. I say nothing as he dips his finger in the sauce and then touches his tongue. His face relaxes as he spears a small piece of "cheese" covered broccoli and puts it in his mouth. I expect to see him start gagging, but instead he just chews. Then he tries another one. I dip my own finger in the sauce and realize it tastes nothing like cheese. I decide it's best if I don't tell him what it's supposed to taste like.

"You like it?" I ask, and fight hard not to grin when he nods his head yes. Outwardly I act as if this is no big deal, but inside I'm throwing a party for one, celebrating that my kid is eating actual grown-out-of-the-ground vegetables. I pick up my phone to text Ethan that his plan worked. I get as far as typing out the first few words before I remind myself—again—that we're not speaking.

Damn, this hurts.

Instead, I text Maren. But the text remains unseen and unanswered. That isn't a surprise since Maren is at a gig—her third one this week. I'm happy for her, but not for me since this means I've been mostly on my own this week.

Finn cleans his plate, even going so far as to lick the "cheese" from the surface until there's nothing left. Then he brings his plate to the sink without complaint. I'm so happy, I undo all the health benefits of the broccoli by serving us both a double scoop of ice cream, topped with chocolate syrup. Finn takes his own bath, which has become our new normal, though he still lets me wash his hair. Then, once he's snuggled in his bed, I read him another chapter of *Mrs. Piggle Wiggle* before kissing him goodnight. I leave the door open a crack and the hall light on, then pad to the kitchen to finish washing the dishes before I start working.

On the counter is a flyer Finn brought home from school, advertising the traveling carnival that's in town right now. I'd noticed them setting up earlier this week in the giant parking lot outside the Sunset Pavilion Strip Mall and thought it might be something fun to do this weekend. Sunset Bay doesn't have a traditional fair like other towns do, and the carnival only comes around every few years. The last time I brought Finn, he was too little to enjoy many of the rides. We'd spent most of our time at the petting zoo, riding the merry-go-round, and eating the container of healthy food I brought while kids around us ate corndogs. But this year I know he's tall enough to ride the roller coasters, and I can't wait to see his face. And maybe I'll also lighten up on the healthy food for one day.

I'd been to the carnival on my own several times as a teen, but only once with my mom. I must have been around Finn's age, and I remember feeling annoyed that she brought Hal, a guy she was seeing at the time. What

I remembered most about him was how handsy he was. If he didn't have his arm around my mom, he was always rubbing my shoulders, playing with my hair, or trying to hold my hand. Every time he touched me, I'd move a little further away, only to have him laugh at how shy I was. At one point, he tried to sit me in his lap, but my mom told him to save our table near the live music while she took me on some rides.

I clung to my mom's arm as we navigated the crowd. She purposely chose rides we could go on together, including the huge Ferris wheel at the end of the park. We rode so high we could see into the backyards of the neighboring houses. Mom would point things out, but I was too busy watching her face. Often when she smiled, it disappeared somewhere in her cheeks, and her eyes held a distant look. But on that Ferris wheel, my mother's laugh radiated over her face, her eyes crinkling as the breeze caught her chestnut hair and swirled it around her face.

Growing up, I never really thought about whether my mom was pretty or not. She was just my mom. But the mom of that moment was the most beautiful woman I knew, and I spent years trying to find that smile again. It never came. It disappeared just as quickly as Hal did after that day.

I finish straightening the kitchen, then spend another hour in my office epoxying keychains and magnets for one of my regular authors. The Romance Lovers Book Expo is happening in San Francisco in a few weeks, and while spending this week alone has been torture on my nerves, it's been excellent in getting ahead of schedule so that all the authors who have ordered through me will have their swag ready in time for the event.

I work until my eyes start burning and the back of my neck aches from hunching over. Rolling my head to relieve the pressure, I head to bed, grabbing my phone on the other side of the room on my way out of the office. I've started doing this to keep from checking it every five minutes, which has allowed me a reprieve from wishing Ethan would just break the silence. When I glance at the screen, the only text I have is from Maren, answering my earlier text.

> Maren: I hardly think vegan cheese is a win, but whatever makes you happy.

I grin, then text her back about the carnival tomorrow.

> Me: Do you want to go?
> Maren: Can't. Work, and then I have another gig at Hillside. Want to come see me after the carnival? I'll save you a table.

I'm tempted. I still have a lot of work to do before the

expo, but I'm also way ahead. I'm about to tell her yes, but then I read it again, seeing where it's going to be. *Hillside.* My thoughts immediately move to Ethan. He's sure to be working, since it's Saturday night.

Me: Can't.

I don't give any reason, and I know Maren knows why— especially when I see the three dots signaling she's typing, then see them disappear, then see them appear again.

Maren: OK

Ugh. Why do people ever type *OK*? There's so much loaded into those two letters, including all the things she's said about our situation over the past week. Mostly, she thinks I should break the silence and apologize for treading on his past, but also let him have it for dating a single mom and not preparing himself to meet my kid.

What Maren isn't saying is that I should move on. I know if this were her, she'd drop him in a heartbeat and already have a date lined up for the weekend. But it took too many years for me to get to this point of actual dating, so I know she won't suggest I forget about him and find someone who's open to dating with kids.

And I don't want to find someone else. Beyond the whole DNA thing, I see something in Ethan that he obviously doesn't see in himself. When I'm with him, I know I have his full attention. It's like he studies me, wanting to know everything there is about me. I think back to our date at the bookstore, how he "cheated" by having the clerk tell him which book I wanted. I love that he did his research instead of just assuming his opinion would be right. Like I did with my ulterior motive book. Ethan isn't like this, though. He asks questions. He moved his schedule to fit around mine. He respected every boundary I had when it came to Finn. If he would just lower his walls a little, he would hit it off great with Finn, and probably be the dad Finn deserves.

It kills me that I have to push that last thought away when it comes to Ethan because no one should have that kind of pressure before they're ready...even if Ethan *is* Finn's dad.

Maren doesn't text back after her paragraph of an OK, and I let that word close our conversation. My mind is swimming with wishes and regrets, but my heavy eyelids tell me to let it go until the morning. So I put my phone on silent and roll over, staring into the empty darkness of my room until sleep finally takes over.

Chapter 17

Morning light streams through my window, easing me out of sleep and into a reality of Finn's feet at my back. *Again*. This kid. I scoot him over as he remains asleep, and then stretch to ease my aching pretzel spine. Then I reach for my phone to see the time. 7:40 a.m., and a text from Ethan.

My stomach does a slow roll, and I fight the urge to open it right away. I need coffee. I need to get my wits about me before I read whatever he has to say.

Scenarios scroll through my mind on the short walk from my bedroom to the kitchen. He could be breaking up with me. He could decide silence is overrated, and he's now ready to tell me off. Or maybe he's just letting me know when I can gather the various things I've left at his apartment, from my yoga pants to the toothbrush he gave me.

I pour my coffee, one eye still on my phone as if it's going to do something. Part of me doesn't even want to open the text. I sit at the kitchen table, placing my phone in front of me, and then clutch my coffee as I take a cleansing breath in and then let it out slow. Finally, I grab my phone and unlock it, then click the message open.

Ethan: We need to talk.

Oh my God. This is the most infuriating text ever in the history of texts. Maybe even more than texting *OK*. This tells me nothing, and only makes me believe the worst. We need to talk? About what? About the end of whatever this thing is between us?

And suddenly, I'm angry. Why the hell am I putting myself through this torture when I literally owe him nothing? I have been raising his kid all on my own, and even when I discovered who he was, I never expected anything from him. I don't even expect anything from him now that I know he's Finn's dad, and he should be glad of it! He doesn't want kids, and I'm not burdening him with one. So what more do I possibly need to give him?

Me: I think we've said enough.

I put the phone down and get up, pacing across the

kitchen as I clench and unclench my hands. I shouldn't be surprised when my phone starts ringing, but I am. I want to detach from him, to just let him go and get back to simpler times when it was just Finn and me. But I don't let all that stop me from retrieving my phone and answering his call.

"Don't hang up," Ethan says. I sputter a laugh.

"That's rich, coming from you."

He sighs into the phone, and the wounded side of me wants to indeed hang up and then ignore him for a week—just to give him a taste of his own medicine. But even stronger is my curiosity over what he wants, even if it's to twist the knife a little deeper.

"I'm sorry," he says. The apology smooths the jagged edges of my need for revenge, enough that I'm willing to hear him out. "I shouldn't have hung up on you. I was mad."

"I didn't ask for Nina to tell me about your da...about your past," I say.

"No, that's not what I was mad about. I mean, yeah, I was mad that she told you, but I wasn't mad that you knew. What I was mad about was the fact that...." He pauses, and I wait him out. I can hear him breathing, recognizing the emotion in his jagged breaths. "I was mad that my dad, who I haven't heard from in over a decade, is still getting in the way of me moving forward with my life. I just..." He pauses again, and I can feel the last strains of my anger flutter away. "Claire, I need to see you. Today. I have so much to say to you, and I really don't want to do it over the phone."

"I can't," I say, wincing when I hear him breathe out into the phone. "I want to, but I can't today. I promised Finn I'd take him to the carnival and I really need to focus on him." I hesitate, but then continue. "The past few weeks have been amazing, but I've been really off balance when it comes to Finn. This week was especially hard not hearing from you, but it was also a wakeup call that I've been losing myself in you and neglecting my obligations as Finn's mom." I close my eyes and take a few deep breaths; thankful he doesn't speak. "Look, I think you and I just aren't going to work." I keep my eyes closed, even as the tears drench my lashes before spilling over my cheeks. "I care for you. I love who you are and how you make me feel when I'm with you, but I don't know how to balance being in a relationship with you and being a mother."

"It doesn't need to be two separate things," he says.

"Right, like how my mom was?"

"You're not your mom."

"And you're not your dad," I point out. "But those ghosts are constantly going to haunt us, aren't they?" I wipe my eyes, trying my best to keep the tears out of my voice. "I don't blame you for taking a step back. I understand all too well how a parent's missteps can affect their child's life. This is why I need to take my own step back. For Finn. I owe him this."

"Please don't do this, Claire. Just let me see you, let me talk with you."

"We *are* talking, Ethan. But I have to do this." My chest feels like it's caving in on itself. Of anything I could be saying to him, I never thought it would be this. It's the right thing though.

"Mom?"

I look up and see Finn standing in the doorway, wiping the sleep from his eyes.

"I have to go." I hang up before he can say anything else, then I turn my phone off for good measure, not wanting to face his repeated calls back to me.

"Hey bud," I say, getting up as I swipe away any lingering tears, "are you hungry?"

He nods, sitting at the table. His feet still aren't long enough to hit the floor, and he swings them even as he lays his head on the table.

"Did you see that flyer the school sent home with you?" I ask, nodding my head at the paper he's lying next to. I warm up the pan as he sits up and brings the flyer toward him, and grin when I see his face light up.

"The carnival? Can we go?"

My heart still aches, but I brush aside the pain as I soak up my son's hopeful face.

"As soon as we're done eating and your room is

clean," I say. He groans, but I know better. The best time for me to get him to do his chores is when he wants something. I would have hated having a mom like me.

No. I wouldn't have hated it.

I make us sausages wrapped in crepes, and Finn wolfs them down in five minutes flat. Then he races from the table, leaving his plate behind, so he can start on his room.

"Wash your hands!" I call after him. The carnival gates won't open for two more hours, but I won't tell him that. Instead, I eat slow, trying to resist the urge to turn my phone on as I sit by myself. I can hear Finn's toys being thrown in his bin. Other than that, it's quiet.

How can I feel this alone when it's been like this most of my life? I don't need Ethan. What the hell did I do before I met him?

When we arrive at the carnival, I have a backpack full of healthy food and a wriggling six-year-old's hand in mine. He's full of ideas on how we'll spend the day, from the roller coasters to visiting the animals at the petting zoo. The way he talks, it's obvious he remembers what the carnival was like, and I'm amazed at his memory. It was only a few years ago, but to him that's half a lifetime.

"Can we get corndogs?" he asks.

I shake my head, ignoring his immediate groans. "You saw me making bento boxes," I say.

"I know, but I thought they were for you. I want regular food."

I laugh. "This was regular enough for your lunch yesterday," I remind him. "You didn't seem to complain when you brought it to school."

"I traded for Brie's turkey sandwich."

"Well, obviously Brie got the better end of the deal."

Finn looks up at me and rolls his eyes.

"Mom, no one brings food like this. They have normal food like chips or cookies or sandwiches."

"I would have killed for a lunch like this when I was your age," I tell him. "Back then it was called Lunchables, and every cool kid had them."

"Did you?" he asks. We reach the line to the ticket counter and wait our turn to buy tickets. It occurs to me right then how lucky I am to have the money to bring him here. I'm not rich by any means, but I have enough to splurge at a carnival. I have enough for groceries so we can eat healthy food, to pay the rent so we have a place to live, and all our bills are paid with money left over.

"No. I was on a special lunch program," I tell him. "I ate the school lunch."

"Lucky," he mutters. But he doesn't know what it's like to hand over the telltale tickets—the one that labeled my family as poor—while everyone else had a packed lunch from home. But if it weren't for those tickets and the bland hot meal I received in return, there were days I wouldn't have eaten.

Finn stays with me until we're through security. Then he's off, running toward the first roller coaster ride he sees. He's all wiggles and smiles until they strap him in and cinch the belt tight. I see his smile fade, and he looks at me with round eyes.

"What if I fall out?" he asks, his voice shaking. I smile, covering his cold hand.

"You won't," I promise, though secretly I had just been thinking the same thing. This carnival was up and running in a day, and they'll tear it down just as fast once the weekend is through. How secure does that make me feel? I peer over at the carnival worker who's still tightening belts. His skin is weathered and dark from the sun, and his beard reaches the middle of his chest. He wears his hair in a ponytail, and the toothpick in his mouth could easily be a cigarette in his off hours. Does he know our lives are in his hands?

The ride starts and Finn grabs hold of my hand, squeezing it as if I'll anchor him if we hurtle into space. Each half second is marked by the click of the tracks and the slow ascent up the steep hill. Finn squeezes his eyes shut, and I nudge him to get him to open them again.

"You're missing the whole ride."

He squints at me, then finally opens his eyes. He even looks over me to see the carnival getting smaller below us. But that's when we reach the top and whip around a corner.

"Mom!" His grip is surprisingly strong as we jerk side to side. But then he loosens his hand before letting go, grabbing hold of the plush bars over his chest. I look at his face and see he's laughing, the fear completely gone as we climb and drop before the ride comes to a quick end.

"Can we do that again?" Finn asks as he trots beside me after the ride.

"Maybe," I say. "But there are a bunch more rides to go on."

"Finn!"

We both turn to see Brie, Finn's friend from class, running toward us. Her mom is behind her, and they wave hello.

"Hi," Brie says to Finn, who is suddenly leaning against me like he's afraid of her. He peers up at me, and I realize he's shy. I nudge him, just like I did on the roller coaster, and he hides a small smile.

"Hi," he says to the ground.

"Hey, Claire, great to see you here," Brenda says once they reach us. "We were just thinking how much more fun this would be if Brie had a friend to go on rides with."

I like Brenda. She sometimes volunteers with me in Finn's class, and she's always so kind and patient—even with the kids who like to follow their own path instead of going with the flow of the class. She's at least a decade older than me, which is the norm for all the parents of Finn's classmates. They're also all stay-at-home moms with husbands who work.

I start to speak, but a familiar face just past her catches my attention.

Ethan.

He stands at a distance, but he's looking right at me. My breath catches, and Brenda looks over her shoulder to see what's caught my eye.

"I was thinking the same thing," I say, and she turns back to me. "But I, uh." I swallow hard, my attention still distracted. "Brenda, I really have to go to the bathroom." I wince, realizing how stupid that sounds. "I mean, I can't take Finn in there, he's too old. And, uh…"

"Say no more," she says. "Let me take Finn with us, and you can catch up with us once you're done." She looks over her shoulder again, before turning back to me with a small smile. "Take your time."

I bite my lip, my face burning red. But she just laughs and ushers the kids away.

Chapter 18

Every bone in my body wants to close the space between Ethan and me, even as my brain reminds me that I broke things off with him for a reason. For Finn. I take the middle ground and stay where I am, letting Ethan be the one to come to me.

"Hi," he says.

I breathe him in. God, why does he have to smell so good?

"Hi," I say.

"Can we—"

"How did you—"

Ethan gives a light laugh, but I can sense the underlying tension. He motions for me to continue.

"What are you doing here?" I ask.

"You said you were going to be here, and I figured it was the best way to get you to talk to me." He ducks his head, rubbing the back of his neck before looking at me with sheepish eyes. "Now that I'm here, I realize how creepy this probably is."

"It's not creepy," I say. And it's not. The truth is, I'm glad he's here. It never even crossed my mind that he'd come to find me. Then again, I'd never had anyone fight for me before—if that's what he's doing, that is. "Why, though? You don't owe me anything, and I don't owe you, either."

"Owe me? Are we keeping score about something? Because if we are, I forfeit."

"That's not what I mean," I say. "I don't know what I mean. I guess I just felt like I was holding you back."

"How? All I want is to be with you. You're incredible, and if anyone is holding you back, it's me."

I look around us, realizing we're having this huge conversation in the middle of a moving crowd. Then I scan the rides until I see Brenda with Finn and Brie. She nods at me, then waves me off, indicating that she's fine with Finn. I turn back to Ethan.

"Let's go sit out of the flow of traffic," I say, then lead him to the picnic benches near the petting zoo. He sits across from me, his hands folded in front of him as he leans in. "I think we came into this not sure what to expect," I say. "I haven't dated anyone but you since Finn was born, and my experience with my mom wasn't the best example about how that's supposed to go. I came into this without a clue about how to juggle parenting and dating, and completely fearful that I'd do Finn wrong."

"But you wouldn't do that, Claire. You're a great mom."

"How would you know, though? You've never seen me with him," I point out.

"True," he says. "But I see how much you care about him when you're not with him. I see how your home is dedicated to him, and it's obviously a safe place for a kid to grow up. I know that you put him first, even willing to break things off with me so that you can focus on him. But Claire, I know that's not what you want."

"You don't know anything about me," I say, even as the tears spring to my eyes.

"I'd like to think I know some things about you," he says carefully. He reaches toward me and his finger catches my tear, then he caresses the side of my face with his palm. I know I need to stay strong, but I can't help leaning into his touch. "I know your heart and how you let it lead in everything you do. I know your brain and how insightful and brilliant you are. I know your soul thrives on creativity. I know you're loyal to anyone in your inner circle, which is small but very dear to you. And I know I broke your trust after you let me into that circle when I cut off all communication."

His words penetrate the small bit of stubbornness I've

been holding on to, and I reach to his hand on my cheek. He grasps my hand, pulling it toward him as his thumb brushes my skin. "Please tell me what you wanted to say before." I squeeze his hand, and he squeezes it back with a small smile.

He tells me everything Nina already told me about his dad's other family, but I hear it from the boy who was rejected by his father.

"He chose them over us," Ethan says. "I know I can't take it personally, but it feels personal." He laughs, shaking his head. "I have all these altered memories of what it was like before he left, like he was some devoted dad or something. But the truth is, he was a shitty father before too. He was always away for his job, or maybe with his other family. When he was around, he didn't do anything with me. I was always in his way, or too loud, or too messy. Just too much, you know? So when he left, I had all these complicated feelings that I couldn't name. But I've also had years to think about it. I realized that a lot of me was angry that he left, and part of me was sad that I'd never see him again. The worst feeling, though, was relief. And that made me feel terrible, like I wished him away or something. I didn't know how to even talk about it, because what would that say about me? That I was glad I didn't have a dad?" Ethan's eyes tear up, and he releases my hand to brush away the moisture. "My mom struggled to keep things together. We had to accept handouts from my uncle, and I know that killed her to need anything from my dad's brother. I was an angry kid, and I took a lot of it out on my mom. To her credit, she never got down hard on me about it. Uncle Steve did, though. He was kind of an asshole, but I think he was also trying to make up for his deadbeat brother." He takes a deep breath in, then looks at me with red-rimmed eyes. "Sorry. This is a super long-winded way to talk about why I shut down last week. You didn't deserve that. But I realized that if we were going to take things further, I needed to be able to talk about this with you, and I've never talked about this with anyone."

"Not even a therapist?" I asked. He tilts his head, as if the answer is obvious.

"Hello, we were dirt poor. Even at reduced rates, my mom never would have been able to afford therapy for me."

"What about now, though?"

"Maybe," he says. "I don't know. It feels like it was so long ago, what's the point?"

"The point is that you've held on to something since you were young, and it's still preventing you from moving forward. Maybe a therapist could help you start to talk about it. Have you even talked with your mom? I mean, is she still around?"

"She's still around," he says with a smile. "She lives in town, and I see her at least once a week. But no, we don't talk about it."

I'm silent for a moment. His hand has found mine again, and I turn it over so I can trace the lines of his palm.

"You're going to have a very long and wonderful life," I say, smirking when he starts to laugh. "Oh, it says here that you're going to meet someone new, very soon."

"I've already met her," he says, closing his hand over mine.

"Not me, silly. A doctor for the heart and brain."

"Really. And have you ever met a doctor for the heart and brain?" he asks.

"Yes, and she saved my life." I don't see Susan anymore, but she was an instrumental part of helping me learn how to be a good mom to Finn. She'd been recommended by Finn's pediatrician when she saw how much I was struggling, and she knew I needed therapy more than I needed parenting classes. "If I hadn't worked out my issues with a therapist, I probably would have repeated some of my mom's mistakes."

"I doubt that," Ethan says.

"You're biased," I laugh. "Seriously, though. Maybe I wouldn't be drunk all the time like my mom, but I was young and lonely, especially in those first few years. Susan helped me to know my worth and gave me the tools I needed to ensure my son grew up in a healthy environment."

"Which is why you didn't want to date," Ethan muses. I nod.

"I didn't know how to. I ended my therapy session a few years ago when I thought I was fine, but I'd never broached the subject of dating because I'd made a vow not to. Then I met you, and well, everything changed."

"I'd like to meet Finn," Ethan blurts out. Then he shakes his head. "Not now, because you have your day planned with him, and I've already stolen enough of your time. But tonight. Your place. I'll bring dinner."

"You don't have to work?" I ask. I feel a little guilty at even considering this since I already turned down Maren's invitation to see her perform at Hillside. But I also know she'll understand.

"I'll call out," he says. "This is much more important than waiting tables."

I bite at a smile, knowing this is a huge step for him. "Are you sure you're ready?"

Ethan doesn't answer. Instead he stands up, still holding my hand. He tugs, bringing me to my feet in front of him, then he cups my face in his.

"Claire, I'm falling in love with you."

I gasp when he says it, but he brings a finger to my lips. I can't fight the grin that breaks through.

"I'm falling in love with you," he repeats, and this time he's smiling too. "It not only scares me to death, but it feels like the most natural thing in the world. I want to be with you, and I cherish everything about you, including your son who I've never met. And so, Claire Myers, would you allow me the honor of meeting your son in exchange for some damn good takeout?"

"It's a deal," I say. "But I think you're giving a lot more than food." I'm bubbling inside, and I long to tell him what he just told me—that I'm falling in love with him too. But I don't want him to think I'm saying it just because he said it to me. So instead, I step on my tiptoes and meet his waiting lips, sighing as he parts them with a deeper kiss.

When he's gone—when I'm back with Brenda and watching the kids crash into each other on the bumper cars—I still feel his kiss, and I can't help tracing the memory with my fingers.

Chapter 19

The house is still clean from my weeks without Ethan, and yet I can't help running the vacuum over the spotless carpet and a dust rag over the shining bookshelves.

"Ethan," Finn mutters at the table, running his race car over the table. It's the third time he's said his name, and I know he's figured out that there's something different about our coming guest. "Why is he coming here?"

"I already told you," I remind him. "He's my friend, and I want him to meet you."

"But he's not *my* friend," Finn mutters, continuing with the car.

I'm not sure what I was expecting from him in all of this. I'd sprung the news on Finn on our way home from the carnival, which was strike number one. He was tired and crashing from the corndogs and soda I caved and let him have, and he took the news like I'd told him I was taking away the television. Then he had normal questions, like what we were having for dinner (*I don't know*), and what Ethan looked like (*he's tall with dark hair like yours*).

But then came the harder question.

How did you meet him? (*He's a friend of Maren's*—which was kind of true)

And, of course, why Ethan had to come over in the first place.

"Go put your cars away and wash up for dinner," I say when I see Ethan's car pull up to the sidewalk. Finn glances outside, then groans.

"Why is he coming here?" he asks for the millionth time in a row.

"Because I'm selling him all of your cars, and your racetrack too."

Finn rolls his eyes at me, but I see the glimmer of a smirk before he scoots away from the table.

I open the door before Ethan walks up, then shut it behind me. His hands are full, including a bouquet of dahlias for me. My favorite. I take them out of his hand, then stand on tiptoe to brush my lips against his.

"Warning, the kid is onto us," I say.

"Oh?"

"Oh. I think he knows our friendship is different than the one I share with Maren, and he's determined to hate you."

Ethan laughs, then lifts one of the bags he's carrying. I peek inside, then nod approvingly when I see a few packages of model cars. Finn doesn't own any of these ones, another sign at how perceptive Ethan is. Still, I know my kid. Even new cars won't break through his stubbornness.

"If he's ungrateful or rude, I apologize in advance."

Ethan leans down and kisses me again. "Don't," he says. "I'm the stranger on his turf. I have to earn his respect."

"He's six," I remind him.

"And he's been the only male here for six years," Ethan shoots back. "Until he knows he can trust me, I'm a threat. Let him figure this out for himself."

I start to protest, but he shakes his head.

"Do you trust me?" he asks.

"If I didn't, you wouldn't be here."

"Right. And how long did that take?"

I smile. Then I grab one of his bags.

"Point taken," I say, then lead him into the house.

Finn is nowhere to be seen, but I can feel his presence close by as I clip the flowers and arrange them in a vase. He's probably in his room with his ears turned up.

"So, what's for dinner?" I ask Ethan, starting to pull down plates. He nudges me away from the cabinets.

"Nothing healthy," he says, which I gathered from

the enticing smells coming from the bags. He nods his head at the table. "Go sit. I'll dish up."

He sets down plates and silverware for all of us, then starts pulling boxes from the bag. My mouth waters when I realize it's Chinese food, even more as the smells get stronger. I'm about to call Finn, but when I turn my head, I see him lingering by the kitchen door. I smile, beckoning him in.

"Finn, this is Ethan," I say. Finn doesn't say anything. He comes closer, and I can see he's itching to lean into me. But something changes in his face. Determination. Maybe defiance. He juts his chin out and sits at the table.

"S'up, Dude," Ethan says, nodding his head at Finn. And that's all he does. He doesn't give him any special attention. Doesn't call him "Little Buddy." Doesn't do anything other than a head check, and then goes back to pulling the last of the boxes out of the bag.

I'm a different story, internally unraveling just seeing the two of them together. If I had any doubts before, they've evaporated now that Finn and Ethan are breathing the same air. I hold my breath, wondering if Ethan notices his own eyes looking back at him—or rather, avoiding him. Finn is doing his best to pretend Ethan isn't there, though I see him sneaking peeks when Ethan's back is turned. Then Finn zeroes in on the cars lying on the counter. He looks at me, and I can see the question eating at him. *Are they mine?* But he doesn't ask it.

Ethan sets a glass of milk down for each of us before sitting, then grabs a container.

"Dig in," he says. Finn looks at me again, his eyes wide. I usually plate his food for him. But this time, I hand him a container, not even sure what's inside.

"Make sure you leave some for the rest of us," I say. Finn can't hide his grin as he works at the top of the container. It tears a little, and some sauce spills on the table, but I pretend not to notice. I'm too busy trying not to get all sappy over seeing Finn's walls come down.

By the time we're all done, Finn's plate is full of sweet and sour pork with a little bit of white rice and an egg roll. He skipped the broccoli and beef, but I also see he's eyeing it with intrigue. I wonder if he's thinking of the broccoli I made him last night. I want to urge him to try a little, but then think better of it. He's swinging his feet. He's happy. I'm not going to ruin the moment by *momming* him.

"Have you ever played 'What's your favorite'?" Ethan asks me.

"No," I say slowly. "What is that?"

"It's easy. One of us asks a question, like 'What's your favorite dinosaur,' and then everyone takes turns answering it. I'll go first with that question. What's your favorite dinosaur?"

"I don't really know my Dinos—"

"Velociraptor," Finn pipes in.

"Wow, good one," Ethan says. "I'm going to have to go with the Psittacosaurus."

"Oh dude, I was going to say that!" Finn says. And I smother my smile at his use of the word *dude*.

"You just made that up," I say to Ethan. He pulls out his phone and starts typing. Then he holds it out to me. Sure enough, there's the Psittacosaurus, which looks like a cross between a parrot and a lizard.

"You really don't know your dinosaurs?" Ethan asks.

"I know a few," I say. "I wouldn't say I have a favorite though."

"Pick one."

I mull it over for a moment. "Brontosaurus?" I say meekly.

"Solid. All right Finn, your turn to ask."

"What's your favorite…" He tilts his head, trying to think. His eyes gravitate towards the cars on the counter again, and I'm certain that's what he's going to say. But instead he blurts out "TV show."

I name *Outlander*, and both Finn and Ethan groan. I laugh, then nudge Finn. "How do you know about that show? I never watch it when you're awake."

"Because you and Aunt Maren are always drooling about it," he says. He turns to Ethan. "And I like *Jesse Starr*." This time, it's my turn to groan.

"That good, huh?" Ethan says.

"That bad." It's a show about some kid who became a rock star at a young age and goes on all these totally unbelievable adventures—probably because he's filthy rich. It always ends with him on stage singing some cheesy song. But Finn loves it and sings along to it whenever it's on. "It's total trash," I say.

"Hey!" Finn says. But he's smiling.

"Well, I like football. Does that count as a TV show?"

Finn nods. "I like football too," he says. He gives a quick glance to me, then ducks his head to eat more food. The kid has never watched a football game in his life, but I'm not going to out him.

"Your turn, Claire," Ethan says. I look at him, and he gives me a wink. I can't believe a silly game like this has totally opened Finn up.

"What's your favorite vegetable?" I ask.

"None of them," Finn shouts.

"Don't yell," I say, rolling my eyes.

"Broccoli," Ethan says, then takes a huge bite of the broccoli and beef, then chomps it with an open mouth. Finn giggles, then eyes the broccoli again. He still doesn't take any.

"I love huge salads," I say. Finn acts like he's going to throw up. "You have to pick one," I say.

"Fine. Broccoli," he huffs. I know he's just saying it because Ethan did, but I test it by placing one small piece of broccoli on his plate. Finn pushes his plate away.

"Dude, you don't know what you're missing. When you eat broccoli like this," he pauses to take off his flannel, revealing his tatted arms under his white t-shirt, "you get guns like these."

Finn's eyes widen. "You have tattoos?"

Ethan lets Finn get close to look at all his tattoos, and I'm somewhere between charmed at this interaction and horrified that Finn might think tattoos are cool enough to get one of this own. It's one thing to think Ethan looks sexy with them, it's a whole other thing to think of my son's beautiful skin covered in ink.

"My turn again," Ethan says. He looks at me, then shifts his eyes at Finn. I glance over just in time to see Finn eat the broccoli, then get a thoughtful look on his face. He takes the container, and it takes everything in me to say nothing as Finn spoons a small helping of broccoli and beef onto his plate.

We play a few more rounds, then retire to the living room for a movie—Finn's choice, which is *How to Train Your Dragon* for the millionth time. Ethan still hasn't mentioned the cars on the counter, and I know Finn is dying to know.

"Ethan?" he asks. He's sitting between both of us, sidled up to me. I notice that he keeps his legs kicked to the side to keep Ethan as far away as possible. "Who are those cars for?"

"What cars?" Ethan asks. His face is serious, but I give him away by laughing. Finn looks at me, then rolls his eyes.

"The ones on the counter," he says.

"Oh! I forgot!" Ethan jumps up, bringing the cars and the vase of flowers.

"These are for you," he says to Finn, holding out the flowers. Finn takes them, his eyebrows furled as he eyes the cars in Ethan's hands.

"And these are for you," he says to me, handing me the cars.

"Hey!" Finn says, but his smile proves that he gets the joke. He hands me the flowers, then grins wider as he takes the cars. He looks them over, then drops to the ground to tear open the packaging. I'm about to remind him to say thank you, but he looks up at Ethan.

"Thank you," he says, and it's so full of sincerity, I think I hear the trust that comes with it. Sure enough, once he has the cars unpackaged, he sits on the other side of me, putting me in the middle.

"Scoot over," he says, and I gladly move toward Ethan, Finn leaning against my thigh. I stealthily move my pinky toward Ethan, brushing it against his hand. He squeezes it, and without looking at me, offers a tiny side smile.

That's all the contact we have for the next two hours. But once Finn is in bed, Ethan and I cuddle on the couch, making up for lost time with small caresses. His arm is around me, and I'm overwhelmed by the sexual tension that's built up inside me—tension I know we won't relieve tonight. It's probably from seeing Ethan interact with Finn, and all the relief that came with it.

"You were a natural," I tell him, looking up into his dark eyes. He kisses the tip of my nose.

"Finn's an easy kid to like," he says. I laugh.

"Right. Easy." I lift an eyebrow, and he smirks.

"Fine, but he wasn't unpredictable. If you were my mom, I'd tell everyone to be hands off too." He tilts his head. "That didn't sound right. What I mean is that Finn loves you and is protective of you. He needed to make sure I'm not going to hurt you."

"He let us sit next to each other," I point out. Ethan grins.

"I think that was my favorite part of the whole night."

"What, sitting next to me? Or Finn letting you sit next to me?"

He leans in and kisses my nose again.

"Both."

Chapter 20

Monday morning, Ethan shows up at my house a few minutes after Finn's bus has left, just like old times. What isn't like old times is the amped up anticipation I feel as he walks toward the door. I guess that's what a week apart will do, plus the fact that we barely touched the night he met Finn. So when he opens the door, I launch myself at him. He catches me easily, his mouth on mine in a shattering kiss as he tugs at my shirt and the waistband of my yoga pants. We leave a trail of clothes to the bedroom where he follows me to the bed, his hands on my body, my hands in his hair, our mouths searching each other.

"We should talk, right?" he breathes against me as we collapse on the mattress. I shove the condom in his hand and shake my head.

"Yes, but later. Don't stop."

And he doesn't. He rips open the package, slides the condom on, then slides just as easily into me. I arch my back as an involuntary gasp escapes my lungs. Then we're moving, my hands clutching his hips in an effort to bring him closer while he tugs at my hair and devours my neck. He smells so goddamn good, like salt and earth, and I bury my face in his chest to inhale his whole being. Every nerve in my body is electrified, so much that the simple stroke of his hand on my skin has me erupting in goosebumps, makes my body shake, and brings me closer and closer to orgasm. Then I shatter, coming completely undone as he thrusts harder. His skin is covered in a thin sheen of sweat. I nip at his arm to keep myself anchored, tasting the salt of his body as I cry out against him, followed by his own shuddering grunts.

Once the final tremor subsides, we stay connected as our breathing slows to a steady, identical pace. I wrap my arms around him, stroking his back, feeling the fullness of his weight on my body. I feel like I can breathe easier with his body covering mine.

He slides off me, disposing of the condom before facing me again. He traces lazy circles on my belly, between my breasts, over my arms. A smile tugs at his lips as his touch leaves a trail of more goosebumps.

"I think you like that," he murmurs.

"I think we spent too long apart," I say, leaning up to give him a slow, sensual kiss. His hand cups my cheek as he deepens the kiss, but he keeps the unhurried pace. Now that we've released that built-up tension, it's nice to just be here, tangled in the sheets with nowhere else to be. I'm grateful for the amount of work I've done this past week, affording me a day of absolutely nothing but lying in Ethan's arms.

"So…" he starts.

"So…" I repeat, lowering my eyes. There's a glimmer of awkwardness between us, and I know it has everything to do with him meeting Finn last night. "How are you feeling?"

"I'm fine," he says. "The question is, how are *you* feeling?"

I check myself then. There's still a small pit of uncertainty in my belly, but I attribute it to the fact that I still haven't told Ethan everything. But as far as how last night went, I couldn't have expected better, and I tell him as much.

"What was your biggest fear?" he asks, and my mind immediately thinks of my mother disappearing to the bedroom with some nameless guy. But when I look in Ethan's face, I realize just how different this is. I know him. At least, I know this isn't some casual fling.

"I guess I was afraid of Finn feeling like I was abandoning him," I say. Ethan strokes my arms, his lips curving into a soft smile, but he says nothing. "And I was afraid I'd lose myself in you and really would abandon him."

"You'd never do that," he said, squeezing my arm.

"Yeah, but I think I understand how easy it is. I mean, the way I feel about you…"

I stop myself, but not soon enough for his eyes to widen, his mouth slipping into an easy grin. He pulls back to look at my face.

"And how is that?" he asks.

He's already confessed his feelings at the carnival, and even though I've been feeling the same way, I haven't been able to tell him. I want to, but it doesn't feel right to say those words when I still haven't admitted my biggest secret to him.

"That I think you're pretty special," I say lamely, and I try to ignore the flash of disappointment that crosses his face. "And I can see this growing into something so much bigger than it already is."

It's only a fraction of what I'm feeling, and I can't help hoping he'll see through my careful words to know how I feel. He nuzzles my neck, sliding his arm across my waist before he climbs over me again.

"How much bigger," he whispers, then lowers to my mouth. My phone on the nightstand starts ringing at the same time, and I groan against him.

"It could be Finn's school," I explain as I roll out from under him to reach my phone. On the display is my mother's name. I frown, wishing I could just ignore it.

"Hello?"

No one speaks, but I can hear breathing on the other line. I sit up in bed, switching the phone to my other ear.

"Mom? You there?"

"You need to get over here," a gruff voice says.

"Duke?"

I'm sure it's him, but I don't get to find out for sure because the phone goes dead. When I turn to Ethan, the alarm must be painted across my face because he gets up and starts pulling on his shirt.

"It's my mom," I explain, grabbing my sweats from the floor. "I just…" my hands won't stop shaking. I'm used to my mom calling me, but never Duke.

"I'll drive," he says, taking my hand in his. I nod, thoughts racing through my head, but the words unformed.

My leg bounces as I navigate, and I'm glad he's the one behind the wheel. No one is in a hurry as we enter the freeway, and we're stuck in place as traffic moves at a crawl.

"Get off at the next exit," I say. "We'll take the side streets."

There's a break in the line of cars, and he makes his move to merge onto the offramp. That's when I notice the plume of smoke in the direction of my mom's neighborhood.

"Oh God," I breathe.

"It might be a coincidence," Ethan assures me, but I know it's hers. Especially as we get closer. My voice breaks as I give him directions, my leg hopping from adrenaline. "Claire…"

"Don't you dare tell me to calm down," I say.

"I'm not," he says. But he doesn't say anything else after that, just takes my hand in his. My leg settles, and I allow his touch to be my anchor.

He takes the final left, then a right. His hand squeezes tighter as the firetrucks come in view, smoke pouring from my mom's house. I let go of his hand to strip off my seatbelt, and I'm jumping out of the car before he comes to a full stop. I run toward the house, tears streaming down my face, a cry lodged in my throat.

"Miss, you can't be here," a firefighter says, catching me by the hand as I reach the front door.

"My mother!" I scream. I can hear Ethan calling my name, but I'm too busy trying to wrench free from the man gripping my hand. Another firefighter grabs me around the waist, pulling me back from the front door.

"She's not in there," he shouts in my ear. Smoke pours out the open door, and I turn my head as if it will reach out its filmy fingers and pull me inside.

"Where is she?"

"Claire!"

The firefighter loosens his hold on me as I turn toward Ethan's voice. Next to him is my mom sitting on the curb, an oxygen mask over her face as a paramedic stands nearby. I break free and run toward her.

"Mom! Are you okay? What happened?"

Her glassy eyes rise to look at me, and I notice how dilated her pupils are, along with a yellow sheen to the whites of her eyes. I want to pretend it's the smoke, but I know better. I look away, a sinking feeling replacing my ebbing panic.

"Where's Duke?" I ask, turning my head to scan the faces of the neighbors watching my mom's house as if it's a movie. Not one of them have come over to see if she's okay, or are even looking in her direction.

"She needs to recover," the paramedic says, her voice void of any real concern. I turn to the woman, and I don't miss the look of annoyance on her face, as if standing here is a waste of her time. I'm ready to say something, but I look at my mom instead. Her eyes are now closed, her pale skin the color of butter. Her head drops to the side, and I grab her shoulder so that she jerks awake again. Her eyes turn toward me, and I can tell it's taking everything she has to focus. Then she falls to the side. I leap toward her, catching her before her head hits the pavement.

"Mom!" I shake her slightly, her frail body feeling like it will break within my grasp. Two more paramedics are at my side, and somehow, I'm maneuvered away from her. Ethan moves in, grasping my elbow, and I'm shocked back into remembering he was here. A moment of embarrassment passes through me as I realize he's seeing the mom I know. Then I'm ashamed that I'm even concerned with anyone's judgment. Maybe everyone thinks it's smoke inhalation. Maybe it really is.

"Do you know what your mom was using before the fire?" the first paramedic asks me. I turn to her, shrinking under her appraising eyes.

"What do you mean?" I ask. I glance sideways at Ethan, then back to paramedic. She sighs, shifting her weight from one foot to the other.

"I don't have time for pretend," she says. The other paramedics are now wheeling my mother into the ambulance. Everything is happening too fast, all at once.

"I got here just a few minutes ago," I spit out. "For you to accuse my mom—"

"Look lady, we're going to test her anyway so we know how to treat her. But things will go a lot easier if you just tell us what you know."

I'm torn on what to do. I want to run to my mom and protect her as she goes to the hospital. But a larger part of me is repulsed, wanting nothing to do with her. I glance at Ethan again. I feel small, like I'm the one who's been using. I don't know what he's thinking, and for a moment I worry that this dose of reality will change the way he feels about me. But then he leans down and kisses my forehead. He lingers there, and I close my eyes, drawing strength from the warmth of his lips against my skin.

"It's probably crack," I say, turning back to the paramedic. I recall the crack pipe I found the last time I saw her, and the cigarette she'd left burning. I tell the paramedic all this as Ethan wraps his arm around my shoulder. "I told her if she wasn't careful, she'd burn the house down." I laugh lightly, and then out of nowhere, I'm crying. Ethan pulls me close as I shudder in his arms.

"We're taking her to Sunset Bay Medical Center," I hear the paramedic say as I bury myself in Ethan's chest. I don't miss the softer note in her voice.

An inspector asks me a few more questions before I leave, though there isn't much I can share except for what I already told the paramedic. I feel like I'm ratting my mom out, but I decide being honest is probably my best bet. As it is, I learn the fire was concentrated to the living room where my mom usually slept during the day.

"We got here early enough that, besides smoke, the rest of the house was unaffected. But the living room is uninhabitable. The couch and floorboards were incinerated, but it didn't go much further than that."

I realize what he's saying, recognizing the danger she was in if the couch caught fire.

"Where's Duke?" I ask once again. "Did he… I mean, was he…"

"No one else was in the house," the inspector says.

"Your mother is lucky she got out in time."

I recall the state my mom was in last time I saw her, along with how she was just now before the ambulance took her away. She did not get out of that house alone. I don't know Duke well, but I know the kind of guys my mom attracts. He just lost his free lodging. We'll never see him again, but at least he had enough decency to call me before he took off.

Chapter 21

Ethan and I head to his car and drive in silence toward the hospital. His hand rests near me, and while I long to take it and soak up some of his reassurance, I keep my own hand in my lap. Instead I stare out the window, drowning in a whirlpool of emotions, unable to decipher a single one. Mostly, I feel numb. Tired. A glance at the clock, and I know my time is severely limited. Finn will be out of school soon, and I have to be there to get him. It's only one more way my mom has complicated my life. I should feel bad for my resentment, but I don't— especially since I know my mom started this fire.

The parking lot is full when we get there, so Ethan drops me off at the entrance to the ER.

"Tell them you're looking for Judy Myers," I say before rushing off to find my mom's room. After confirming I'm her daughter, the nurse buzzes me into the back where I'm led to a curtained area. Behind the curtain is my mother, her wispy hair spread out around her, an oxygen mask covering her nose and mouth as she lays with her eyes closed. I watch her for a moment, taking in her sleeping body. She looks so small in the bed, like a child with a weathered face and a mess of tubes and wires. I knew she wasn't doing well, but seeing her now, I know it's beyond that.

I move the curtain, and her eyes open. She tilts her head until she finds me, and I see the smile in her eyes even if I can't see her face. She fumbles with the mask, drawing it down.

"Hey, girl," she croaks. I move forward and replace the mask.

"You need that, Mom," I insist, but she shakes her head, slipping it back off.

"I'm fine," she says, though her voice sounds like it's coming out a whiskey barrel. "What a day, huh?"

I take a deep breath in, studying her face to see where she's at. "Do you know how the fire started?" I ask. She shrugs.

"Anyone's guess," she says. A bolt of fury electrifies me, and I clench my hands. But then I take another deep breath, letting it out slow as my fists unfurl. None of us know how it started, I only have my assumptions.

"Well, you're very lucky," I say. She nods. Her head rolls to the side, and I think that maybe she passed out again. But her eyes are open.

"He's gone, isn't he?" she says softly.

"Who, Duke? I didn't see him there, if that's what you're asking."

My mom nods but doesn't say anything else about it. For a moment, I put myself in her shoes, understanding how it feels to lose someone without saying goodbye. But for me, I've been losing my mom for years.

"Judy Myers?"

Both of us turn toward the doctor. His name tag reads *Dr. Miguel Carrillo, MD,* and he states it for us as well. He comes in the room with a smile as if unfazed by my addict mother. I appreciate this game of pretend. It's better than the judgmental paramedic.

Dr. Carrillo goes over my mom's chart with both of us, confirming the results of my mom's failed urine test as if he were confirming a pulled muscle. Cocaine, though I already know it was crack. His only comment is to recommend a treatment program, but he says it breezily enough that I know he doesn't expect either of us to take him seriously.

"We'd like to keep you overnight, Ms. Myers," he says to my mom.

"Just Judy," she rasps out. "And for what?"

"You inhaled a lot of smoke," he says, "and your system is weak. I'd feel better if we could monitor you for at least twenty-four hours."

"I'd like to go home," my mother says, trying to sit up in bed, but falling back after only a few seconds of struggle.

"You can't, Mom," I say. "Your house burnt down." Technically, just the living room is damaged, but I know she can't live there. Even more, I have to figure out what to do with her once she's out of the hospital. I can't have her move in with me, but I might not have a choice. I need the time to figure this out, and a hospital stay is my saving grace.

My mom doesn't argue after that, and I help fill out the necessary paperwork before leaving.

"I have to be home for Finn," I tell my mom. Even though it's the truth, I feel fortunate for the excuse to get out of there.

Ethan is in the waiting room when I come out. He stands up like an expectant father, which is a silly thought to have in a moment like this.

"Everything okay?" he asks.

"Yeah," I say, nodding. "They're going to keep her overnight." I look at the clock on the wall and wince. "Finn is going to be home in five minutes, let's get out of here."

As Ethan drives, I text Beth—the neighbor I know the best—and explain the situation. When she texts back, she says she'll bring Finn to her house until I return. With that taken care of, I can finally relax. I rest my head against the window, releasing a deep breath, feeling my body completely let down from an afternoon of stress.

"You're probably wondering how you got mixed up with such a messed-up girl, huh?" I say, letting out a forced laugh.

"Don't do that," he says. I look toward him, but I'm too tired to brush any of this off with a smile. None of it feels funny.

"It's true, though. Isn't it?"

"Right, and I'm Mr. Perfect over here," he says. "Neither one of us are our parents, even if they've done a great job trying to fuck up our lives."

"And for me, it's never going to stop," I point out. "My mom is going to continue fucking things up, and I'm always going to be the dutiful daughter, ready to bail her out. What happens when it affects your life too? She just lost her home. What if she has to move in with me?"

"Then we spend a lot more time at my house," he says.

"You don't understand. If she moves in with me, I can't leave her alone. Ever! The next house she burns down could be mine."

Ethan reaches for my hand, but I pull it away even though I'm not mad at him. No, I'm just mad in general. I breathe hard, focusing on the cars we pass as he drives. Eventually, my breath slows, and my thoughts start to form into something I can touch.

"I don't want her to move in," I whisper.

"I know you don't, baby. There are other options. When we get back to your house, let me help you with some research."

The last thing I want to do is spend any more energy on any of this. I want to curl up in bed and sleep away the rest of the day. But I've been gifted twenty-four hours to come up with some solutions, and if I throw it away, I will be making up a foldout couch for my mom and saying goodbye to my peace of mind.

When we get home, I gather Finn from Beth's house, then set him up at the table with a snack and his homework. He has a lot of questions about his grandmother, and I tell him what I can without getting into the darker details of her addiction. Finn doesn't know my mom as well as he should, thanks to my boundaries with her. Still, I feel terrible seeing his brow crinkle with worry. He does his homework without complaint, and when he's done, I let him watch TV in the other room.

Ethan and I get to work on researching solutions. He seeks out care homes in our area, and I make phone calls to every promising place. Most want me to come in and tour the facility before giving prices, but a few bypass that step when I explain the situation. All of them are out of my price range.

"So, we have your mom sell her house," Ethan says.

"Does she have a mortgage on it?'"

"No," I say. It's something we were fortunate to have, even when everything else was out of our reach. My grandparents died before I was born, and my mom got their house. All she's owed is annual taxes, and a modest trust took care of that for a while. But the trust ran out years ago, and she's lived on borrowed time and money for years. Mostly, *my* time and money. "Who'd want to buy a partially burnt home, anyway?"

"You'd be surprised what people will buy," Ethan says. "I saw a news article recently about a fire-damaged home in Northern California that sold for over a million dollars."

That gets my attention for a moment, but then reality sets in. "She'll never sell it," I say. Of all the things my mom is, one of them is fiercely loyal to the memory of her parents. An only child, my grandparents doted on her until the day they died. Even though I never knew them, I'm well aware of the ghosts that live within the walls of my mother's home. The memory of them runs deep, from the photos of them on the walls to the furniture from my mom's childhood. Including the couch she just burnt.

Ethan mentions a few more avenues we can take, including a possible intervention. I feel like the walls are closing in. He takes one look at me, then closes the laptop. Without a word, he gets up and makes me a cup of tea. Once the steaming herbal liquid is in front of me, he stands at my back and gently kneads my shoulders. Despite my feelings of hopelessness, I lean into his touch, rolling my neck as he loosens the knots in my muscles.

"We can tackle this in the morning," he murmurs, then smooths the hair from my neck so he can place a gentle kiss on my skin. His hot breath creates a trail of shivers down my spine. "It's not like we're accomplishing anything right now, anyway."

I'm grateful for his help. I also feel the weight of truth in his words. We haven't accomplished *anything*, except to see how much is out of my reach. Tomorrow will be no different. Meanwhile, my mom will be released from the hospital tomorrow, and the only logical place to take her is here. My home. Which she will taint with her addictions, because I'm just not strong enough to fight her on them.

I rest my hand on Ethan's, my shoulders sagging in defeat. "Thank you," I say.

Chapter 22

Ethan stays for dinner, and then stays the night after Finn goes to bed. I make a place for him on the couch, but I end up joining him on the tight space. He wraps his arms around me, pulling me flush against him. He's wearing only a t-shirt and his boxers, and I can feel him grow hard against me. But he doesn't act on it, seeming to sense my need for comfort over passion. I drift away to the feel of his heartbeat against my back and the sound of his slow breath as we both succumb to sleep.

I'm still in his arms when I wake, and for a moment I forget everything from the night before. I'm so comfortable in the cocoon of his body, and I burrow closer to him, rousing him as he wraps his arms tighter around me.

"Good morning," he murmurs, and it's at the same time that I recall my mother in the hospital, the state of her home, and the impossible situation I'm now in. I turn, groaning as I crush my face against Ethan's chest, wishing I can bury myself until everything works itself out. He strokes my hair, neither of us moving in the dim light of morning. But when I hear the coffeepot start on its automatic timer, I know I need to get up and face reality. At the very least, I need to get Finn ready for school. But I'll have to deal with my mom today too, and I still have no clue what to do.

I pour us both a cup of coffee, then join Ethan again in the dimly lit living room. He inhales the steam from his cup, then rests his free hand on my knee.

"Thank you," he says. "How did you sleep?"

"Surprisingly well."

And it hits me how natural it feels for him to be here—as if I could wake up to his face every morning and greet the day together over a cup of coffee. In the midst of my busy mind, I'm grateful he's there. His presence has a calming effect on me.

"I'm still not sure what to do about my mom," I admit, and he squeezes my knee.

"Let's hear what the doctor has to say," he says.

I warm at his use of the word "let's," at his insinuation that this is *our* problem, not just mine.

For so many years, I've done everything on my own. I've had no one to rely on. I was forced to use my best judgement and ignore my fatigue as I figured out how to make ends meet when the work wasn't coming in, or how to add more hours to my day so I could work and meet all of Finn's needs, or still take care of my mother when I didn't even want to be around her.

Maybe I'm done having to figure things out on my own.

Ethan takes over breakfast duty as I get Finn ready for school. By the time Finn's hair is combed, the table is set with three plates of runny eggs and toast. I'd clued Ethan in on Finn's preferences beforehand, and he did it perfectly—including the blonde piece of toast smothered in butter. Finn chatters easily over breakfast, unlike his usual grumpy morning self. I stay quiet, brushing aside the worries I have over my mom as I witness the cadence of Ethan and Finn's conversation. It seems Finn's let go of any resistance he initially felt over Ethan, and Ethan seems to have forgotten his hesitation over kids. At one point they both laugh, and my heart leaps at the similar way they throw their heads back and then end it with a dimpled grin.

If Ethan notices, he doesn't say anything. When we say goodbye, Finn seems to hesitate at the door, glancing at me and then Ethan. My breath catches, and I wonder if this is the moment he'll decide he's not okay that I'm dating.

"Do you think…" he starts, and then stops. That's when I realize what he wants…and that he doesn't know how to ask.

"If it's all right with you, I think we'll wait with you at the bus stop," I say, and his face lights up. He puts his hand in mine—and I do my best to act like this is no big thing. Seriously. No big thing that my independent son is actually wanting to be near me, actually holding my hand. Then he looks at Ethan and grins, and I just about melt into a pile of lovestruck mush. But if I so much as tear up, I know I'll totally ruin the moment by embarrassing Finn. So I just let him hold my hand as he rehashes his favorite carnival rides he went on with Brie. Was that only a few days ago? Now we're here, seeing Finn off like we're a family.

It's a sign. My heart lurches as I realize I need to tell Ethan the full truth. He deserves to know, and seeing how he is with Finn, I know it's the right choice. Ethan is the right choice—for both of us.

The bus comes, and Finn hugs me even though everyone can see. He pauses when he looks at Ethan, who puts his fist out for a bump. Finn grins, pushing his fist against Ethan's, and I have to look away so he can't see the tears forming in my eyes.

As the bus moves away, I gather my courage with a few deep breaths. Ethan glances down at me, his face twisting into a question when he sees my emotional state. I take his hand, leading him to the house as my heart beats wildly. My hand feels sweaty in his, and I hope he doesn't notice.

"We need to talk," I say, my mouth feeling like it has marbles in it as I search for the right words. But I get no further than the door when I hear my phone ringing on the kitchen table. *Mom.* I release Ethan's hand and race for the phone, reaching it just as it stops ringing.

"Damn," I swear, picking it up. It's the same number, multiple times. I hit the number, listening to it ring until it reaches an automated voice from the hospital. I listen as the voice goes through my options, but it's interrupted by someone ringing through on the other line. I end the call and switch over.

"Hello?"

"Get me the fuck out of here," my mother croaks in my ear. I grimace, glancing over at Ethan. *My mom,* I mouth to him, and he nods. He busies himself with cleaning up the breakfast dishes.

"What does the doctor say?" In my head, I'm right back to square one, wondering what the hell I'm going to do with her.

"I don't care what that idiot man says. I want out of here. Why aren't you here? You're never around when I need you."

I clench and release my fist multiple times, feeling my resentment build like rushing water in a bursting dam. "I had to get Finn off to school," I say, but I can't expect her to know that. What I do know is that her words are clearer than I've heard her speak in a long time, more forceful. When was the last time I'd experienced my mother sober? "We're on our way," I say. "We just have a few things to clean up before we leave the house."

"We?" she asks, just as I realize my mistake. "I thought Finn had to be at school."

"I'll be there soon." I hang up before she can ask any more questions.

Ethan drives us there, and I'm silent the whole time. If the doctor releases my mom, I have no choice but to bring her home. Will she sleep on the couch? Do I give up my work studio? What happens the first time she brings drugs into my home? Because it's not a matter of *if*, but *when*.

"How you doing?" Ethan asks as he shuts the car off. I offer a shaky smile as my answer.

"Come with me?" I ask, and he nods. He leans over, cupping my chin in his hand as he presses his lips gently on mine.

"I'm not going anywhere," he promises. I press my forehead against his, letting out the breath I'd been holding. I don't know how I'd face this without him.

He holds my hand as we cross the parking lot, and he doesn't let go as we reach the front desk of the nurse's station. The woman behind the counter directs me to my mom's floor and room number, and then we're in the elevator. I feel like a kid again as I grip Ethan's hand. Scared. Unsure which mom I'm about to encounter. Who I'm going to bring home with me.

But when I reach the right corridor, I'm surprised to see a police officer outside the room the nurse told us to go to. I slow my steps as the police officer looks at me.

"Claire Myers?" he asks.

"Let her in!" I hear my mom scream from inside the room.

"What's going on, Officer," Ethan says, stepping forward while still holding my hand. I hang back, unsure what to do. The officer ignores Ethan, his focus on me.

"Your mother is charged with reckless burning under Penal Code 452 PC," the officer says. All the while, my mother is screaming obscenities inside the room.

"But she didn't do it on purpose," I say, finally finding my voice.

"She was under the influence when it happened," the officer says. "If convicted, she faces up to six months in jail."

My mouth drops open. My mother will not last a week in jail, let alone half a year.

"We have a few options," a voice says behind me. I turn to see Dr. Carrillo, the same doctor I talked with yesterday. "Please excuse us," he says to the officer, then ushers Ethan and I down the hall. I can still hear my mother screaming, but it's not as loud from over here.

"Your mother's in bad shape," Dr. Carrillo says honestly, "her liver is pretty shot. You can see it in the yellowing of her skin and eyes, and with how swollen her abdomen is."

I'd noticed both before, but hadn't paid either any attention. She just always appeared sickly, and I assumed her sallow skin went with it.

The doctor goes on, sharing how my mom will not survive if she continues drinking or using.

"You think I know how to get her to stop?" I blurt out. He shakes his head.

"No, I don't," he says. "And it's not your responsibility, either. But there's a place she can go to get help." He tells us about Mountain Vista, a treatment facility up north that would take her on an emergency basis. "There's a spot available for her," he continues. "It's not cheap, but I know many patients who have completed the program and have remained sober."

"How long is the program, and how much is it?" Ethan asks.

"It's a six-week program. Some insurances may cover it, but out-of-pocket it can run up to $50,000, sometimes more."

My heart sinks at the number. I know she doesn't have that kind of money, and I definitely don't.

"If she completes the program, she may avoid jail time," the doctor continues.

"She'll do it," I say quickly.

"I can help you," Ethan offers, but I shake my head.

"No," I say. "I have some savings, and I can take out a loan to cover the rest." I turn to the doctor. "Does my mom know?"

He nods. "She hasn't agreed to it, but I don't think she understands the situation."

"I'll make her see," I say.

The doctor hands me a pamphlet from the facility, showing me the number to call and the person I need to speak with. "They're expecting your call," he says.

My mom has quieted down by the time we reach her room again. The officer is still standing guard outside her room when we come back. I look to Ethan, my hand tightening in his. He nods, letting me know he's not going anywhere. He enters the room with me, and I cling to him for strength.

My mom's eyes are closed when we walk in, but they snap open as soon as she hears our footsteps. Her gaze is hard, but it softens when she sees my face, then curious when she glances at Ethan. I'm worried about what she'll say in front of him, but I'm not willing to be alone with her. I don't know how I'm going to break the news to her.

"I talked with the doctor," I start, and her face lifts into a sneer.

"That asshole doesn't know what he's talking about,"

she says. "I'm not going to Mountain Vista or any other shithole treatment center. I don't have a problem." She lifts her hand to brush the wisps of hair from her face, and that's when I see she's handcuffed to the bed.

"Really, Mom?" I nod to her handcuffed arm. "And what's your alternative."

"That I go home and take care of myself, just like I have all my goddamn life."

"You almost burned your goddamn house down," I say, my voice raising as I release Ethan's hand. I clench my fists into tight balls at my side, feeling the heat rise in me as I stare down my mom's defiant face. "You've been high or drunk every day of my goddamn life. I can't even let you around your grandson because you're a fucking mess."

"And you think you're any better?" Her lips curl into a smile, her eyes narrowing on Ethan. "Did she tell you she's a whore?" she asks.

"That's enough!" I scream. I turn to Ethan, shaking my head. "I'm sorry. Can you wait outside?"

"Are you sure?" he asks. "She can't say anything that will make me love you less."

"She doesn't even know who Finn's father is," my mom snarls.

"Please, just wait outside," I say, suddenly aware of what a mistake this was. I can't get him out of here fast enough. "I'll be okay, I promise. I'll just be a moment."

He leans over and kisses my cheek, then without even glancing at my mom, he turns and steps outside the room. I move closer to my mom, but not close enough for her to touch me.

"You are going to Mountain Vista, and that's final," I hiss.

"I will not," my mom says.

"And then what will you do? Rot in jail? Because that's where you're going if you don't get help. You think you'll get drugs in jail? You think it will be easier than a treatment program? You've run out of options Mom, and it's time you faced facts."

"I won't go," my mom insists, but her voice wavers. I see the seed of panic in her eyes, the fear over what happens next. But I harden my heart. I won't do this anymore; I'm done saving her.

"You don't have a choice," I tell her, even though it's a lie. "They're releasing you to the treatment center as soon as the doctor clears you to leave. After that, you're on your own to figure things out. I'm done, Mom."

"What are you talking about, Claire?"

But I really am done. I turn to leave.

"Don't you dare leave, Claire," my mom shouts after me. "Get back here."

I don't. But I don't leave either. I pause on the other side of the curtain where she can't see me, my hands shaking as I try to compose myself.

"You think you're better than me? You goddamn whore, Claire!"

My insides twist at her voice. I'm seventeen again, coming home to her stumbling down the hall. *You goddamn whore, Claire.*

"You didn't even know his name," my mom laughs, but I hear the crackle in her voice. "A masked lover. I wonder if he even knows he has a kid."

I want to march back in there and retaliate against her words. I want to tell her all the ways she failed me. This is what she's going to hold over my head? What about all the ways she failed me? Or that she doesn't know who my father is? Or how I've been the one making sure she survives?

But I'm done. I unclench my fists and swipe at the moisture forming in my eyes. Then, with a deep breath, I leave the room.

The officer is still there, but Ethan isn't. I look at the officer and he nods his head down the hallway.

"Thanks," I murmur, then head in the direction he indicated. When I round the corner, I see Ethan sitting in a chair in the waiting room, his head bowed and his hands folded in front of him. I step closer, placing my hand on his shoulder. He looks up, and my breath catches at how pale his face is. For the first time, I notice his hands shaking.

"Is it true?" he asks.

Chapter 23

It's like the floor drops from under me, like the room is getting smaller around us.

He knows.

"Ethan…"

But he's up, heading for the elevator. I follow, but he turns at last minute and barrels through the doors of the stairwell. I let the door slam shut without following him, even though I want to. Instead, I take the elevator, my own hands shaking as tears spill down my cheeks. I reach the lobby and he's not there. But in the parking lot I see his car, and I see him hunched over, getting sick next to the driver's side door.

I rush to him, but he brushes me off.

"Did you know it was me?" he grunts out, looking up at me as he clutches his stomach.

"Not at first," I say.

"Was this your idea of fun? Was Nina in on it? Your friend, Maren?"

"No, Ethan, I swear!"

He groans, lurching forward, but nothing comes up. I reach over to touch his arm, but he jerks out of the way.

"Don't touch me," he growls. "How long did you know?"

"Our first date," I admit, and his mouth drops.

"The book," he says, shaking his head.

"That was a mistake," I plead. "It wasn't a joke, I swear. I wasn't trying to do anything but coax you into knowing the truth."

"If you wanted me to know so bad, why didn't you tell me?"

"Because you told me you didn't want kids!" I say. He glares at my raised voice, and I lift my hands as I do my best to calm down. "I didn't want to scare you off when it was obvious there was a huge reason."

"Yeah, one you went behind my back to figure out," he shoots at me. I have nothing to say to this. "How many other secrets are you keeping from me, Claire? How many lies have you fed me?"

"I haven't lied to you!"

"No, you just omitted the truth." Ethan wipes his mouth, standing up straight even though he still appears a pale shade of green. He opens his mouth to say something else, then shuts it, shaking his head again.

"Get in the car," he finally says.

"What?" I look at him in confusion. "Where are we going?"

"I'm taking you home, and then I'm going back to my house."

I shake my head, backing up. I pull out my phone.

"I don't need you to do anything for me," I say, opening the Uber app. He reaches over and grabs my phone.

"No, that's your way, isn't it?" With my phone in hand, he opens the car door and gets in. I narrow my eyes, but also realize I have no ground to stand on here. I also have no choice. I circle the car and get in the passenger side.

We drive in silence, though he's driving a little faster than usual. It's like he can't wait to be free of me. But instead of driving me home, he exits the freeway early.

"Where are we going?" I ask.

He doesn't answer, but I can already tell. He takes the left into my mother's neighborhood. But we don't stop at her house. My eyes stay on the house as we pass it. If I didn't know about the burned living room and ignored the caution tape wrapped around the house, I wouldn't even know it had been on fire.

Ethan reaches the end of the street, then turns right. We're at the dead end. *The* dead end. He turns off the car, and I start to unbuckle my seatbelt to get out.

"Stay," he growls, and even though my heart is beating wildly, I don't move. I stare straight ahead, the memories of that night we first met clashing with this moment now.

"This is the place, right?" he asks.

I nod, and he lets out a rush of air. Both of us are silent for a moment, the sound of our breathing filling the small space.

"I thought about you so many times," he whispers.

I'm afraid to speak, and so I don't. But my thoughts are filled with what I want to tell him. That I thought of him too. Not just because he was Finn's father, but because he was the lifeline I needed that night, and a lifeline I wished I could grasp when times were hard.

"Do you have any idea what you've done?" he asks. I turn to him, confused. "You made me just like my father." His angry eyes are filled with tears, but he doesn't brush them away.

"I only just found out," I say.

"And you didn't tell me!" I flinch as he slams his hand into the steering wheel, his horn sounding with the impact.

"It's not that simple!"

"Really?" he asks. "Hey Ethan, I think we knew each other seven years ago, and by the way, you have a kid."

"Right, and then you'd either disappear again, or you'd try to take my son away from me."

"Our son!" he yells, and a sob escapes his lips. He clamps his hand over his mouth, just as surprised by the sound as I am. "Our son," he repeats, this time softly. "And if you think either of those things, you don't know me very well."

"You're right," I say. "There's still so much to know about you. But back when I found out? I didn't know you at all. In fact, the moment I found out you didn't want kids, I was ready to never see you again. But when I realized you were Finn's father, I wanted to give you another chance."

"Gee, thanks," he says. "I guess you were in charge the whole time."

"It's not like that," I say.

"That's exactly what it's like."

"When you have kids…"

"What, Claire? Because I *do* have a kid."

I breathe through my nose, turning away from him as I collect myself.

"You don't get it," I say slowly, then look back at him. "I raised Finn all these years on my own. My job has been to protect him from harm, and that includes emotional harm. I had no way to know if you were a good guy or a bad one. I already swore I wasn't going to date anyone until I was done raising Finn. You changed my mind, first because of who you are to Finn, but second because of who you are as a man. I wouldn't have found out if you were the right man for either of us if I'd told you about Finn that night. So I'm glad I didn't tell you, because then I wouldn't know what it feels like to fall in love with you."

The words tumble from me, and I try to catch them as they land between us. His mouth opens, and I think I see his face soften. Then he looks away. I brush my pinky against his hand on the center console, and he jerks as if to move, but his hand remains. I wrap my pinky around his, and he grips it back. I can see the tears rolling down his cheek, even though he's trying to keep his face from mine.

"My biggest fear," he finally says, then sniffs as he wipes his face, "my biggest reason for not having kids, is my fear that I'd do to them what my dad did to me."

"Finn grew up happy," I say softly. He looks over at me, his face shining with tears.

"Without a dad," he says.

"But happy." I take his hand in mine, and he lets me even though his grasp is loose. "It wasn't my ideal choice either," I tell him, "especially now that I know you. Finn would have loved having you as a father. I mean, he'll love having you as a dad now," I correct myself. The words scare me to death, especially as I see the shift in his face. "Do you *want* to be his dad?"

He takes a shaky breath, and his hand is moist with sweat. Or maybe it's mine. My heart is beating a million miles a minute. I've never been good at sharing, and right now I'm letting go of so many trust issues when I don't even know where Ethan and I stand.

"Yes, I want to be his dad," he says. "No kid should have to go without his father."

I know Ethan is coming from a place of hurt, but I can't help feeling slighted by the statement—as if somehow Finn suffered under only my care.

"He's been okay all these years," I say carefully. Even still, Ethan's eyes flash as he looks at me, taking his hand from mine.

"I'm going to be his dad," he repeats. He starts the car again, putting it in reverse. The conversation is over, but there's still so much to say. Yet neither of us speak for the duration of the ride. We reach my house, and he pulls in front without making a move to get out. I unclip my seatbelt, taking long enough to see if there's anything else he wants to say. He stares straight ahead, his jaw pulsing as his eyes flash. I don't know what to think. I want to say something—anything—but nothing feels appropriate. We've gone in circles enough, and I wish I'd found a way to tell him about Finn before it came to this. Would it have been better? I'll never know.

I step outside the car, my feet feeling like lead as they hit the concrete. I turn, pausing in the moment to see if there's anything left. He shifts the car in drive. The message is clear. I close door, and he squeals from the curb, leaving me behind.

Maren is at my house fifteen minutes after I text her. She'd been working her shift at Insomniacs, but she left early due to a family emergency. I suppose this is exactly that, especially since I'm a crumpled heap on the kitchen table.

"He's just reacting to something surprising," Maren assures me. "Knowing what he's been through, he's probably dealing with some trauma. He'll come back around. Didn't he come around last time?"

"Yeah, but this is so much bigger. It's not like snooping into his life. I hid his own son from him." I bury my head in my hands again, wishing I could take back the past few months and start fresh, this time with only the truth.

"You had your reasons," Maren reminded me. "When you made that decision, you didn't owe Ethan anything. You did what you had to do to protect your son. Don't you think Ethan would have done the same?"

"I wouldn't know," I say, "I never even let him be a parent."

Maren groans, then takes my hands. "Claire, get a grip. Ethan is angry right now, but once he calms down, he'll see things from your side of it. He has to. You were only doing what was best for Finn, and Ethan cannot blame you for that."

"I know." I wipe my eyes, then sigh. "This just doesn't feel good. It feels like I keep messing everything up with Ethan, and all he's done is be wonderful."

"Except for seeing things from your perspective," Maren points out. "He's a great guy and all, but he's having a hard time seeing anyone's side except his own. And if anything, he should be thanking you."

"Why?" I sniff. She rolls her eyes.

"Claire, you raised a wonderful little boy on your own for the past six years. You didn't seek him out to make him pay, you just did what you needed to do to make sure Finn had the best childhood ever. You've gone to great lengths to make sure he's been protected and happy. That's not a small feat, especially with where you came from. You had all the ingredients to be a messed-up mom to him, and you weren't at all. Finn is lucky to have you, and when Ethan comes to his senses, he's going to realize he was lucky to have you raising his son too."

"But he's not going to ever get there because he was stripped of the chance to be Finn's dad."

"By circumstance," Maren says. "Look, we can go round and round in circles about this, but the truth of the matter is you made the best decision you could make with the limited information you had." Maren picks up the pile of tissues I have on the table and throws them away before washing her hands with a good amount of soap. She fills a glass of water, and then sets it in front of me. I sip it gratefully. Even though I still feel weighed down by my guilt, the load feels a little lighter after talking it out.

"Now that Ethan knows, what are your thoughts on how things will go forward?" Maren asks.

"I don't know." I've been so consumed by my missteps, that I haven't had a chance to think about the reality of this new situation. Before, I'd figured things would go smoothly with the two of us working together. This morning was a great example of how good it could be. But now, I wasn't sure we were even together. I could possibly be facing a custody battle of sorts.

"No, you won't," Maren says when I tell her as much. "Only your name is on that birth certificate. As of right now, he has no rights and will have to go through you for anything regarding Finn."

"This sounds so mean and awful," I moan.

"And it's reality," Maren says. "Hopefully Ethan comes to his senses about the two of you. But if he doesn't, you need to keep your wits about you. Don't go getting soft just because of your feelings."

"I won't," I promise, and this is one promise I know I can keep. I might have feelings for Ethan, even love him, but my love for Finn is ingrained in every cell of my body. I would move mountains for that kid, and no man is worth more than that.

Chapter 24

A few days pass before I hear from Ethan again. He texts me with a request for joint custody, which at this point, feels so incredibly cliché. Perhaps it's because I was already prepared for this conversation. I've had days to think up worst case scenarios and have researched every law there is that could affect my custody rights over Finn. I shoot back a text informing him that he has no rights, but if he'd like to set up a more casual visitation schedule, I'd be happy to work with him in any way that is best for Finn.

My phone rings immediately after that, and I don't even fight the wry smile that springs to my lips.

"Hello," I sing sweetly into the phone. I hear him chuckle on the other end, and my shoulders relax from their defensive state.

"I'm not looking to take Finn from you," he says.

"That's good, because I'd never let you do that." I keep the smile on my face, but my eyes narrow as I wonder what he has up his sleeve. I no longer trust him, and that is also thanks to several days of silence. I've spent those days considering how he'll use this newfound information about his son.

"This is new to me, is all," he says. "I don't know what I'm supposed to do, but I just know I want to do the right thing."

"The right thing would be to understand that, to Finn, his family is perfect the way it is, and any change to that is going to feel like an intrusion."

"I know."

His answer surprises me. I'd expected to have a big fight on my hands, but so far he seems to be waiting for my lead on this. Even though I'm relieved, it makes me feel slightly off balance.

"Do you think we can meet for coffee or something?" he asks. "We have a lot to figure out, and it's not so easy to do over the phone."

"I think that would be best."

"Not Insomniacs," he blurts out, and I laugh.

"Not Insomniacs," I agree. "But there's a place called Brew on the other side of town that serves beer and coffee."

"Even better," he says. "With how this week's gone, I think both of us could use a beer."

That's an understatement, of course. In the midst of everything that's been going on with Ethan, I've had to hire people to help clear out the burned portion of my mother's home, plus consider what I'll do with it. There's no fire insurance, and I don't have the money to fix what she burned, and I know my mom doesn't either. One of the days I was there, a real estate agent approached me with his business card, telling me he had buyers who would purchase it "as-is" if I was interested. Of course, I'm interested. But I don't know if I'll ever convince my mom. She's been at the treatment center for two days now, and even if she was allowed to call me, I know she wouldn't. In her mind, I betrayed her. And standing strong in all of this is taking every ounce of energy I have left.

I need a beer like a fish needs water.

I meet Ethan at Brew the next day. I wear a pair of yoga pants and an oversized sweatshirt, my hair in my regular messy bun. I'm doing my best to look like I don't care how he sees me, though I also put on mascara and clear gloss. I mean, I can't go full slob. Besides, I know he likes the way my ass looks in yoga pants.

He shows up looking better than ever. He's wearing tight jeans and a white button up shirt. His sleeves are rolled up, revealing his tattoos, and his beard is trimmed perfectly. I can't tear my eyes away. When he gets close, my mouth drops as soon as the smell of his cologne hits my nose. Holy hell, this man is going to make things hard, especially when I see the appreciative way his eyes roam over my body—as if he finds something appealing in my weekend wear.

"What are you having?" he asks. "I figure I owe you six years of child support, so I might as well start paying by getting you a drink."

"Sit your ass down," I say just as the waitress get there with the beers I already ordered and paid for. He raises his eyebrow, a smile tugging at his lips as he takes the seat across from me.

It's hard to know what to say in a moment like this, so I sip my beer. He does the same. I'm not sure where to look, so I study our surroundings, glance back at him, look away, stare at the table. Our eyes finally meet, and it's like a magnetic pull. I can't look away, and he doesn't either. I feel my breath go shallow as a ball of warmth grows in the center of my chest, expanding throughout my body until my fingers and toes tingle. How does he do this to me?

He clears his throat and I finally find the strength to close my eyes, gather my wits, and remind myself why we're here.

"Finn still has no idea that you're his father," I say. "For now, I think it's best we keep it that way." I look away after saying this, unsure how he'll take this. He taps his fingers on the table, and when I peek at his expression it's unreadable.

"I guess I can respect that," he says slowly.

"It's not that I want to keep it from him forever," I explain. "It's just that this is a big deal, and he still hardly knows you. I think it will be easier for him after the two of you have a more established relationship."

"*Will* we have a more established relationship?" he asks.

"Of course," I say. "That's why we're here, right?"

He tilts his head, and I can tell he's being cautious. We both are. But underneath that caution, the distrust remains. We both have something to lose here, even if it's just our ego.

"What would be okay for you?" he asks.

I think about this for a moment. The truth is that none of this feels okay. I don't want to set up visits away from me, or think of Finn spending weekend with Ethan, or any of the other scenarios that come to mind. How do I share my son when I've spent the last six years as his only parent?

"I don't know," I admit. I wrinkle my brow as I look at him. "I'm having a hard time knowing how to be fair, because right now I'm feeling very protective over my son." I shake my head. "*Our* son," I correct.

He nods slowly, looking out the window as he takes another sip of beer. Then he looks back at me. "I guess I can understand that," he says. "Or at least I can respect it. I'm nervous about this too. I haven't been around a lot of kids, and like you said, I don't really know Finn. But I also know it has to start somewhere. So, what would make you feel comfortable as we move forward?"

I appreciate that Ethan is keeping me in the lead on this. As well as I know him, I'm sure he has some ideas about what he wants. But the fact that he's taking a backseat on all of this is reassuring to me.

"Why don't we start out with what we were already doing? You come to my house for dinners, we can go on outings together, like to the zoo or the park, and we just slowly get him more used to being with you."

"So, the three of us," he says.

I'm stung by the look of disappointment on his face, and I clench my jaw as I try to come up with a fair response.

"It's not about you," he rushes in. "I mean, I don't…" He looks away, and I wish he'd finish that thought because I have no idea where we stand. "I just kind of hoped to get to know him on my own," he finally says.

"We'll get there," I promise, even though it feels like a hard promise to make. "But can we ease into it?"

"Do you think I'll do something to hurt him?"

My eyes widen, and I shake my head.

"No! Not at all. It's just that…" I pause. Am I doing

this for Finn or for me? "I know you'll be just fine with Finn, in fact, I think you and Finn will get along famously. I already see so many similarities between the two of you…"

"You do?" he interrupts, "Like what?"

My face relaxes into a smile. "You have the same laugh," I say, "and sometimes you two stand the same way."

"We do?" He grins, ducking his head.

"That!" I laugh, "Finn does that too."

"What?"

"That thing you do when I've said something that both pleases and embarrasses you. When Finn feels that way, he grins and lowers his head, and it's the cutest thing ever." As soon as I say it, I realize I've just revealed that "the cutest thing ever" applies to Ethan too. My cheeks flush, but then I brush it away. Who cares? We may be in this weird spot of our relationship, if there even is a relationship, but he can't just expect my attraction to him to go away—and neither can I.

"The other day when you had dinner with us, Finn kept mimicking what you were doing. I'm not sure if you noticed since you haven't been around him a lot, but I did. I could tell he looked up to you, so I know it will be no time at all before he's comfortable being with you without me. It's just that…" I pause, embarrassed as I feel hot tears spring to my eyes. I swipe them away, but they keep coming. "This is hard," I say. "My whole entire life is wrapped around Finn, and just the thought of sharing him is sending me into a humiliating turmoil. It shouldn't be this big of a deal, but it totally is. I can't imagine my life without Finn, and this feels like I'm letting him go."

Ethan reaches over and takes my hand. His thumb rubs over the back of my hand, and even as the tears are coming steadily now, I find relief in this small show of affection.

"I will never get in the way of your relationship with Finn," Ethan says. "I appreciate how difficult this is for you. Let's start things your way and see how it goes, okay?"

"Okay," I sniff. I turn my hand over to get a better grasp of his hand, but he pulls it away. The move is slight, but enough to send a message. Still, I find myself in a tug of war over needing clarification.

"What about us?" I finally ask, losing my inner battle of wills. He looks away.

"I don't know," he says, "I need time to think."

"Ethan, I didn't mean to…"

"I know, Claire," he says, looking back at me. "I know there are so many layers to this situation, and there are things you had to do that I couldn't possibly understand. But it doesn't make it hurt any less. We've only known each other a short time, and I feel like there have been so many secrets and hidden truths. I'm not sure that's a foundation any relationship can be built on."

"But…"

"I know," he repeats. "Can we just focus on Finn for now?"

I nod. It's not what I want to hear, but it's the most mature thing to do. It also gives me a slight sense of shame that he's the one suggesting it and not me.

Chapter 25

Even though things feel weird between us, Ethan and I agree to start our casual visitation thing this afternoon. He joins me at the house while we wait for Finn to get home from school. He even stopped at the store before he arrived so he could pick up a few snack supplies—celery, peanut butter, raisins, and some flavored water to drink. I'm relieved he's in line with my attempts to keep Finn healthy. Or maybe he's paid attention to what I do for Finn. Either way, I'm impressed.

Finn gets home and is thrilled to see Ethan there. He immediately wants to show Ethan the additions to the racetrack in his room, but Ethan puts on the brakes.

"I'll see it in a bit," he says, "after your homework is done."

Finn looks to me, his expression twisted with confusion.

"You know the rules," I say, though I feel for the kid. Ethan is supposed to be Mommy's fun friend, not the rules guy. This is probably messing with Finn's world. Still, he sits at the table and pulls out his homework with a sigh while Ethan starts making his snack.

"Mom, can you help me with the word problems?" Finn drapes himself over the homework sheet, and I start to go toward him.

"Math?" Ethan asks. "That's my specialty. What you got, Dude?" He places the snack plate on the table then takes the chair next to Finn.

I want to stick around for all of this, and I feel a little lost in what my role should be. But I know I'll just be in the way of what these visits are for, so I excuse myself and leave the room. The Romance Lovers Book Expo is this weekend anyway, and I still have a few things left to do before I send the swag packages to Cass, the event coordinator. I usually send items directly to the authors, but thanks to Cass's immense generosity to the authors, this works out best for all of us. She'll make sure they're there at each author's table, and the authors will have one less thing to lug to San Francisco.

Really, I just have to add a few personal touches to the boxes before sealing them. I always include Chapstick with my logo on it, because who doesn't need a good tube of Chapstick? I also add some sweets and a handwritten thank you card. Once the boxes are complete, I seal them with pink and black personalized tape that says "Bookish Magic" in large letters and "Cast by Claire Myers" in a smaller font below that.

All the while, I'm listening in on Finn and Ethan's conversation in the other room. At first, it's just Ethan showing Finn a trick on how to solve the word problem, and I tune in and out on what they're saying. But I hear Finn mention Brie's name, and I pause what I'm doing to hear the full conversation.

"Do you like her as a friend?" Ethan asks, "Or do you *like-like* her?"

I purse my lips, hating the direction of this conversation. Isn't six a little young to be thinking about *like-liking* someone?

"I *like-like* her," Finn says. "But she doesn't like me like that at all. She likes Ollie because he's more popular than me."

"How so?"

"Well, his mom packs him cool lunches with chip bags and cookies."

"And your mom doesn't, huh," Ethan muses.

I roll my eyes. I'm not about to resort to crap food so that my kid will feel popular.

"No, she makes all the food herself instead of buying it at the store."

"How mean of her," Ethan laughs, and I hear Finn giggle. "What else?"

"Ollie is better at kickball, and he's always chosen first, and he walks home from school instead of taking the baby bus."

"Those are okay reasons to be popular, but I'm not convinced that's why a girl would go for a guy."

"What do you mean?" Finn asks.

At this point, I've abandoned my work. It's done anyway, but I'm not about to leave the room and stop this conversation.

"Having good lunches or being great at sports can be cool and all, but girls want more than that. They want someone who's nice to them. They like to feel special when they're with him."

"So, how do I do that?"

"Well, the most important part is to just be yourself," Ethan says. "Don't do things that aren't like you, because then she won't get to know the real you."

"I already do that," Finn says, "and she doesn't care."

"Because that's only part of it. The other part is to do kind things for her. Tomorrow ask her what she did after school, and then listen. Find out what kind of shows she watches, and then watch them so you know why she likes them, and maybe even have something to talk about with her. I mean, do you know some of the things she likes?"

As they continue, my mind wanders to the ways Ethan has followed this advice himself. Our first date, when I went on and on about *Frankenstein*, which then led to questions about my childhood. Our date to the bookstore, where he uncovered my obsession over a certain book series. The way he roped me into showing him the way I dress my hot dog. All of these were simple things, but they were part of his plan to get to know me better and make me feel special—and around him, I *do* feel special.

I have no doubt Ethan still has feelings for me, even if they're dulled by the secret I had to keep from him. But now everything is in the open, and while I won't get in the way of his focus on getting to know his son, I can also use this time to turn the tables on him. Plan outings based on Ethan's interests. Make him feel special. Help him see that he not only has a family with Finn, but with me too.

"Wait, is this the girl you were hanging out with at the carnival?" Ethan asks.

"How did you know?"

Finn never even saw Ethan there, and I grin waiting to hear how Ethan will get out of this one.

"Your mom mentioned it. So, is it?"

"Yeah, that's her."

Ethan chuckles.

"I hate to break it to you, but I think that girl is into you. Just keep being nice to her. By next week, she won't even remember Ollie's name."

Ethan stays through the evening, insisting on making us dinner from what I have in the fridge. He keeps me out of the room while Finn helps, which is fine by me. I use the time to take a bath with a book and a glass of wine, believing I could get used to this. I keep my music on but can still hear clanging pots and pans over the sound of Novo Amor crooning through my phone speakers. I ignore it, nestling in with BA Warner's latest book, the one she's debuting at this weekend's event. By the time I'm a prune and dressed in sweats, I can smell something delicious wafting from the kitchen.

"Finn is washing up before dinner. Don't look at the sink," Ethan warns as he sets a plate of roasted carrots on the table next to a bowl of white sauce. I dip my finger in, squealing as he swats me away, then lick the sauce to taste.

"Tahini?" I ask.

"For the carrots," he says. Then he lowers his voice to a whisper. "Finn already had a carrot when I told him how it helps me see in the dark."

"Oh my God, what happens when he finds out you're lying?"

"What do you mean?" he asks. "I totally see in the dark."

I roll my eyes, but have no time to offer a retort as Finn walks back in. He goes to my chair and pulls it out.

"Sit here, Mom," he says, gesturing to my normal

seat. I raise my eyebrows at Ethan, but he's busy giving Finn a thumbs up. Then he hides his hand, rubbing the back of his neck as if pretending nothing happened. I laugh, then go to the chair. Finn grunts as he tries to push the chair in, and I scoot to help him.

The rest of the dinner is roasted chicken thighs and mashed potatoes, and everything smells incredible.

"Here, Mom," Finn says, picking up the plate of carrots with unsteady hands. I grab it before he drops it.

"How about we keep the platters on the table and I hold my plate closer to the food, would that be easier?" I say this as I eye the heavy plate of chicken, imagining it all over the floor.

"Okay," he says, looking disappointed.

"But you can put the food on my plate," I say, and he perks up. As he serves me, I glance at Ethan. *Thank you*, I mouth, and he nods. I see the pride in his face.

After dinner, Finn and Ethan clean up while I sip a glass of wine at the table.

"We should do this every night," I joke, then laugh when I see the way Finn's face lights up. He's standing on a stool at the sink, his hands submerged in soapy water while Ethan rinses—and re-washes—the dishes before setting them in the drying rack.

"Maybe not every night," Ethan says. "But we can definitely do this again. I like hanging out with you."

"And Mom too?"

Ethan looks at me over Finn's head, and I feel my cheeks burning. I'm waiting for the answer too. Ethan's face softens into a small smile, then gives a slow nod.

"Your mom too." He sticks his hand in the soap and piles it on Finn's head, who squeals before grabbing a handful and tossing it at Ethan.

"All right, enough," I laugh, and Finn groans at me, though he's smiling.

After Ethan leaves, Finn takes his bath and I keep the bathroom door open, my ears perked while I finish straightening the house. I'm almost done piling the swag packages by the door when Finn calls me to wash his hair. When I enter the bathroom, Finn's face is serious as he sits in the water. I kneel down, grabbing the pitcher and filling it with water. I study his solemn face, which he tilts up as I pour the water over his hair.

"Everything okay?" I ask. I fill my hand with shampoo and massage it in his hair. He keeps his eyes closed tight as I do.

"I'm okay," he says. But I can tell his mind is full. I know mine is. When Ethan left, he gave Finn the usual fist bump, but I could tell he was aching for more. Something fatherlier, like a hug. When it came to me though, I got a smile and a wave. I'm not sure what I was expecting. Maybe not a makeout session, but a kiss on the cheek would have been nice. Maybe a hug.

Just a few days ago, we were waking up on the couch together, sipping coffee in the morning light, working together to get Finn ready for school while I entertained fantasies of us being a family. Tonight was no different, at least with visions of how it could be. The only thing missing was that charming smile meant just for me.

"Mom, what does love feel like?"

The question jars me out of my head, and I look at my young son. His eyes are still closed, even though I'm done rinsing. I brush the water from his face, and he finally opens his eyes and looks at me.

"I guess it feels like falling, but in a good way," I say.

"A good way?" he asks, wrinkling his nose.

I think about it for a moment, and I realize what a terrible analogy that is. Falling in love doesn't feel like falling at all. Not completely, anyway.

"Okay, how about this. You know how it feels when you're spinning in circles? You spin and spin and spin, and it feels so free and wild, and all you're aware of is your body because the whole world feels like a blur. You know how that feels?"

"Yeah, like when you spin so fast you want to hurl?"

I laugh. "More or less, but not always. It's more like, when you love someone, you're spinning with them and the whole world feels blurry because you're so caught up with them. It feels wild and free, and sometimes you want to hurl. But also, sometimes you want to sit in the dizziness with that person and just laugh because everything feels so silly and wonderful. That's love."

Finn smiles, ducking his head as he looks at the water. I smile, smoothing the back of his head the way I used to do when he was younger. He usually stops me, now that he's older. But this time, he lets me.

"I think I'm in love," he says. He looks at me, his face scrunched up in an embarrassed smile.

"Try not to hurl," I say, and he splashes me with water.

Once he's dried off and in bed, I read another chapter from *Mrs. Piggle Wiggle*. This one is about a boy who gets super-sonic hearing when Mrs. Piggle Wiggle sprinkles magic powder in his ear. This reminds Finn of his super-sonic eyesight, and he makes me turn off the lights.

"I can't read the book then," I say, but do it anyway when he insists. Then he says he can read the story instead. I hand the book over, and even though I know he can't see the words, he pretends he can, making up the rest of the story so that the little boy ends up with laser vision that slices through walls and kills bad guys. It's definitely not the story I remember, but hey, it's been a while since I've read it.

Finn hands me the book, and I kiss him on his forehead.

"I like Ethan," he says. I raise my eyebrows, then take

a moment to sit back on his bed.

"Oh?"

"Yeah. He's nice. I like that he lets me help with stuff and doesn't treat me like I'm a baby."

I frown in the dark. "Do I treat you like you're a baby?"

"No. Kind of. I guess you're my mom, so you have to. But he doesn't."

I nod, even though he can't see me. "Ethan is a good guy," I say.

"Can he come over tomorrow?" he asks.

"Maybe. I'll ask him." I get up, brushing my hand over his hair before heading to the door.

"Mom?"

I pause at the door. "Yes, sweetie?"

"Do you love Ethan?"

I take a deep breath in, not sure what to say.

"I think Ethan is a great guy, and I'm glad we both get to be friends with him," I finally say. I wait for him to ask more questions, but this seems to satisfy him, as the only thing he says next is goodnight.

Chapter 26

Operation *woo Ethan* is in full effect, starting the very next day. I know Ethan likes football, so I dig into my savings and treat the three of us to a USC game. It's a bit over my budget, but it's worth the cost when I see the look on Ethan's face every time they score a touchdown. Or is it a goal? Whatever. Ethan is in his element, and Finn feeds off his energy, jumping up every time Ethan does. The two of them spend the whole game giving each other high fives and bear hugs. I spend the game trying to not be a sappy girl as I watch my guys have an evening of bro moments.

We end the night at a burger bar, where Ethan and Finn go over the highlights of the game. I realize how much Finn is missing out on by being raised by his bookworm mom. I hardly watch TV, and when I do, it's sappy love stories or family-friendly movies. It's never sports. But seeing Finn with Ethan, and the way his eyes gravitate to the highlights recap on the TV in the corner, I realize Finn actually likes stuff like this. I should keep the game on at home. Or, you know, have Ethan over more often.

It's hard to beat a night of football, but the next night I do my best by suggesting we go to the zoo once Finn is out of school. Finn is in absolute heaven, and it seems that's enough to make Ethan happy. I make it a point to hang back, letting Ethan take the lead with Finn. But Finn still calls out to me whenever something cool happens.

"Mom, look at the size of that bear!"

"That kangaroo is cute, huh Mom?"

"Oh man, elephants have huge poop! Did you see that, Mom?"

I try to be nonchalant, to let Ethan have more of a spotlight. But as fun as the afternoon is, Finn is more interested in showing me.

"Give him time," I murmur to Ethan. I get a tight smile in return.

By the end of the night, Finn is happy but exhausted, and Ethan looks ready to go home. I feel like an epic failure.

The next day, I text Ethan to see what he thinks about a day at the park. It's not exactly a woo-worthy spot, but it's Finn's favorite place to play.

Ethan calls me instead of texting back.

"I have a better idea," he says. "Why don't I pick Finn up after school, and I'll plan an afternoon for just the two of us?"

"Without me?" I ask. I hear him sigh, and I know I'm being ridiculous. "But what will you tell him?" I'm grasping at straws here, but I don't care. "He might think it's strange to go out with you without me."

"Maybe," Ethan says. "Or maybe he'll think nothing of it at all. Come on, Claire. I'm trying to build a relationship with Finn, but I can't do it if you're hanging around."

My mouth drops open at this. "So, you're saying I'm a third wheel."

"Yes," he says. "Wait, no! I mean… Come on Claire, you know what I meant. I just want Finn and I to get to the place where I can finally tell him that I'm his dad."

Something about the words hit me differently. All this time, I've been dreaming of having the two of them get to this point. But now that we're here, I feel an ugly, selfish part of me tugging at my mind. The days of just Finn and me are over. Now—forever—I will have to share Finn with someone else.

I brush the feelings aside as soon as they come, forcing a smile even though Ethan can't see it over the phone.

"Of course," I say. "It will be good for the two of you

to do something without me in the way."

"You're not in the way, Claire."

"No, I know. I just mean that it will be easier for the two of you to bond if you hang out on your own. That's what you're saying, right?"

"Yes?"

I force a laugh even though this doesn't feel like my favorite idea. But I appreciate what he's doing. Even now, even when we're in this weird limbo, he's being careful of my feelings.

"It's fine, Ethan. Finn will love it. Do you want me to drop him off?"

"Actually, I was thinking I could just pick him up from school, if that's okay."

"Oh. Yeah." I start to spiral again, but I stop myself just in time. "I'll have to call the school first, let them know Finn isn't taking the bus. You may need to get him in the office since you haven't picked him up before."

"I can do that. Just tell me where to go."

I give him directions and the time Finn's school lets out, and by the time I hang up, I feel more alone than ever. The house is quiet. Empty. I have a full day to do whatever I want for as long as I want to.

And I hate it.

I call the school and let them know about Finn's pickup change and find out all the security details so that Ethan can get our son. I spend the next hour sitting on my couch with a book, but I barely see the words on the page. I text Maren, but she's busy working at the coffee shop. I realize I haven't seen her in a while, so I grab my bag and head out the door.

Insomniacs is bustling as usual. I step inside the shop, greeted by a whir of machines, metal spoons on porcelain cups, and the clatter of conversation. Maren looks up as I enter, and her face breaks into a grin. She nods toward an empty table in the corner.

"Grab it," she calls out over the noise. "Coffee's on me."

I do, waiting for a lull in the line of coffee fanatics before she can finally reach me. She yanks off her apron and sits across from me, handing me a latte with a line of hearts on it. I take a sip, sighing in appreciation at the taste of almond milk with a touch of honey.

"Finn is hanging out with Ethan today after school today," I blurt out.

"Is he excited?" She sips her mocha, coming away with a lip of whip cream that she licks away.

"He doesn't know," I say. "Ethan is picking him up from school, and they're going to do something without me."

"And you feel left out."

My cheeks burn as tears spring to my eyes. Why am I crying over this? "I'm being stupid, I know it."

"No, you're not," Maren says, patting my hand.

"You've spent years as the biggest person in Finn's life. It's only natural that it feels hard to share him."

At this I burst into tears. I try to hide it, to control it in some way, but once the tears start, I can't stop them. "This is so dumb," I snivel. "I mean, I wanted this. But now that we're here, I don't. And I don't even know how Ethan feels about me. So is this how it's going to go? Finn will split time between me and Ethan forever, and that's just the way it is?"

"I don't know," Maren says. "I think you're getting ahead of yourself."

"But I have to!" I wipe my nose on my sleeve. "If I don't, then I'll be completely unprepared."

"And you'll drive yourself miserable by living so far into the future instead of just focusing on the here and now. You are still Finn's primary parent. You still get the final say in everything he does, how he spends his time, how he cuts his hair. Everything."

I sniff loudly, swiping at my eyes, then my nose again. "I know." I look at her, my head aching from an emotional hangover. "But what do I do in the meantime?"

"Right now? We get dressed up in our hottest clothes, then we go to the bar and grab a real drink. We listen to some live music, and we eat up all the attention we're going to get because, damn girl, you're a hot mess right now, but you still got it going on."

I look down at my usual yoga pants, then back to her. "I mean, with a little work you do," she laughs.

We end up at Water's Edge, a cool oceanside bar with open air seating that allows you to be a part of the live music inside while also enjoying the waves just across the beach. It's still early enough that the sun is out, but it doesn't make the nightlife any less. The place is crowded with tourists, and we're lucky to have scored a table on the patio. I'm wearing one of Maren's jumpsuits that leave little to the imagination in the way of curves. The front dips all the way to my navel, and I'm super grateful for the tape that's holding it all together. Maren is in a short skirt with thigh high boots and a sheer top. Both of us look like we're ready to mingle, judging by the amount of heads that keep looking in our direction. I cross my arms in front of me, keeping my head down. Maren just laughs at me, knocking my hands out of the way.

"Own it, Claire. Stop being selfish with your hotness."

"That doesn't even make sense," I say, but I put my arms down and do my best to ignore the unwanted attention, focusing on the music in the corner. It's some guy who came to play all the instruments, starting with the harmonica and bongos. It's a strange combination, but it kind of works. I nod my head in time with the music, sipping a lavender vodka lemonade while Maren drinks a Coke. I used to think it bothered her to be at places that serve alcohol when she didn't drink, but she always claims this is where her people are.

The waiter comes to our table, delivering a refill for each of us, even though I've only taken two sips of the one I have.

"This is from the two gentlemen at the bar," the waiter says. I give Maren a pointed look. She rolls her eyes, then raises her soda to the men grinning at us from across the room.

"Thanks, but we're together," she shouts loudly, then she slips her arm around my waist and giving me a squeeze.

"Maren," I laugh, smacking her arm as I pull away. Her declaration does nothing to dissuade them, judging by the way their eyes bug out, but they eventually turn around.

"I hope you're happy. I just made sure neither one of us can get laid."

"You're still getting laid," I point out, referring to Maren's fuck boy. "I have no one." I look toward the two guys at the bar, who have already moved on to other girls, and I hiss my disgust. It doesn't help that the guys in this place look especially hot. But still, all I can think of is Ethan. I take another long sip of my drink, hoping it will help me forget him so I can actually have some fun. But the more sips I take, the more his face crosses my mind. And this place sucks. The music seems too loud, and I feel way too naked to be out in public. I just keep sipping on that drink, waiting for a slight buzz to help me loosen up, all while I fill Maren in on how Ethan is getting to know Finn better.

"And then you know what he said to me?" I ask, sipping from my fourth drink of the night. Maren sighs, pulling the drink from my hands.

"Babe, eat something, will you?" She pushes a plate of nachos toward me, and I grab a huge handful.

"He said I'm a third wheel," I say around the chips in my mouth.

"You already said that." Maren sighs, tilting her head at me.

I can't get enough of these nachos. I don't think I've ever tasted anything so good. I grab another handful, liking the way they crunch in my mouth underneath a ton of cheese. Why aren't I making these for Finn? He'd love them. I wash it down with the rest of my drink, then flag the waiter down for another. Maren waves the guy away though, and I frown at her.

"You are a sad drunk, Claire. You know that?"

I shake my head, smiling, ready to argue. But as I shake my head, it feels like the room is spinning around me. I stop, and I have to hold the table until everything stills.

"Fuck. I'm drunk? I can't be. I need to get home in…" I grab my phone from my purse, squinting at the moving numbers. Then my eyes widen. "Fifteen minutes! Shit!" I move to get up, but stumble over the high heels I borrowed from Maren and land on my ass. She stands over me and pulls me up, and I realize my eyes won't focus.

"You're the biggest lightweight I know," she laughs, holding on to me while I get my footing. "I haven't had a drink in seven years, and I bet I could still drink you under the table."

"Not funny," I mumble. I grin sheepishly at her. "Thank God I have my DD, right?"

"That's what I'm here for, to get you drunk then drive you home."

She keeps a tight grip on me as we walk through the bar. Some guy shouts something obscene in our direction, but I'm too focused on making it to the door without falling that I can't hear what he says.

"Fuck off," Maren growls, and I'm grateful she's in charge.

Somehow I manage to keep my food down on the drive home, but my stomach starts churning as we pull up in front of my house. I open the door and heave nachos onto the sidewalk while Maren gets out of the car.

"She'll be okay," I hear her say, and I look up to see Ethan standing next to her by the car. I hang my head, too nauseous to acknowledge him, though my embarrassment is greater.

"Give me her keys," Ethan says, and Maren reaches into the car and grabs my purse.

"Stay here," Maren says.

"What about Finn?" I croak.

"He's in my car, don't worry. Just stay put, and I'll bring him in the house."

Hot tears blur my vision as I hear Ethan chatting with Finn up the pathway to my house before they disappear inside. I shiver, the night air penetrating my exposed skin. My stomach feels empty, though I heave a few more times before I think I'm done.

"You okay?" Maren asks. She has a blanket and helps me stand so she can wrap it around my shoulders. I nod.

"Where's Finn?"

"Ethan is getting him ready for bed. Let's go inside and get you some water."

She leads me into my house, and I sink into a chair at the table while she fills a glass with water and grabs a few ibuprofens. I slip the pills in my mouth, then take a tiny sip of the water. Ethan comes out of the hallway, catching my eye. His mouth twists into a smile, and even though I feel like crap, I can't help but smile back. My eyes are having a hard time staying open though, and my head feels heavy.

"Whoa there," he says, leaping forward as I tilt to the side.

"It's my fault," Maren admits. "I know her limit, but she seemed intent on drinking away her regrets."

"Regrets, huh?"

Even though I'm blitzed, I don't miss the way Maren shrugs, flashing an innocent grin.

"I'm probably telling you too much," she says, waving a hand as if wiping the words away. "I should get her to bed though."

"It's okay," he says, "I'll take it from here."

"Ethan." There's a warning in Maren's voice.

"I'm fine, both of you," I say, moving to stand. But the room spins around me and I moan, afraid I'm going to throw up again. Ethan pulls me to him, and I bury my face in his chest, inhaling. God, he smells so damn good. I could lick every part of him. Just the thought makes me cling to him tighter, hoping he's the one to put me to bed.

"She'll be fine. And safe," Ethan assured Maren.

"Hm."

I hear Maren's keys as she heads to the door.

"Call me tomorrow, Claire."

I make some kind of noise that must sound like an agreement, because the door clicks closed soon after.

"Come on, let's get you to bed," Ethan says.

"Are you coming too?" I peer up at him and grin, my heavy head flopping back. He shakes his head.

"I'm helping you get into your bed without waking Finn or breaking an ankle." He leads me through the living room and down the hall, then to my bed. I sit on the edge and then collapse backwards. The room is still spinning, but it feels good to lie down. I close my eyes and it helps to keep the room still. I feel him take off my shoes.

"I have to pee," I say, my eyes still closed. I tug at the jumpsuit, realizing there's no easy way around this. He chuckles, then grips my hand to pull me up again.

"Don't get any ideas," he says. He places my arms on his back for support, then pulls the jumpsuit down so that I'm wearing nothing but my underwear. I hear him take in a sharp breath. His warm hand rests at my waist, and I feel his pinky finger tugging at the hem of my underwear. I hold my breath as I wait. But when I run my hand along his back, he clears his throat.

"Hold on to me, and I'll get you to the bathroom."

I lean on him for support as we walk. I know I should be embarrassed, especially when I sit on the toilet completely naked while he stands nearby to make sure I don't fall. When I'm done, he helps me back to my bed, pulling the covers over me.

"Stay," I whisper, my eyes closed.

"I don't think that's a good idea." I can hear the longing in his voice though. I smile, peeking one eye open to him.

"Please? Just for tonight?"

He doesn't say anything for a few moments. Honestly, I think I fall asleep for a second. But I jerk awake when he says, "Okay."

He disappears, then comes back with a pot and a glass of water.

"Just in case," he says, placing both on my nightstand. I hear him undressing before he slides into bed with me. I scoot up to him, feeling that he's still wearing a t-shirt and his boxers. I also feel him harden against my backside. He starts to scoot away, but I inch closer. Finally, he sighs. He slips an arm around my waist, drawing my back against his chest.

"We're just sleeping," he growls in my ear. I grin, nestling even closer. And in minutes, I'm out.

Chapter 27

The room is too bright when I open my eyes. Blindingly bright. I grumble at the open curtains, shielding my eyes as I search for my phone to check the time. 7:45 a.m.

"Shit!" Finn's bus comes in ten minutes. I sit up, and my head quickly reminds me that I drank too much last night. I feel like my temples are caving in on each other, and my mouth is a sand dune. I look to my nightstand, noting the water and two aspirin. That's when I remember Ethan.

The bed beside me is cold, which proves he's been gone for a while. He didn't even text me or anything. Then I hear voices in the other room—Ethan's and Finn's.

I take the aspirin and sip the water slowly. My stomach seems much better than last night, but I'm not taking any chances. I find a pair of sweats in a heap in the corner, then pull a robe on over it. Unable to stand the taste of my own mouth, I hurriedly brush my teeth in the bathroom. But when I look up the mirror, I stop in my tracks.

I see my mother.

My mascara pools around my eyes and streaks down my cheeks. My lipstick is smeared across my mouth. My hair is ratted in all directions. Even my skin appears sickly and pale.

I sink to the bathroom floor—no longer on a mission to leave the room—and pull my knees to my chest. My shame envelops me like quicksand. Outside the room, I can still hear my son's small voice, followed by Ethan's deeper one. I hear the front door open and close, followed soon after by the whining brakes of the school bus. The bus leaves, I hear dishes in the sink, and then Ethan's footsteps approaching my bedroom door.

I don't move, even when he creaks the door open. From where I'm sitting, I can still see him as he peers around the room before spotting me in the bathroom.

"Hey," he says, pushing the door open further. "You feel okay?"

I don't answer, just continue staring straight ahead. He joins me, dropping into a cross-legged position just outside the bathroom.

"Does Finn know?" I whisper.

"Know what?"

I look up at him, not wanting to say it. I finally gesture to myself, looking away as I do.

"No," he says. "He knows you're not feeling well, but he doesn't know why."

I close my eyes, hot tears welling in my lashes.

"Hey, it's okay." He scoots next to me, wrapping an arm around my shoulder. I want to pull away, feeling undeserving of his attention. At the same time, it's like rain in a drought. I've missed his touch terribly. I lean against him, and as I do, an involuntary shudder moves through me.

"Tell me what you're thinking," he says.

"I'm thinking that I let my son down completely." I fold my hands in my lap, twisting my fingers into each other. "I'm thinking how I have one job that matters in this life, and that's to make sure Finn is cared for and safe, and I failed to do that."

"That's not true," Ethan says, running his hand on my shoulder. "I was here with him the whole time. Never once was he unsupervised or left to fend for himself." He squeezes me against him, then brushes my hair away from my face. I can't look at him though. I want to evaporate, cease to exist. "Claire, you didn't do anything wrong."

At this, I jerk away. I scramble to my feet, closing my eyes briefly as my head catches up with the motion. When the room stills, I glare at Ethan.

"I did everything wrong," I hiss. "What if you weren't here? He never would have woken up or made the bus. What if he got sick last night or fell out of bed and hurt himself? I wouldn't have been able to care for him. I know better. I can't put him through that too. I can't…" I break off, my voice cracking as hot tears blur my vision. Ethan moves to stand, and I put my hands up to keep him from coming close.

"You enjoyed a night out," he says. "When was the last time you could hang out with Maren and not worry about being a mom?"

"It doesn't matter. I *am* a mom!"

"And you've done a wonderful job," he says. I shake my head, but his words only make me cry harder.

"I'm just like h…"

"No," he says angrily, this time closing the space between us and taking hold of my shoulders. He leans down, his face close to mine so that I can't look anywhere else. "You're nothing like her," he growls. "Finn will never know what you went through because he'll never experience it. You went out for one night, and you had too much to drink. Do you think you're the only parent who's ever done that? Do you know how many times I've had too much to drink? I can't even give you a number, and that doesn't make me a bad person."

"But you weren't caring for a child," I point out.

"And neither were you."

I start to argue, but he shakes his head.

"Claire, Finn was with me. He was safe, and you were free to have some fun."

I take a shaky breath and nod my head, but I can't shake my feelings of failure.

"Look at me," he murmurs.

I do, my lip trembling as he wipes the tears from my lashes. I turn away, wiping the rest of them on the sleeve of my robe. Then I look back at him.

"You're a good mom," he says. "Probably one of the best. Finn is lucky to have you, and you're not alone anymore. I'm here, and I'm not going anywhere."

My heart lurches at this, my lips parting as his words wash over me. I realize how much I've missed him, and how much I'm craving his touch now. Last night is still foggy, but I remember curling into him, sleeping while his arm was wrapped around my waist.

He reaches out and brushes my hair away from my face, then swipes his fingers across my cheeks to catch my tears. I look at him through blurry eyes, catching the way his gaze softens.

"You're so beautiful, it's distracting," he murmurs. My mouth drops, and while they're nice words to hear, I don't believe him.

"I look like shit," I say. He shakes his head.

"Claire, I don't care if you're dressed to the nines or you just woke up. You're the most beautiful woman I've ever known."

"Right, like all those models you used to date?" As soon as the words leave my mouth, I feel stupid. It's not like Ethan and I have ever discussed his dating past. I also know he couldn't possibly find me attractive right now. But then he tilts my head back so I'm looking at him, his mouth tantalizingly close.

"You don't even know how gorgeous you are. How can you not see how attracted I am to you?"

I shake my head. "It's hard to tell when you've been keeping a pretty good distance from me," I point out. "You had plenty of opportunity last night, but you didn't try a thing."

He smirks, then runs his thumb over my lip. "Do you have any idea how hard that was? How hard it's been to be angry with you?"

"Are you still angry?" I whisper.

His eyes remain on my lips, his face darkening. "Furious," he says, then he claims my mouth. I cling to him, pulling him closer until he lifts me in his arms and carries me to the bed. His mouth returns to mine as he slides my robe off my shoulders, his fingers trailing over my skin until he tugs at my pajamas. I break from him to undress, then watch with hungry eyes as he rips off his t-shirt.

He collapses on me wearing just his jeans, his buckle digging into my tender belly, and his chest pressed against my naked breasts. He devours my mouth and trails wet kisses across my neck and collarbone, his hands wrapped in my hair. Then he nips at my skin, the pain filling a carnal need deep inside me. I arch my back, clutching his hair as he bites every few inches on me. I moan loudly, needing the pain, needing his closeness—needing him. He catches my nipple in his mouth, his teeth grazing the tender flesh as his eyes meet mine.

"Do you like that?" he asks.

"Yes," I whisper. "More." He increases the pressure, his teeth sending sharper pains through me, reaching my core. It unearths something in me, undoing the past few weeks of heartache and loss. I press against his punishing mouth as he trails lower. Then he finds his destination, his tongue replacing the graze of his teeth, and I arch my back as he works me with his warm mouth. His fingers grip my thighs with brute force, but his mouth is tender, coaxing me with slick caresses until I'm shuddering beneath him, crying out his name. His fingers take the place of his tongue, filling me so deliciously as he slides in and out, and I'm gone. My body at his mercy as I ride out the euphoric waves.

He slips his fingers from me as I pant against my pillow, my eyes closed as I recover. I hear his jeans drop to the ground, and then the sound of him ripping open the foil package.

"Open your legs," he growls low. And I do, watching

him with hooded eyes as he climbs onto the bed, then I suck in my breath as he plunges into me. There is nothing gentle about it as he takes me with the same urgency I feel. His hands grip my skin, pull at my hair, latch onto my shoulders with each thrust. I cling to his back, pulling him closer as I move with him.

"You feel so good," he breathes against me. "I've missed you." He buries his face in my neck, cradling the back of my head. I don't know if it's the relief of his words or the feel of him swelling inside me, but soon the pressure releases and I'm coming. I throw my head back, crying out as he quickens his pace.

This is different than every time we've been intimate. This isn't making love; this is both of us taking. This is making up for lost time. This is filling the space that was left when we couldn't be together. When I look in his eyes, there's something wild reflected in them. I know I harbor the same beast. He unleashes something inside me that I never knew existed, and now that I've had a taste, I never want to lose him again.

Ethan tangles his hands in my hair, pulling my head back as he claims my mouth. I feel him swell inside me, my own orgasm building when he cries out against my lips, then collapses on my sweaty body. We stay still for a moment, just breathing into the empty space of the room. I can still taste the salt of his skin and can't help but rain soft kisses against his shoulder to taste more of him. He runs his hands through my hair, rolling to his side so he can look at me.

"You are so beautiful," he whispers, his fingers lacing through mine. I offer a smile, but I'm suddenly more tired than ever. And hungry, as my growling stomach reminds me. Ethan laughs, patting my belly.

"Can I fix you some eggs?" he asks.

I wrinkle my nose at the thought. Even though he'd jostled me plenty just now, I'm not sure my stomach can handle a full breakfast.

"Just toast," I say, "and some coffee. No cream."

"Anything for you," he says, kissing the tip of my nose. "Don't move. I want you just like this when I come back."

I flash my breasts at him as he pulls on his boxers, and he groans.

"Hurry back," I tease.

While he's gone, I roll over and grab my phone. Maren has already texted, asking if I'm still alive. I grin, then unlock it to answer.

> Me: *It was a rough morning, but it's better now.*
>   *;-)*
> Maren: *He's still there, isn't he?*

I can hear clinking in the other room, and then the sound of Ethan's feet padding toward my room.

Me: Gotta go. He's serving me breakfast in bed.
Maren: Fuck, I need a real boyfriend.

"Maren says hi," I say, placing my phone back on my dresser and then sitting up so I can take the coffee from his hands. Even though it's more bitter than my usual creamy coffee, it's just what I needed. I can feel my nerves waking up.

"The delivery guy dropped off some packages on your porch," he says, placing a plate with toast in my lap. "I didn't get them, though. I figured your neighbors don't need to see your naked boyfriend."

"I'd like to see my naked boyfriend," I say, then giggle when he strips again and climbs into bed with me. I take a bite of toast, then offer him a bite. He takes a small nibble, then pushes it back to me.

"I already ate with Finn. You eat."

I do, enjoying the way it feels to be wrapped in his arms while eating. I don't usually butter my toast, but the healthy serving he layered on it tastes so delicious, I feel like a changed woman.

I'm also unsure what was delivered. As far as I know, I'm not expecting anything. The Book Expo was my last big job, and I've enjoyed a slight reprieve since mailing the packages a few days ago.

But the idea of boxes staying on my doorstep bothers

me. I trust my neighbors, but there's always the chance of porch pirates looking for an opportunity. So as soon my plate is empty, I slide away from Ethan and pull on a robe.

"So soon?" He gives me a tempting smile, rubbing the bed next to him. God, I could look at his body all day, and it takes everything in me not to forget the packages and head for his package instead.

"Give me a few minutes," I say. "I'll just bring the boxes in, and then I swear, I'm all yours for as long as you'll have me."

"Promise?"

I lean down, my robe falling open as I kiss him. He pushes his tongue inside my mouth as his hand grasps my breast, and I moan as my yearning awakens once again.

"I promise," I sigh into his mouth before pulling away. His chuckle follows me out of the room.

But when I open the door, all my yearning disappears. There are several large boxes, the same ones I packed up and shipped a couple days ago for the book expo—which is tomorrow. I'd even paid extra to make sure they arrived in San Francisco by today. Instead, they're on my porch, more than three hundred miles south of where they're supposed to be.

"Fuck."

Chapter 28

After several phone calls, it's obvious there's nothing that can be done. It's a mistake on the post office's end, but they don't have a solution to fix it except to refund the money I spent on shipping.

Ethan sits with me at the table, now covered in boxes. He joined me as soon as he heard me swear, and I can tell he feels helpless as I try to figure out what to do.

"You can deliver it yourself," he says, and I bury my head in my hands. It's really the only solution, and I know it. But tomorrow is Friday, and Finn has school. He could skip for the day, but I know he'll hate it. He'd rather be with his friends than take a road trip.

"Finn can stay with me," Ethan says, as if reading my mind.

"No." It slips out of my mouth before I can even think of what I'm saying. I see his jaw flex as he takes in the word, and I momentarily feel bad. But I also can't allow this. "Finn has never once in his life spent the night away from his home," I explain.

"That's fine, but that was before he had a father."

I get up from the table, turning from him as his words sink in. There's so much that's unresolved about this, and I know it's a conversation we need to have. I'm just not ready. Will I ever be ready? I'm not sure.

"We haven't even told him yet, and you already want him to stay at your house."

"His house now, too, Claire. He has two parents, even if he doesn't know yet."

My hands clench, my chest feeling like it's going to cave in on itself. "You can't do this," I say.

"I'm not doing anything. I'm just offering to take him for the weekend."

"And then what?" I ask, my voice filling the small space. "First he stays overnight. Then a week? Then we're in court figuring out split custody, and Finn is in a different home every week? I won't do that to my son."

"Our son," he reminds me, and I glare at him. "And I'm not asking for joint custody or a split schedule, or anything like that. I want to be with you, Claire. This isn't some casual fling. I know the stakes here and what it means to be with you. But I also want time with my son so we can get to know each other better."

"And you can tell him you're his dad," I mutter.

"Well, yeah," he says. I whip my head in his direction, ready to yell, but he holds his hands up. "Not yet," he assures me. "But I'd like to tell him soon. I'd like us to tell him together. I wish he knew now, but I'm respecting your wishes. I'm respecting all your wishes with Finn, Claire. But you need to give me a chance here."

I look down, playing with the sash of my robe, unsure what to say. He's right, of course, one overnight isn't a lot. But where does it stop? What if I keep loosening the reins and end up losing Finn in the process? I think of Finn's little voice this morning, the excitement I could hear even from the bedroom. It's only a matter of time before we're telling him that Ethan is his dad, and I'm not ready yet.

For a brief moment, I wish I'd never met Ethan at all. My life would be back to predictable, and I wouldn't have to worry about losing Finn. But when I look into Ethan's eyes, I realize how unfair I'm being. I nod, looking down, then yelp when he jumps up and swings me around the room.

"You won't regret this," he says, and kisses me full on the mouth. I smile against him, pressing on his chest so I can catch my breath.

"I just have one request," I say. "Well, several. But one big one."

"Anything."

A burst of emotion wells up inside me, and I bat it away. He's so enthusiastic about this. Meanwhile, I feel defeated.

"Can you stay here instead of at your house? At least for now? It's just that I won't be able to prepare him for staying at your house, and…" I wipe at my eyes, "I know I'm being ridiculous, but it will make me feel better knowing he's in a familiar place."

"I can stay here," he agrees, folding me into a hug. I lean my head on his chest, closing my eyes. "I think that's a great idea anyway," he continues. "I can call out of work and…"

"Oh God, your job!" I lift my head up, peering into his face. "I'm sorry, I didn't even think."

"It's fine, Claire, really. There are plenty of bartenders looking to pick up a shift or two. It's no big deal."

As I pack, I go over the list of important details, including contact information for Finn's doctor and dentist, phone numbers for Maren and my neighbor, the books he likes to be read, all the immunizations he's had so far, and his blood type. If I'm being over the top—and I know I am—Ethan says nothing. He simply types it all into a note on his phone.

I call Cass to tell her what happened with the packages, but only get her voicemail. In a rushed message, I explain the mix up and how I'm fixing it.

Then I load up my car with Ethan's help.

"Have Finn call me as soon as he gets home," I say, taking my house key off the ring and handing it to him, "and before he goes to bed."

"We'll be okay," Ethan says. "Finn will be fine."

I'm trying to believe that myself, but I can't help feeling like I'm abandoning my son. And then there's the other thing…

"Please don't tell him you're his father."

He's silent for a moment, but then nods. I can see the unease on his face though, and I realize I have to let go at some point.

"Not yet," I say. "Let's plan it for when I come home, okay?"

He nods again, but a small smile works its way to his mouth.

"I'll wait. I promise," he says. He wraps his arms around me, pressing his mouth against the top of my head as he holds me close. "I'll miss you."

I relax in his arms in that moment. Everything between us has shifted. We're in this together. It's time I let him in completely.

"I'll miss you too," I say. "Have a wonderful time with your son."

He grins at this, and I know they're the right words. They feel right.

"Drive safe, my love," he says, then kisses me sweetly.

It makes it hard to leave, but I know I need to go if I plan on reaching San Francisco at a decent hour. I watch him from my rearview mirror, waving until I can't see him anymore.

Then, I'm on my way.

Even though I knew Finn is in good hands, I can't help the thoughts ping-ponging through my head as I drive. Will Finn feel like I abandoned him? He hasn't seen me since yesterday morning, thanks to my drunken night, and now he's coming home not expecting Ethan. I'm not going to disrupt him at school with the news, but I go back and forth on whether this is the right decision.

"Of course it's the right decision," Maren says through my car speakers. I called her once I'd been on the road for an hour, unable to stand my own thoughts.

"He's going to hate me," I moan.

"Are you kidding? You should have seen him with Ethan last night. That kid was eating up everything your boyfriend handed him. He's going to be thrilled when he finds out Ethan is there and you're not."

"That's worse!" I say, which only makes her laugh. "It's not funny. If he ends up liking Ethan more than he likes me, I'm never going to forgive you. I never should have started dating."

"Right," she says, still laughing, "and I'm sure you felt that way while you and Ethan were making up this morning."

I bite back my smile, the memory broadsiding me in the midst of my regrets.

"Secondly, Finn will never love anyone more than he loves you," Maren continues. "That kid adores you, even if he doesn't always show it. Trust me, he'll probably spend the whole night talking about you."

"You think?"

"I know. On the nights you were out with Ethan, Finn started almost every sentence with 'My mom said' this and 'My mom does' that. The kid thinks you hung the moon, so don't you worry about the stars he has in his eyes for Ethan."

It's what I needed to hear, and her words stay with me even when Finn calls me a few hours later, obviously unfazed by my not being there. He's only on the phone for a few minutes before he hands it to Ethan to watch TV.

"Not too much TV," I warn, and he laughs before telling me to stop being a mom. "It's not something I can turn off," I say, but I feel better now that I've talked with my son.

I only stop once on the way to San Francisco, filling up my gas tank before buying a sandwich from a nearby deli. I reach San Francisco by early evening, then let my GPS guide me through the maze of streets until I find Cass's apartment. She'd called me back on the drive, and when she found out I was going to try and find a motel, she insisted I stay with her.

Cass is on the sidewalk when I pull up. She gets in the passenger side so she can instruct me toward a parking spot a block away.

"I've already paid for it with Spot Hero," she says, holding up her phone. "It's the least I can do for your trouble."

"There shouldn't have been any trouble," I mutter, but her enthusiasm is contagious. Soon we're at her kitchen table, killing a bottle of wine between us as we gab about our favorite book boyfriends and the movies that were actually better than the book. Maren isn't much of a reader, and after the *By the Bay* book fiasco, it's no joke that Ethan isn't either. So it's a relief to know someone as passionate about books as I am.

Finn calls me in the midst of this, just before he's going to bed. He tells me that Ethan bought him the first *Warriors* book—a series about a clan of feral cats—and already read him the first chapter. He obviously loves it, and I can't help feeling a little jealous. I know it's a lot more grown up than *Mrs. Piggle Wiggle*, and I regret not being the one to introduce him to it first.

"When you get back, can we finish *Mrs. Piggle Wiggle*?" he asks then.

"What about *Warriors*?" I ask.

"We can read that too, maybe when Ethan comes

over. But *Mrs. Piggle Wiggle* is ours."

I hang up even more reassured. Funny how a six-year-old can do that.

The next day, I help Cass deliver the different swag packages to the right author tables. My plan had been to leave just before the Expo started, but Cass slipped a VIP pass around my neck and convinced me to stay for a few hours.

This means, for the third day in a row, I won't be home for Finn when he gets home from school. But when I talk with Ethan, he encourages me to take my time.

"Finn and I had a blast last night, and I already promised him burritos for dinner if I'm still here," he says.

I cringe, sure that Finn's growth will be stunted by all the junk food he's had the past few days.

"Does he even miss me?" I can't help asking it, even if it's a pathetic question.

"He does," Ethan says. "He talked about you all night and wouldn't even let me open the *Mrs. Piggle Wiggle* book on his dresser, which is why I needed to buy him a book for just us."

"He said we get to read it together when I'm back," I laugh.

"I'd like that," he says, and it's so full of feeling, I can't help thinking about what our future will look like once I'm back in town.

The rest of the morning is spent helping Cass keep the authors happy with food and water, plus visiting a few of the authors I only know by email. I've never actually been to a Book Expo, and seeing the looks on readers' faces when they talk with their favorite authors is like nothing else. I realize the bubble I've been in since learning I was pregnant with Finn, and I make a vow to attend the Book Expo for real one day.

But not this year. I leave by noon, after lots of goodbyes with many new friends, and a huge hug from Cass who promises me a free pass and a couch to sleep on next year. I take her up on it.

The drive home takes forever, but only because I miss Finn so much. Ethan too. I'm also nervous, because I know that once I get back, we're going to have to discuss how to tell Finn the truth. It's time, and I know it. I'm not sure if Ethan and I have a future. I hope we do, but I can't count on it. What I can count on is the fact that he takes fatherhood seriously and won't let Finn down. Regardless of where Ethan and I land, he will be in our lives forever as Finn's father.

I pull up to my house as the sun is setting, noting that Ethan's car isn't there. I start to text him that I'm home, but he pulls up behind me. I get out of the car, my smile wide as I see a grinning Finn leaning forward from the backseat. Ethan turns to him to say something, and I see

Finn's smile falter and his eyes lower. I start to walk over, but Ethan gets out, handing Finn the bags of food and the house keys.

"You know how to use these, right? Take these inside, and we'll be right behind you."

My mind is racing at what's going on, especially as Finn avoids my face when he walks up to the house.

"Can I help with your bags?" Ethan asks. I shake my head, pulling my duffel bag from the backseat, an uneasy feeling washing over me as I take in the serious look on his face.

"What's going on?" I ask. "Did he do something bad?"

"No," he says. His eyes shift from my face, focusing on the space between us instead. "He knows, Claire."

Chapter 29

It takes a moment for his words to sink in. But then, they hit me full force.

"He *knows*? What do you mean he knows?" The rage washes over me like a tsunami, and I grip the handle of my bag, tempted to swing it at him.

"It was a mistake," he starts, but I'm already heading for the door. "Claire!"

I stomp inside, dropping my bag before bursting into the kitchen. One look at Finn's wide eyes, and I take a deep breath to compose myself.

"Mom?" The food is still in bags on the table, and it's obvious he's been watching from the window. I realize I don't know what to say in this moment. Ethan comes in, moving around me to stand next to Finn. My son looks up at him, and Ethan pats him on the shoulder in reassurance.

I'm an outsider in my own home.

"Well, I guess you know everything, don't you?"

It's my mother's voice. I hear it coming out of my mouth, and I feel the shame coursing through me when I see Finn's face fall. But I'm so angry, I can't stop myself.

"And you just had to tell him, didn't you? Well, I hope you're happy. Congratulations. You have a son, and I'm just the nobody who's done everything for the past six years of his life."

I turn around and leave, heading to my bedroom where I lock myself inside. I expect Ethan will follow, and I brace myself for what I'll say. What I'll yell. But no one comes. They stay in their area of the house, and I stay in mine. I can hear them talk over burritos, and it's obvious it's already started—Ethan is the hero in Finn's story, and I'm no longer needed.

Hot tears form in my eyes, but I swipe them away. I will not cry over this. Further, I should not be locked away in my bedroom when this is my house, not Ethan's.

I storm out of the room, glaring at Ethan as I approach the table.

"Finn, Ethan and I have a few things to discuss, and then he's leaving. You can eat your dinner in front of the TV if you'd like, but I need you to leave the table."

"Claire, can we just sit and discuss this?" Ethan looks at me, then nods his head toward Finn, as if he's more concerned about my son than I am.

"That's what we're about to do," I say through clenched teeth.

"Mom."

I look at Finn, my eyes blazing until I see the way his eyebrows are furled, how torn he appears. It puts me in my place, softening my resolve as I loosen my fists and sink into a chair at the table.

"I'm just…" I don't know what to say.

"I know what you're feeling," Ethan says, and I narrow my eyes at him.

"What could you possibly know?" I ask. I glance at Finn, biting the words I want to say. How Finn is mine and not Ethan's, and he's just stolen my whole world in a matter of a weekend. "You just couldn't wait for me to leave so you could spill the truth," I finally spit out. "Well, now it's out. It doesn't even matter that I've been the one to pick up the pieces all these years while you…"

"Mom," Finn cuts in, and I shut my mouth, "it wasn't his fault. I figured it out on my own."

I tilt my head at Ethan, shooting him a look of disbelief.

"Mom, listen!"

Then Finn tells me how they'd stopped at Ethan's house and his photo albums were out.

"I'd been looking at them beforehand, trying to see the similarities between Finn and me, and forgot I'd left them on my coffee table," Ethan explains.

"And I thought they were pictures of me," Finn continues. "When Da…" He stops himself, glancing at Ethan before looking back at me, "Ethan said it was him as a kid, I thought it was weird that he looked like me."

"And you just asked him if he was your dad?" I shook my head, still not buying it.

"I hoped he was," Finn says quietly, looking down. He speaks gently, as if he's protecting my feelings while guiding me to the truth. I'm struck in the moment at how levelheaded my six-year-old son is being in this moment, as if he's grown up in the one night I've been gone. In contrast, I feel frantic and out of control. All along, I'd hoped Finn would like Ethan enough to want him as a father. We didn't get here the way I wanted, but we got here just the same.

"When Finn asked, it put me on the spot," Ethan says. "I knew you wanted me to wait until we could do it together, but…"

"But you didn't want to lie to him," I finish. I fold my hands in my lap, looking down at the table. I'm still upset that I couldn't be there for this conversation. But now I've taken what was supposed to be a really special moment for my son and ruined it because my ego got in the way.

"We got you a burrito, if you want one," Ethan says, pushing a foil wrapped package toward me, his fingers brushing across mine. I linger for a moment, my eyes meeting his before I accept the food. Finn begins sharing about everything he did with Ethan while I was gone, chattering happily as if some huge bomb didn't drop over the weekend. I listen as I take small bites, realizing just how hungry I am—for food, and for this…normalcy. The three of us. A family. By the time I'm halfway through the burrito, I feel more alert and less on the defense.

"Finn, how do you feel about Ethan being your dad?" I ask. I glance at Ethan, seeing the small tug of a smile on his mouth. When I look back at Finn, he's beaming.

"I think it's cool," Finn says. "I've never had a dad."

"Well, you did. You just didn't know him yet."

He looks between the two of us, his mouth twisting with thought.

"Does this mean you're getting married?" he asks.

My eyes widen, and I look back at Ethan, who's trying his best to look serious. He's failing, though. I see the laughter in his eyes.

"It just means you have two people who love you very much," I say. I hesitate a moment, then I slip my hand in Ethan's. "And we care about each other too."

Ethan helps me put Finn to bed, reading another chapter from *Warriors* while Finn and I listen. He even does the voices, much to both our amusement.

Once Finn is tucked in, Ethan and I retreat to the living room. I sit a few feet away from him, but he pulls me to him. Despite every ounce of drama that's still tugging at my spirit, I laugh and then sink into his embrace. I'm flooded by relief as I close my eyes and bury my face in his t-shirt, inhaling his scent.

"I feel terrible how Finn found out," Ethan says, his hand smoothing over my hair. I shake my head against him.

"I wasn't sure how to tell him anyway." I fiddle with the hem of his shirt, lightly touching his smooth skin underneath. I feel his sharp inhale, and I find it humorous. "Honestly, I put so much into this, thinking he'd be mad at me for not telling him, or even abandoning me for you."

"He'd never," Ethan says.

"No, I know. But I guess I expected way more of a reaction, and he didn't seem to think it was a big deal at all." I look up at him then, realizing how callous that sounds. "It's a big deal, though. I'm sure he realizes that."

Ethan shakes his head, then kisses the tip of my nose. "He was surprised when he found out. But I also don't think he understands the gravity of it, at least not the way you and I do. To him, having just a mom is the normal version of family. I'm just a novelty at this point, which is fine. With time, I think he'll understand what it means to have a dad."

I reach up, touching his cheek.

"You're a great dad," I murmur.

"And you're a great mom," he says, but his eyes immediately well up with tears. He gives an embarrassed laugh as he wipes them away. But I know.

Both of us are fighting similar monsters, created in us by the people who were supposed to love us best. Ethan's dad failed him when he abandoned their family. My mom did the same, but through drugs and men. Maybe this is why I loved the story of *Frankenstein* so much. I could relate with the creature and how much he longed for love.

For Ethan and me, isolation is at the root of everything that went wrong in our stories.

But now, here we are. We have this chance to fix all the broken things in ourselves, and we can ensure Finn will never know.

"I have something to show you," Ethan says, leaving me on the couch to retrieve something from his bag. He pulls out a picture album, and I excitedly sit up, ready to see Ethan as a child. When he opens the album, I'm startled at the similarities between him and Finn. They could almost be the same person. I pause at one of Ethan playing on the beach with his dad, my finger touching his tiny face. It's like looking at Finn with Ethan, and my eyes fill up with tears.

"You look so happy," I say. But what I'm really moved by is seeing what's to come for our family. Except Ethan is a man we can depend on, who will always do right by our son.

Our son.

I start to put the book down, suddenly feeling the need to be close to him.

"Wait, there's more," he says, and I groan. He flips a few pages and then stops. "Finn hasn't seen this one yet. I wanted you to see it first."

I lean closer, studying the people in the photograph. It's dark and it looks like everyone is in costume. Then my eyes land on a masked girl in the background, sitting on the floor as she looks up at the boy holding her hand.

"It's us," I breathe, peering closer.

"It's the moment we met," he says.

"How?" I ask. "Where did you find this?"

"My friend Brayden posted it to his Instagram the other day," he explains. "He posted a bunch of photos from the grad party he threw back then, and this was one of them."

I study our youthfulness, the innocence of this moment. "We had no idea how much that night would change our lives," I muse.

This time, Ethan is the one to close the album. He cups my chin in his hand, looking into my eyes. It makes me think of that night, and I feel the same spark as I see myself reflected in his iris. He presses his lips to mine, and I sink into him. We only stay there a moment though. He gets up and takes my hand, helping me to stand before leading me to my bedroom. As he closes the space between us once again, his skin melting with mine, I realize for the first time that this is what forever feels like.

I'm ready for it.

Chapter 30

One year later…

"Can I get the double bison burger with fries?"

Finn points to it on the menu, and I cringe at the description of heavy meat and cheese, but nod my head.

"For your birthday, you can have anything," I say, taking his menu and stacking it with the rest.

"All right, one of those too," he says, pointing to a blended daiquiri at the next table over.

"You have a few more years before that," Ethan says. "But how about a regular milkshake? I'll have the crew add a few cherries on top."

"Thanks, Dad," Finn says with a grin.

"How about you, Mom? You ready for the meatiest burger of your life?" Ethan turns to the slight woman sitting next to him, and she nudges him.

"You know I won't eat that stuff," Stacy says, crinkling her nose as she points to a salad, no meat, on the menu.

Stacy has quickly earned a special place in my heart. The first day she met me and her grandson, Stacy turned on her maternal charm and we've been close ever since. She's even succeeded in feeding Finn vegetables—since every meal at her house is vegan—and her fake cheese sauce *actually* tastes like cheese.

Ethan signals to Jordy, one of the waitresses on deck tonight, that we're ready. But I put my hand on his arm, holding up the text on my phone.

"Wait a few more minutes, she says she's almost here."

I glance at the entrance as the waitress approaches, and Ethan explains that we'll need a few more minutes, but asks her if she can get a milkshake started.

"With lots of cherries," Finn pipes in, and she salutes him.

"Sure thing, boss," Jordy jokes. It's what she always calls Finn, just like she calls his dad, who's now co-owner of Hillside Brewery as of three months ago. Ethan's boss is getting ready to retire and sold half the business to Ethan while he trains him up. Once Pete officially retires, he'll sell Ethan the rest, fulfilling Ethan's dream of owning his own bar.

It's not the only exciting thing going on in our lives.

Around the same time, Ethan and I closed on our own house together—one that's just a short walk to the beach and almost twice the size of my last home.

It's not normal for two people our age to be able to afford a house and a business in Sunset Bay. Truthfully, we have Ethan's father to thank. Well, *thank* may be too strong of a word. Ethan will never forgive his dad for walking out on him. When we found out he passed away, Ethan refused to grieve. He did spend the whole day playing songs about shitty fathers; "Father of Mine," by *Everclear*, "Had a Dad," by Jane's Addiction, "The Story of My Old Man," by *Good Charlotte*. Plus, he accepted the inheritance that came his way—enough that he could invest in the restaurant and a down payment on our house.

"She's here," Ethan says, nodding toward the entrance. I look up in time to see my mom, a wide smile on her face as her eyes land on Finn. My son gets up from the table and runs to her, and she envelops him in a hug.

For as long as I live, I will never get over this. The change in my mom. The relationship they both share. The way my mom's smile reaches her eyes, her cheeks are filled out, and her words are now clear.

"Hi Judy," Ethan says, leaning in to give her a kiss and a big hug. She pats his cheek with her hand, and I'm moved by their obvious care for each other. She sits down next to Stacy, who wraps an arm around my mom's shoulders, then she leans across the table toward Finn.

"Tell me, kid," she says, "what's good here?"

As Finn goes over the menu he's memorized, I glance at the table next to us, at the huge daiquiri still sitting half full amongst a pile of abandoned dishes. We've been here a few times since my mom got sober, but I still worry if it affects her.

"You're doing it again, aren't you," my mom says, leaning over to me. I drag my eyes away from the daiquiri, and wrinkle my nose at her. "You know those fruity drinks were never my thing," she points out.

"No, but it still seems strange to be at a brew pub when you're coming up on a year."

"Girl, these are my people," she says, her hands gesturing around her at the tables surrounding us. "Well, maybe not that guy," she says, nodding at someone stumbling for the bathroom.

"I'll take care of that," Ethan says, standing up and following the guy, his phone to his ear. I know for a fact he's calling a cab, a responsibility he takes seriously as a bar owner. I also know the bar pays the bill for the ride.

"You *were* that man," I say, and she nods in agreement.

"And thank God for my stubborn daughter, or I wouldn't be here today." She reaches over and takes my hand.

When I forced my mom to live at the rehab center, I thought for sure it was the last time I'd ever see her. I also didn't believe it would work. But the day they released her, she called me. Not for a favor. Not to move in with me. Not for anything other than to tell me how sorry she was. She was six weeks clean at this point, and we both knew she had a long road ahead of her. Which is why she now lives in a sober house with a bunch of really great people. She ended up selling the house she'd lived in since childhood, saying goodbye to the past as she welcomed a new kind of future. With the proceeds from the sale, she paid me back the money I spent on her rehab, set some aside for Finn's college, and now lives on the rest as she focuses her energy on volunteering at a program for troubled youth. I asked her about it once, and she explained that when she helps kids, especially those struggling with problems at home, she feels like she's making amends to me.

According to my mom, her job will never be done.

"Well, I'll be. Is that Maren?" Mom cranes her neck and peers at my raven-haired friend behind an electric guitar, making a statement on the small Hillside stage. She then starts telling Stacy about the karaoke station Maren and I had set up in our living room, and for a moment, I think of my childhood as something that was normal and good. This time, though, it's not with the same feelings of wistfulness. We did have some good times, just like we had some bad times. But right now? I'm just glad to have my mom back in my life—in all of our lives—as we move further and further from the past.

"That girl's got chops, doesn't she?" my mom asks, turning to me.

"She sure does, Mom."

I glance back at the stage, looking at Maren instead. She looks amazing, wearing a slender black dress that slits from her ankle to mid-thigh, revealing stocky boots with a four-inch stiletto heel. Her black hair is in waves around her face, and her lips are a pouty brick red. She catches my eye, then blows me a kiss.

The song ends, and Maren takes the microphone out of the stand and walks to the front of the stage.

"Thank you, everyone, for coming tonight," she says, then waits out the applause, plus a few screams from the galley of girls. "Tonight is a very special night. It's my nephew Finn's seven-and-a-half birthday, which doesn't come around every day."

I laugh as she points toward our table, and the crowd politely claps. What they don't know is that, in our family, we have a lot of birthdays to make up for, which is why we've started celebrating the half birthdays too. To commemorate the occasion, a half a birthday cake sits in the center of the table. Paired with Finn's milkshake, I'm pretty sure my son will be bouncing off the walls when we try to put him to bed. I think I'll let

Ethan know it's his turn to wrestle with the seven-and-a-half-year-old.

Speaking of Ethan, he still hasn't returned from helping that stumbling guy get home. I search the faces around me, looking for him just as Maren leads us all in a "Happy Half-Birthday" song. When it's over, Maren quiets down the cheering, then gets a serious look on her face.

"Before we start the next song, I want to tell you about someone special to me." Her eyes are still on me. I settle back in my chair, my head tilting to the side as I wonder what my friend is up to now.

"I've known Claire since I was seven years old, the same age as Finn."

My cheeks redden as I feel a million eyes on me. I have no idea what she's doing, but I hate the attention.

"Claire has been like a sister to me, even in times I didn't deserve it. She's shared her kid with me so I don't have to have any." There were a few chuckles from the crowd. "And Finn is the best nephew any auntie could ask for. This is why I'm thrilled the two of them have a man in their life who supports their dreams, believes in equal partnership, and who loves both of them unconditionally."

"God, Maren, are you going to write my wedding vows too?"

I whip around, and there's Ethan holding a

microphone, his eyes shining as he looks straight at me.

"What is going on?" I mouth to him. He just grins, then looks sideways at Finn, who gives him a nod. Suddenly, Ethan is on one knee and my hand is in his. He turns off the microphone, then looks back at me. Meanwhile, I am fighting the tears and losing miserably.

"This is just for us," he says, setting the microphone on the ground. He takes both of my hands in his. I can feel the crowd around us leaning in, but I'm too consumed by what's happening to care. "I think the first time I realized I was in love with you was when I heard you talk about that book you love, *Frankenstein*." He grins as I laugh through my tears. "It wasn't the book," he continues, "it was the way you talked about it. I had never known someone with so much passion. You made me want to know everything you loved, and to love all of them too. Every day I've known you, you make me feel more alive. You never do anything halfway. Not even half birthdays." He grins, nodding at the half birthday cake. "You give everything your all, especially with the way you care for people. All of us who are lucky to call you family know that you love us with your whole heart."

Ethan glances at both our moms standing on the other side of the table, and I can't help but look too. Stacy's smiling wide, her hands clasped at her chest. But my mom is a mess of emotions. Her eyes are filled with tears, and her fingers are touching the smile on her lips.

It occurs to me how lucky I feel that she gets to be here for this, that both of us get to share this new beginning.

"Claire, you are everything to me. You have my full heart, and have had it since the first day I laid eyes on you. And if you'll have me, I'd like to make you the owner of my heart forever." At this, he nods to Finn, who pulls a box from his jacket pocket and places it in Ethan's hand.

"You stinker," I laugh, swiping at the mascara under my eyes. "You knew the whole time, didn't you?"

Finn shrugs, but his face is beaming.

"Claire Gertrude Myers…"

"That's not my middle name!" I laugh, then shoot a glare towards Maren.

"Will you marry me?"

Ethan opens the box, and inside is a rose gold ring with leaves weaving toward a small diamond. It's absolutely stunning. But I'm more moved by the realization that this is forever, and I get it with him. I throw myself in his arms, crying against his neck.

"Is that a yes?"

I pull myself away, placing my hands over his face as I look into his eyes.

"Yes, Ethan. 100% yes!"

He breaks from me just long enough to take the ring from the box and place it on my finger. I can't stop looking at it, even as the crowd flocks to us for congratulations.

"All right, lover boy. It's my turn with the bride. Move over." Maren is grinning as she faces me, and I playfully push her shoulder.

"You knew too! Did all of you know?"

Maren looks at Finn, then at my mom before turning back to me and nodding.

"Yup, I think you were the last to know. But don't worry, I think this is the last of all the secrets." She narrows her eyes then. "When you're ready to plan your wedding, keep in mind I only wear black."

Later that night, Ethan holds me in bed while my head rests on his chest. I can hear his breathing get slower as he drifts toward sleep, and I'm lulled by the beat of his heart against my ear. I can't help thinking how fortunate I am. Of all the great loves I've discovered in the books I've read, ours is my favorite. The road we took to get here was full of detours and wrong turns, but in the end, fate led the way. Ours is a love that was written in the stars, starting with my very first *yes* when we were only teenagers, and continuing with the *yes* I told him today.

"I love you, Ethan Chance," I whisper. "With everything I am, I love you forever."

"I love you, Claire Myers," he murmurs sleepily into my hair. "I can't wait to call you my wife."

I hope you enjoyed reading Masquerade Mistake as much as I enjoyed writing it. If you did, please consider leaving a review on Amazon and Goodreads. Your support means the world to me!

Coming October 2024

Naked Coffee Guy

Maren's Story
(Sunset Bay, Book 2)

Sign up for updates at
crissilangwell.com/subscribe

Turn the page for the steamy first chapter...

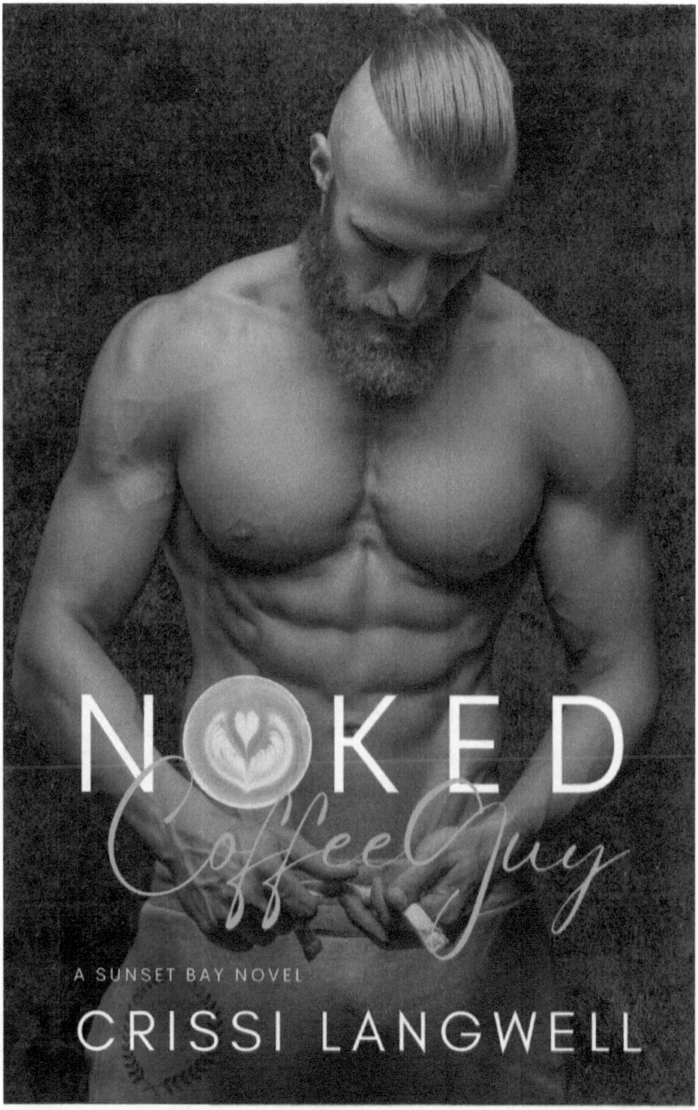
NAKED
Coffee Guy
A SUNSET BAY NOVEL
CRISSI LANGWELL

Chapter One

"Baby." He breathes it in my ear, which should have made me hot. But nothing about Brock makes me even lukewarm. He's just a means to an end, a Band-Aid to my non-existent love life, and the reason I don't feel the need to couple up and settle down. He's also kind of my meal ticket, since he manages the apartment I live in. I have a feeling it's why my rent hasn't raised.

Hey, I don't fuck for money, but I'm not above securing rent control, even in non-conventional ways. Brock has been eyeing my ass since I moved in, and a year ago I finally gave it to him. Consider it my cure for California's housing crisis.

He cradles the back of my neck, shifting his weight as he pulls my leg around him. "Fuck, your legs are so long," he murmurs, running his hand over my calf, then my thigh, and over my bare ass before he resumes thrusting into me.

"Less talking, more fucking." I nip his bottom lip, sucking on his lip ring as he groans against my mouth.

"Maren, baby, you make this so hard."

This. Not *me*. I don't slow my pace, because if he's breaking off this casual fling we have going, I at least want to get my rocks off before it happens.

"I hope we can keep this going after you find a new place to live."

That stops me. I still my hips, press my hands on his tattooed chest, my black manicured nails digging slightly into his skin as I fight the urge to carve his heart out.

"What do you mean, find a new place?" I narrow my eyes, daring him to retract his words. He grins, then nuzzles my neck with his nose. It's a move that would normally send shivers up and down my body. Instead, I'm trying to ignore the feelings of repulsion that want to reject his dick that is still hard inside me.

"Consider this your advance notice," he whispers, then rolls his hips as he continues grinding. I wrap my leg around his, grab his forearm, then flip him on his back so that I'm straddling him. His face breaks into a wide grin, his eyes hooded with lust as he licks his lips. "Damn, Maren, you're a good fuck."

"What advance notice?" He reaches for me, but I swat his hands away. When he shifts under me, I thrust down to immobilize him. I can see the impatience washing over his expression, but I don't care. "Brock, what the fuck are you talking about?"

"Hey, you still have thirty days."

I freeze, letting his words sink in. Thirty days. To find a new place. I can barely afford this place, and I know it's below market rate. How the fuck am I supposed to find a new place in a month?

Then I remember the guy I'm sitting on. Despite this sneak attack, he's still hard. And the way he's snaking his hands over my thighs, he thinks we're still fucking.

"You're evicting me while you're inside me?" I slam my hands against his shoulder, pushing him hard against the mattress as I hoist myself off him. I'm deceivingly strong when I want to be, despite my wiry frame, and I find some satisfaction as he grunts from the move, and even more at the red marks I leave behind. I should have clawed his heart out while I had a chance.

"Maren, baby, you'll be fine. With a body like that, I bet you can find a new place in no time."

"I'm not some fucking whore, Brock."

He grins at this, sitting up in the bed. My bed. The one he's been fucking me in for the past couple years. "Come on, Maren. I'm not calling you a whore. But I'm not dumb, either. Why are we even here? It can't be all the non-existent dates we go on, or the sunset strolls we never took. Maybe it's my charm, my good looks, or the way I make you cum every time we fuck."

Not every time, but I'm not taking the time to correct him. Sometimes a girl just needs the guy to finish, and a little fake orgasm speeds things along. Speaking of speeding things along, why is his naked ass still sitting on my bed?

"Do you have a point, fuckhead?"

"Yeah, Maren, I have a point. You're fucking me because you think I can keep your rent low. But the truth is, I don't have that kind of power. The owner is just too lazy to raise rents."

He's had no power over my rent. The fact that this new knowledge makes me regret the last year says a lot. I really am a whore.

I drag my eyes over him, trying to find the part of him I find attractive. His broad shoulders. His chiseled jawline. His solid tattooed chest and tree trunk arms. His giant hands that have been all over my body…

Not one thing attracts me, especially not in this moment.

I snatch his shirt and pants off the floor and throw it at him. "Get dressed and get out. Lose my number, Brock." Then I turn on my heel and head for the shower, not even waiting for him to leave.

He's gone by the time I get out. Not even a goodbye. Sure, this was nothing but a casual fling. And sure, I was using him. But his absence without a fight feels like a rejection.

"No Maren, him kicking you out is a rejection," I mutter as I towel dry my hair. Fuck, I can be so stupid.

I've never done well with rejection. Correction. In my adult life, I have not had to deal with rejection. It's why I don't do relationships, and why I always break things off while things still feel hot and heavy. I'd rather leave them wanting more than to be left behind with a broken heart.

And my heart isn't breaking now. But my security is because I'm one month away from being homeless. Again.

I glance at the clock and groan. 3:23 a.m. Letting that fucktard come over when I had to work the early shift was a stupid idea. One I was going to regret later today, for sure. The coffee shop I work at is called Insomniacs, and at this late hour—or early?—the name is more than ironic.

I have a decision to make. Go to bed now and get an hour and a half of sleep before my alarm goes off, or power through and sleep when my shift is over. I choose the latter, slipping on a pair of yoga pants and an oversized sweater, then grab my guitar and settle onto the couch. The walls are thin, so I can't go ham. But I strum lightly, smoothing out the kinks to a new song I've been working on.

This is the magic that soothes my soul, the thing that makes me forget every single thing from my past and all the stress of my present. When I feel like all the dominoes are about to fall, all I need to do is pull out my guitar and lost myself in the music.

But this time is different. My fingers fumble over the strings, the notes sounding tinny within the four walls of my tiny living room. It's not much, but it's mine. Or was mine. Even with the funky smell I can't seem to find, and the dark spots on the walls that I think might be growing.

Even with the foul-smelling water I can't drink and the wall heater that gives me a headache every time I use it.

I earned this place. I kept myself afloat without the help of anyone. I turned my whole entire life around and found myself a home, supporting myself while most kids were going to college on their parents' dime.

Yet, this is where it got me—evicted without a safety net to land in.

I look at the poster-covered walls that surround me, absorbing the images of Shirley Manson, Hayley Williams, and Chrissie Hynde, trying to soak up the courage I desperately need through osmosis. It's what I do when I'm on stage. I call on my idols like some New Age crystal-toting hippie calling on their angels. It's their persona I put on, like putting on my favorite shirt. It's what keeps me from getting too shy about performing in public and keeps me from hiding away. When I stand behind that microphone with my guitar strapped to my body, I am Shirley, daring the crowd to fuck with me as I glare at them through kohl-lined eyes. I am Hayley, singing the anthem of a generation, my fist in the air. And in the times when I'm alone with my lyrics, trying to find the words to feelings I wish I had, I am Chrissie, the songwriter who probably wrote the best love song of all eternity when she wrote "Don't Get Me Wrong."

I'm hardly into love songs now. All I can think about is that fucktard who came in here and stuck his dick in me only to tell me I needed to find a new place to live.

Fuck him.

What I need is a new song. I play a few chords, trying to loosen some lyrics from my angry brain in an attempt to move beyond the foul mood that asshole put me in, but each strum of the guitar sounds like *fuck you*, which is both juvenile and cathartic. So I go with it.

Fuck you, you fucking loser.
You piece of shit, you two bit poser.
Fuck you, you think you're cute.
Don't act surprised when I give you the boot.
You had your chance, you fucking poodle
I'm tired of your dangling noodle
Grab your things, it's time to go
You're not my prince, I'm not your hoe.

I burst out laughing, even though I'm still mad at that asshole and this impossible situation he's put me in. Okay, maybe not him. It's really the guy who owns this building. But Brock is the messenger, and a shitty one at that. I mean, he had his dick in me when he broke the news. Who does that?

The song is shit, and I definitely can't play it anywhere. At least not at the venues I usually perform at. I think of my friend Claire and her seven-year-old son Finn, who are almost always at my shows when I perform at Hilltop, especially now that Claire's fiancé Ethan owns the outdoor bar venue. Whenever I put the word *fuck* in my lyrics, she can tell me exactly how many times I sang it because Finn sang them with me.

I fucking love that kid.

And I fucking hate this situation.

And, glancing at the clock, it's time to start getting ready for the longest shift ever at Insomniacs. At least it might help get my mind off the mess I'm in.

Naked Coffee Guy releases in October 2023
Pre-sale link at crissilangwell.com/sunset-bay

Want to be alerted to this release? Sign up for my newsletter at
crissilangwell.com/subscribe

Acknowledgements

Once upon a time, I was a single mom of two incredible children. We moved out of a house of hardship and into my parents' home where I laid on the couch and healed while they helped me raise my kids.

I lived within that depression for a year, and then I finally woke up and took back the reins. I got a job, I secured a place to live, and the kids and I set off on our own for a single mom adventure that was nothing like I expected, but held so many things to be grateful for. We barely had any money. Food was slim. We lived to the penny. But the bills were paid, the kids were taken care of, and we bonded as a tight unit of three.

Today, my kids are 25 and 22, and we are now a family of five with my husband (their stepdad) and his son.

But our little unit of three is still tight, and I know it's because we got the chance to grow together in a tough but rewarding circumstance.

I wouldn't change it for the world.

I drew on this experience as I wrote about Claire and her son Finn, and the close bond they share. Like me, Claire was a young mother with no experience when she was suddenly thrust into motherhood. Even more, she had to do it all on her own right from the start, but without the family support I had. Plus, she went through a roller coaster of emotions when considering the possibility of joint custody.

I wrote this book for the single mother I was. And I wrote this book for all single moms out there who are doing their damndest to hold it all together, even when they're spread too thin.

If this is you, this book is for you.

This book would not be possible without several very important people.

First, Summer and Lucas. You are my kids. But you're also my favorite friends. Thank you for letting your old mom do fun things with you. Let's win bar trivia this week, okay?

A big thank you to my editor, Sarah Villanueva of Dear Jane Editing. I am delighted we are working together again, and I can't wait to give you more books to polish. Every book I put in your hands comes back to me so much better. You are the kind of editor every author dreams of having.

Thank you to my workshop buddies, Ana Manwaring, Heather Chavez, and Jan Flynn. You three ladies were cheerleaders when I needed a boost, and ruthless editors when I needed good words. Thank you for your help in uncovering the magical parts of this story.

To my local California Writing Club, Redwood Writers. Being a part of a network of writers has been both inspiring and filled with growth opportunity. I love the friendships I've made, the mentors that have built me up, and the people who come to me for advice. This group is truly made up of writers helping writers.

And my most favorite thank you goes to my husband, Shawn. I had no idea how good our life would be when I said "Here? Now?" when you asked me to marry you. I regret nothing. I love you more than the stars in the sky.

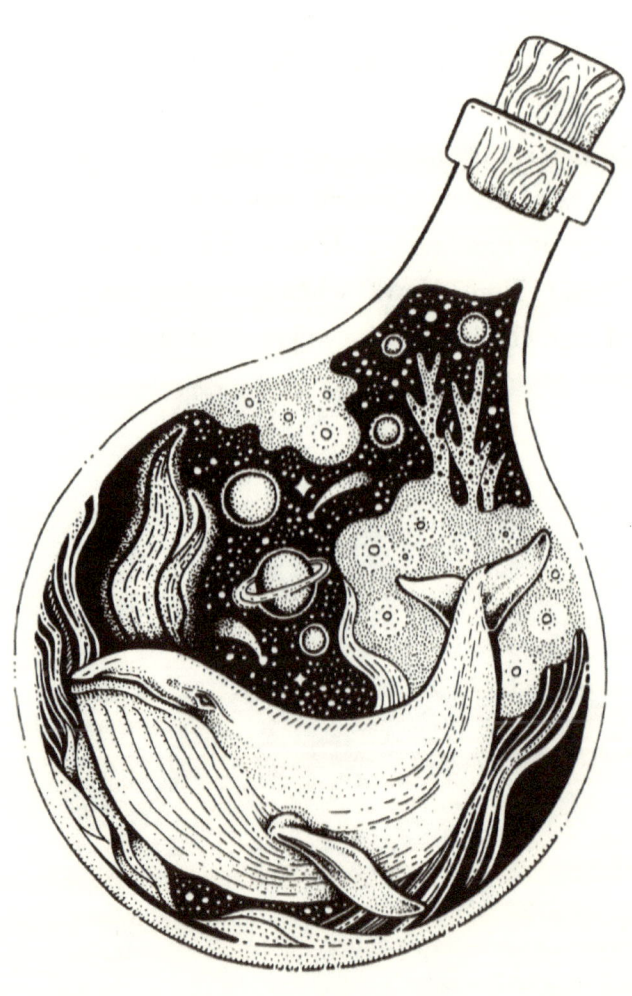

Books by Crissi Langwell

ROMANCE

Masquerade Mistake ~ Sunset Bay 1

Naked Coffee Guy ~ Sunset Bay 2 (Fall 2023)

Savior Complex ~ Sunset Bay 3 (Spring 2024)

For the Birds

Numbered

Come Here, Cupcake

OTHER BOOKS BY CRISSI LANGWELL

Loving the Wind: The Story of Tiger Lily & Peter Pan

The Road to Hope ~ Hope Series 1

Hope at the Crossroads ~ Hope Series 2

Hope for the Broken Girl ~ Hope Series 3

A Symphony of Cicadas ~ Forever After 1

Forever Thirteen ~ Forever After 2

www.crissilangwell.com

About Crissi Langwell

Crissi Langwell writes stories that come from the heart, from romantic love stories to magical fairytales that happen worlds away. She pulls her inspiration from the ocean and breathes freely among redwoods. She lives in Northern California with her husband and their blended family of three young adult kids, and a spoiled and sassy cat. Find her at crissilangwell.com.